IN AN URBAN FOREST

In an Urban Forest

KATHRYN PURNELL

J R Garran

CONTENTS

~ ~

CHAPTER ONE

1

~ ~

CHAPTER TWO

19

~ ~

CHAPTER THREE

35

~ ~

CHAPTER FOUR

49

~ ~

CHAPTER FIVE

67

~ ~

CHAPTER SIX

79

~ ~

CHAPTER SEVEN
97

~ ~

CHAPTER EIGHT
115

~ ~

CHAPTER NINE
129

~ ~

CHAPTER TEN
145

~ ~

CHAPTER ELEVEN
163

~ ~

CHAPTER TWELVE
181

~ ~

CHAPTER THIRTEEN
199

~ ~

CHAPTER FOURTEEN
209

~ ~

CHAPTER FIFTEEN
223

ABOUT THE AUTHOR
240

IMPRINT PAGE

Title: In an Urban Forest
Author: Kathryn Purnell (1911-2006)
First published in 2018
Copyright © J R Garran 2018
ISBN 978 0 6482478 9 0
A catalogue record for this book is available from
The National Library of Australia
www.trove.nla.gov.au

'In the urban forest every house is a tree; every car
a foraging squirrel with sharp teeth, defensive
while the nut is in the cheek. It is easier for the
birds to wait within the shelter of the territorial
tree. Yet still they fly.'

CHAPTER ONE

'There should be a great green circle edging the city from Royal
Park Zoo past the university through the Treasury and Fitzroy Gardens, encompassing the river with foot bridges to swing round and
include the Botanical Gardens and all the green of St Kilda Road.
Then Melbourne would really be a city instead of a patchwork built
around individual and conglomerated greeds. Greed has so little
imagination – should never be allowed to dominate the lives of
three million people in a country where land is plentiful.'

Sims always mused aloud about the city while getting home to
Richmond from the university. When walking by himself, his urban
musings formed deliberately disciplined patterns that he preferred
as a break from the mental strain of his studies. When Paul drove
him home in the M.G., Sims mused orally by way of light conversation and Paul turned the radio off. He found Sims as soothing in
the traffic as pop music since he required no more than a mono-
syllabic acknowledgment from time to time. Paul thought Sims in-
triguing on the subject of the city, although he rarely agreed with
his opinions. Sims was never sardonically clever about the city and,
until recently, Paul was amused to have found the Achilles heel of
his friend. Sims was urban-based and devoid of the desire to escape
to the country, which nagged at Paul. There were times when Paul
thought Sims considered a city to have an identity as real as he had
himself. He seemed to think a city could mould and influence in the
same way as a home and parents, which could, of course, be true for
Sims who was without family, so Paul avoided pursuing that aspect

of cities to the argumentative stage. The repeated green circle idea, however, was something Paul was beginning to find irritating considering the reality of city space, which could be valued in millions. As they pulled up at the red light on Clarendon Street to turn into Bridge Road, he said so.

'I'll tell you this, Sims,' he concluded, 'Your green circle around this city is a pipe dream if the likes of my old man have any say. Money talks big and they'd rather buy themselves a stake at Surfer's or a Collins Street sheep property to escape to than give up one foot of land in the city so the likes of you can stretch your legs. You've said so yourself better than I can, yet you keep right on about your green circle as if it was love. Melbourne is run on greed, like you said in the first place.' He put his foot on the accelerator and they swung round and shot forward. In a way he was sorry he'd come down on Sims' green circle. It was the only dream kind of thing Sims indulged in. If Sims was anything, he was a realist. He had to be; there were times when Paul envied Sims, not only the escape from the silver spoon, but the fast computer ability of words that allowed him to speak his mind under safe cover. This was one of those such times and as usual Paul hated himself for taking advantage. On surface value he had the lot and Sims had nothing. Paul decided that considering his friendship with Sims was based on argument and the attraction of opposites, he was growing peculiarly sensitive to Sims and the city. No doubt it was something to do with Barbi. Lately there had been this unexpected tension. Sims had taken a protective, fatherly attitude over Barbi of the kind that Arthur exhibited with Ruth and it was just about the last thing Barbi needed. Yet Sims was a clever devil and when she was present, acted as natural as the day, did old Sims with all his peculiarities and parent instincts subdued.

'I'll stop at the Greeks,' Paul said to Sims' perceptive silence. 'Sarge won't have eaten yet.'

Sims' digs were in a small Richmond side street that patiently received the traffic dust from Bridge Road and let it lie where it filtered down. The house was one of a row of single-fronted weatherboard dwellings and sported a bay window with a corrugated iron roof. Alongside the front door, the bay window peered across the road into the back entrance of a spare parts factory. Sarge, the landlord, had a three-foot-high picket fence with peeling white paint to protect a six-foot-square of lawn surrounded by straggly geraniums. This he called his garden. The important front room with the bay window was Sarge's bedroom and opened into a narrow, straight hall behind the front door which landed visitors into a twelve-foot by twelve-foot dining room like a jointed funnel with four lead-outs. The first lead was an opening into a doorless kitchen; then Sims' room was behind a door facing the entrance hall. Still another door led down a roofed outdoor passage past a room the same size as Sims', which was locked anticipating the return of old Sarge's grandson, Jimmy. Beyond Jimmy's room was a combination laundry, shower and finally the toilet. At the very end of the yard leaned a propped-up tin shed into which Paul found no reason to venture, although he and Sims often found old Sarge puttering there in decent weather. In the beginning old Sarge had offered to let Sims his front room, but Sims had preferred to dig in like a bear in the room beside the dining room. The old man never went into Sims' room and Sims washed his own bed linen and towel meticulously every week, and hung them with his underwear on the long line under the back passage. In the winter you ducked wet laundry all the way down to the toilet, which embarrassed Paul who was careful to avoid Sarge's back passage. Barbi had been impressed with Sims' den, as he called it, explaining to Paul later that it just went to show what could be done with a ten by twelve feet bedsitter if you had to. Paul could only stare out the small screened open window to the wall of the next house two feet away and long for fresh air, because to him the whole place always smelled rancid. His own stupid reaction to the place upset Paul.

Why did he have to feel embarrassed? Why was he embarrassed even more by his car which he parked half on the footpath and half on the road? Other cars were parked in the street but Paul knew the space in front of Sarge's house was always there because the old man made a nuisance of himself every morning demanding his rights. The space was exactly the dimensions of the house and Sims and Barbi made a great joke of the old man managing to keep it clear. Yet every time Paul parked and saw his car and Sarge's house together, he felt rotten inside.

'Your gas is leaking, Sarge,' Sims said as he and Paul came in with fish and chips. The old man was standing head-down over the Herald. He always read the paper on both feet, bent over from the waist with a space of grey singlet exposed between his cardigan and the trousers hitched up by elastic-sprung ancient braces. When he straightened up he groaned in friendly welcome, one hand pressed to his back over one hip. 'Gettin' old,' he mumbled out of habit, then bared his mind. 'Bloody bastards, them politicians. Strike me pink!'

'Take it easy, Sarge. We are privileged to have company and the guest has brought your lunch – fresh fried from the Greeks.'

'Good-o, son, good-o. Come on in, Paul. Come on in, boy, an' shut that blasted door behind you. Old age creepin' up I s'pose, but I get cold in the back these days.'

'Why don't you have your heater on then, you fantastic old crock?' Sims demanded amicably.

'Didn't think of it, son; 'struth. It's enough fer a man to put up with the bloody news without thinking of a kerosene heater to keep his bloody innards warm.'

'I'll light it,' Sims said. 'Look at that gas, will you, Paul? He probably only half turned it off when he made his tea.'

'I'll put a match to the oven for the fish and chips.' Paul said.

'Look out you don't blow your head off.'

'Okay, it seems to be right. I reckon it's safe.'

The truth was Paul couldn't tell one smell from another in the old man's kitchen. Even though Barbi told him it was only old plumbing and cheap tobacco, it seemed foul to him and every time his nose collided with it, he wondered why the hell he came. Barbi was better than he was. She always got out the soap and washed out the clammy dish-rag, wiped around with it and hung it above the gas stove to dry. But it was the kind of thing that puked Paul and he remembered with shame that once when they came he had almost vomited with the stink of the blocked drain. Barbi had sent him out to buy stuff called Draino and Lavenda disinfectant. He supposed by now Sims would have used all of it. He'd better try to remember to buy another bottle. Before he lit the oven, he sniffed hard, annoyed that Sims could recognise immediately chemical smells and tastes that eluded him altogether.

The kitchen was small, old, inconvenient and cold. Damn a kitchen that had no door into the dining room, which in turn had three doors into the other parts of the house. Who could have designed such a stupid place? Comes of living in luxury in Toorak, you can't take Richmond dwellings. One thing though, he could smell kerosene, that was for sure. The place reeked with it now that Sims was filling up the old Fireside. He realised another thing too: between the oven in the kitchen and the redglow kerosene stove, the small dining room warmed up quickly. The old man thawed out sitting down to the fish and chips that he loved and served out with glee.

'Looks bonza, don't it?' he said, rubbing his hands. 'Pull up your chairs, boys. There's still some of that homemade jam your girlfriend's mum sent, Paul. Bread and apricot jam – can't beat it.' He had scraped the remains of the jam into a glass dish and put it on the neatly set table. He liked his meals nicely arranged and properly set up. 'No slumming here, boys – I never once let Jimmy eat fish and chips out of a newspaper like a heathen. We always sat down to as nice a meal as if he'd had a mum. No beer bottles neither on this table – always had our lager in a decent tumbler in this humpy.'

No crystal either, Paul thought. He had invited Sims home to dinner once, but it had been a mistake. Not that Sims had been unequal to the Carlister's Georgian dining room. On the contrary, his manners had impressed Olwyn past those of most of Paul's contemporaries and his conversation dumbfounded Arthur into the kind of respect meted out to public relations men in the five-figure salary bracket. Sims, supposedly a casual guest, had also put Paul to shame in the matter of exemplary dress – even his hair, shiny from the caress of velvet soap administered with vigour under Sarge's rusty shower was plastered back into a shoulder sweep vaguely reminiscent of Franz Liszt. Olwyn had served a splendid dinner and Arthur produced his imported Cognac with the coffee before Olwyn peppered their hospitality with her bogey of antecedents.

'Sims Flavin, what an unusual name. Where did your people come from, Sims? I'm so interested in backgrounds.' She wasn't really, merely being snobbish. 'What is your father? I don't think I know any Flavins.'

'Which is quite understandable, Mrs Carlister. I don't myself. Unfortunately we lost track of my father before I was born.'

Arthur had made a fuss about refilling Sims' Cognac glass in his best host manner. You could always count on Arthur for that. Funny thing about Arthur, he was as hard as nails in business but on a personal basis, he couldn't stand up to hurt and knew every lurk ever imagined for face saving. Oh well, that was that and he saw Sims every day anyway.

Paul pulled up his chair opposite Sims at old Sarge's table with his eyes lowered to the clean plastic cloth and waited for his friend to bring Barbara back into the conversation. Paul preferred to be walking beside Sims when Barbi made the talk by her absence. When she was physically present the atmosphere was as natural as the day, all in, nobody excluded. It was a gift the Shorman women had. There had been no embarrassing moment when Sims dined at the Shormans'. But Sims wasn't invited all that often to the Shormans' because Barbi Shorman was Paul's girl.

The old man chuckled, making his distribution of hot, salty chips exactly even on each Coles willow-pattern plate. Looked good-o, it did. His thin, pink fingers denied the same pink colour of his tongue's persuasion to pop a chip into his mouth as he usually did when he ate by himself. Sims eyed his temptation with sardonic impatience. 'Hurry up, old man, you're stringing it out. One of these days you'll start cutting a chip in three.'

Seeing his chance to keep Barbi out of the conversation, Paul took on Sims. 'You lay off Sarge. He's doing a good job. Let him take his time.'

Sarge came right back with the expected answer. 'Not that I got all that much time boys, eighty on me birthday an' getting stiff an' cranky.'

'Here we go again,' roared Sims. 'You'll outlive the lot of us. The great mowing machine of the streets is after us young bastards, not you, old man. Why, we were attacked less than half an hour ago, getting across Nicholson Street. We barely withdrew our nose in time. One of these days...'

'Oh, shut up, Sims.' Paul grimaced. 'I'm not all that rotten a driver.'

Sarge was delighted with the turn of the conversation and settled into his lunch with gusto. Sometimes these days he could only eat with company and still those 'do-gooder' ladies wanted to bring him meals on wheels to eat alone – all hot, mucky stuff. Every day, dead on noon they came down his way, they said when they called. He'd declined their offer. He would rather have that Mrs Shorman, Barbi's mother, who sent stuff with somebody to eat it with – like the apricot jam. But he hadn't had much from that source lately, been away the girl said, overseas or some bloody place. Sarge squinted at Paul and Sims having a go about traffic instead of eating their grub like they ought. Not that Sims wouldn't finish every chip when it was stone-cold. Probably take it into his room and swallow it unconscious-like over his books. Paul wouldn't, though. He'd just get up and walk away, leavin' half on his plate. Too bloody affluent, some of these young ones. And so goddam generous he was, like money was nothing. Now that Barbi – she wasn't. Every time she came, she tidied up like and put stuff leftover

on a saucer in the fridge that Jimmy bought him from that outfit in
Bridge Road, out of his first pay.

'And where's Miss Barbi today?' Sarge inquired, continuing his
thought out loud.

The argument stopped instantly and as Sims did not speak into
the silence, Paul was forced to answer. 'It's a big day today, Sarge.
Mrs Shorman is coming home.'

'Barbara missed two lectures this morning, Sims said flatly, in
the voice of reprimand.

'Now Sims,' Sarge said and Paul noticed the placatory tone.
'That's only natural that a girl don't go to lectures when her mum's
coming home. She's been away a long time too. We've nearly finished the apricot jam.'

Sims snapped, 'What's the jam got to do with it?' So Paul added,
'She's been away for two months, Sarge.' Then he pushed his chair
back and got to his feet and said thanks for the lunch and started
out the door. 'But you haven't finished, son,' Sarge complained,
turning to Sims. 'Why don't he finish his lunch when he bought it?'

'He's taking Barbara to the airport to meet her mother.'

Sarge knew the fun was over, but he was too shrewd to ask Sims
why he wasn't going along as well, when Paul had taken the trouble
to bring him home for his lunch. He suspected Sims must be missing
a lecture himself, but there was no use asking the boy about that.
No siree! Sims ran his own show about where and when he studied
– half the bloody night the light was on, just as if it cost nothin'. So
Sarge began to mutter about waste and how when he was young, he
knew what money was, all right – more'n the young snappers did
nowadays, for sure.

Sims stood up, reached over to pick up Paul's plate and empty its
contents on to his own. 'There's no waste,' he said, and taking the
full plate with him, went into his room and closed the door.

The old man shrugged and told himself softly that if Sims had
any sense he'd uv left the door open and got some heat in his room.
It sure was cozy in here now with the Fireside on. The boy sure had

a genius for working the bloody thing, no doubt about that. Well, he might as well have a pipe and enjoy it. He pulled his old leather armchair around a bit, preferring its awkward weight to touching the Fireside. As soon as he had settled himself he fell asleep.

The traffic through the city on the way to the airport was fierce. It was not until they were well down Royal Parade that Arthur Carlister said quietly to his wife, 'Seems to me you are stretching it a bit, coming out to Tullamarine, Olwyn. Dinner would have been quite enough.'

'I could have driven Mother out,' Ruth said, from the back seat.

'You had quite enough, dear, getting Rollo over to his other nana. Arthur just hates traffic.' Olwyn sounded smug.

'Not a bit of it,' Arthur said. 'Not the point, which is that being invited for dinner is adequate. We needn't force ourselves on the Shormans at the airport as well.'

'Force ourselves! You do use the most objectionable terms, Arthur. We are expected.'

'No doubt, but probably not wanted – at least until later, which is something else.'

'You are ridiculously touchy about Linda Shorman's family, Arthur, considering your nephew is married to her daughter. George phoned to invite us particularly.'

'You know perfectly well I consider Mim Shorman a damn fine woman – always have and I expect will continue to do so. However, as I have said, there is a limit that you are inclined to overreach, Olwyn.'

'Thank you, Arthur, and you, for your part could kindly remember that I have allowed bygones to be bygones, for the family's sake. As I said, we are giving moral support to George.'

'In my opinion George never needed moral support, and as for that young fool, Paul, taking it upon himself to drive Barbara out...'

Listening now, and grown sensitive to her in-laws, Ruth made an effort to put herself into the conversation. 'Paul's coming – well that's interesting isn't it?' Mummy was just asking me the other day if I thought Paul was serious about Barbi.'

Arthur grunted, but amicably. 'It would be far more to the point if he concentrated on getting through and left the girls alone.'

'But wouldn't it be interesting – Maddy's sister?'

Arthur grunted again, but this time without follow-on speech. Olwyn took her eyes off the traffic long enough to glance back at her daughter-in-law, her eyebrows raised in the driver's direction. Ruth took the hint immediately and changed the conversation back to Rollo. It was Ruth's private suspicion that Arthur had at one time had a very special interest in Mim Shorman. She had not even a rumour to go on and her own mother had never heard any scandal in that direction, yet Ruth had been forced to the feeling on several occasions and each time had found her husband Mark as clam-like as his father on the subject. Ruth sighed. Actually she wasn't keen on this trip to Tullamarine any more than Arthur was. She hadn't had a letter from Mark in over two weeks and Mummy kept asking for news in that sharp way she had of being polite without real interest. She supposed she was apprehensive that the returning Mrs Shorman might have more recent news of Mark than she had herself.

'You look tired, Ruth,' Arthur remarked, hearing the sigh. 'No wonder – this traffic is hell, isn't it?'

Ruth straightened on the back seat and laughed. She was fond of her father-in-law who always gave her the benefit of extra consideration. 'I'm missing your son and heir,' she said. This was the statement of their intimacy, the friendly joke that had sparked and grown between them since Rollo had arrived to accept the concentrated attention of Mummy and Olwyn.

'It's also the strain of wondering whether you'll have to learn lingo: Cambridge or West-Coast Americanese. You would marry a physicist, you know how they are.'

'And he won't let you know until he's sure of his appointment,' Olwyn added. 'Because that's how he was long before he was a physicist. His letters are always full of nothing. Then you get a short-settled statement.'

'Speak for yourself, dear,' Arthur said.

'I think I'll plump for America,' Ruth said. 'I think I'd rather have central heating for Rollo.'

She really didn't want to go overseas. She hadn't even wanted the grand tour with Mummy, let alone with the other St Cath girls she came out with. She smiled at herself suddenly. For a normally healthy, sports-loving girl, she really was off-colour this last week. Maybe there was a hope she wouldn't have to go. No one could possibly expect her to go if she was sick. Not that she ever was sick, and she hadn't a hope of another pregnancy. Mark had said she could have Rollo almost as a kind of special gift.

Arthur parked his car with deliberate care. Hopping out immediately, while Olwyn stayed a moment to adjust her new hat and admire the new Garbo sweep of the brim. Ruth joined Arthur as he checked the possible safety of his Mercedes from a swipe from the front.

'Looks good enough,' he muttered. 'Not that you can tell the way young fools drive these days, males I mean. Did you write and tell Mark your preference, Ruth?'

'He hasn't asked yet.'

'Not likely to – write and tell him first. Haven't you heard at all, then?'

'Not since he arrived.'

'Hm, thought maybe that was it. Nothing unusual, I shouldn't worry, Ruthie. You'll get it all at once – stamped, sealed and delivered with two days to get your ticket.' He looked at her strangely for a moment and then, on one of his hunches said, 'Tell you what, sweetie, write a long letter and tell him all those little burpings of Rollo's that set Olwyn aglow.'

She smiled straight into his face. She was beautiful. Blonde, wholesome, healthy, slim, and chic, thought Arthur. The works! What more was he always expecting of her?

'Oh, Dad, you're quite superbly fabulous. I couldn't for the life of me even remember, let alone write them down.'

'It seems I heard you were a super prefect at school – they have to be literate.'

'Or play hockey! Through that line of duty I worked really hard for Mummy as compensation for not wanting to be a model.'

'What on earth are you two talking about?' Olwyn called. 'Hurry up.'

Scared she'd miss something, Arthur reflected. He wished to God she wouldn't buy hats that even Ruth would have trouble getting away with. Apparently, as usual, he was wrong.

'Your hat is gorgeous,' Ruth said. 'Dad was just saying I should send a letter with all Rollo's little doings to his doting father. But you know, I'm practically illiterate that way.' She wondered briefly why she always made such compromising statements to Olwyn, playing herself down. She did exactly the same thing with Mummy. She had better mind her tongue with the Shorman clan, who could be so unexpectedly penetrating. She was sure that was one reason Arthur and Mark and Paul found them fascinating and Olwyn hated them. She was terrified of Doctor Shorman, who would be in control. Normally she would try to have a word with Mrs Shorman herself, who always asked kindly about Rollo. Hardly a hope today! A strange wave of nauseous anticipation swept over her and settled like an oncoming heat-wave as Arthur politely stepped back from the automatic glass door into the airport lounge, where it was impossible to miss the Shorman reception committee congregated together with full monopoly of a section of the vinex-covered seats. All were present, it was evident, and attachments as well – even Paul, whose apparel would not allow him to participate unnoticed in any crowd. On this bright afternoon in the glassy, affluent atmosphere invoked by airport terminals, her brother-in-law could only be described as scruffy. She was left to imagine Arthur's comment hearing Olwyn's reply as they closed ranks beside her.

'He's only a boy, Arthur. They all dress like that.'

'Damn it, Olwyn. Don't be ridiculous. He's the only one and what's more it's his intention to be the only one. It's his way of telling them all he's misunderstood at home.'

'Arthur – shhh!'

They approached and the company made room. George put Olwyn into a seat beside Aunt Harriet. Doctor Shorman stepped up stiffly to welcome Arthur. Maddy Amber, who was standing on the other side of Harriet, made room between for Ruth. The ranks closed again. Inside the inner circle, Paul turned, swept the long hair from his eyes, shrugged the shoulders of his unnecessary duffel coat and raised a thin, bony hand.

'Family salute,' he drawled. 'Mother, where in Gawd's name did you find that hat?'

Ruth smiled to herself, noticing how easily he was ignored in the quick buzz of conversation. She stared politely into the wide open blue eyes of Aunt Harriet, who had immediately corralled her. Barbara had certainly sounded excited on the phone, Aunt Harriet was saying. She supposed that Madeleine would have to be big sister as usual and wait to talk to her mother until Barbara and Henrietta were all finished with their problems both individual and combined, as if their university peccadilloes were anything important. She herself would also have to wait, no doubt, to speak to Linda, although her health these days was poorly – age, of course, increasingly poorly.

Then a small pink fist tugged at Maddy's skirt, followed by a high, falsetto voice: 'Is it time, Mummy, is it time?' The beautiful blonde Henrietta Shorman and her latest, equally beautiful blonde young man had brought little Mimi back from a walk to see the planes, so Madeleine Amber, the daintiest of the attractive Shorman sisters smiled and assumed with alacrity her role as mother as she bent to lift up her fair-haired three-year-old in the apricot velvet dress with attached frilly petticoats. Mimi was Madeleine's trump card.

'Nearly time, darling,' she said and looked around to check on the two little boys running the stairs and riding the escalator from one floor to the next as a way to use energy killing time.

Ruth turned, wishing fervently she had brought along Rollo, who was also a beautiful child. She took the opportunity to detach herself from the peppered conversation of Aunt Harriet to say quietly, 'The children must be very excited, Maddy.' It was a remark which Ruth regretted as soon as it was out, so she was surprised when Maddy Amber took it seriously.

'So am I,' Maddy said. 'I'm nearly dead,' and Ruth saw with amazement that the hands holding Mimi were trembling.

A few minutes later, when Mim Shorman came through the customs door, it was not Madeleine and Mimi Amber, or even Barbara and Henrietta who pushed forward to meet her. She saw Aunt Harriet push forward to stand at Doctor Shorman's elbow and then noticed the Shorman girls standing together in a straight row; Madeleine holding Mimi in the centre, with one sister on either side, while George Amber stood behind, gripping the hands of his two sons. Beyond them, far back, Ruth noticed Paul standing by himself. She herself stood beside Arthur, although she had no idea where Arthur had come from. Thinking about it later, Ruth wondered why she should remember such detail, surrounded as she was with people moving around her in excited animation like a Disney cartoon. Yet she couldn't forget how still they stood, the Shorman girls together, Paul by himself, and herself and Arthur.

She was unprepared during the first moment of airport welcome to feel the eyes of Mim Shorman rest briefly on her own face, flicker up to recognise Arthur, flash back to herself, then turn in the direction of Paul before they settled solemnly on the faces of her waiting daughters. To Ruth it was all detached like a second dream, before the closing in of a welcome from which she stood apart.

After that, Mim held Mimi in her arms, the little boys tugged at her coat and her daughters held her shoulders in a procession of brief, passionate hugs and kisses and the welcome was like all other welcomes, Ruth thought – sentimentally overdone. She stood quietly beside Arthur, waiting as he was waiting. Olwyn detached herself from the hovering crowd and told them brightly, 'Linda looks well – tired of course, but very well.' She didn't seem to expect an answer and Ruth, catching a glimpse of Mim Shorman, saw only a middle-aged woman of medium height in a navy blue and green tweed coat of uncertain length who wasn't wearing a hat. So she shrugged and was able to ask a question she hadn't thought of before. 'Why do you always call Mrs Shorman Linda, when everybody else calls her Mim? Not that Linda isn't a lot prettier.'

Olwyn bristled. 'Exactly, darling. Mim is a special, family name, a hangover from one of the girls' baby sayings. It's a ridiculous name for an adult woman, isn't it, Arthur?'

'No sillier than Mum or Mummy,' Arthur said.

'Is that what it is?' Ruth asked, enlightened.

'I suppose that's how it started,' Arthur said.

'They seem to have a thing about names,' Olwyn said. 'Madeleine gets Maddy, Barbara – Barbi, Henrietta – Henny.'

'And the other sister, Eliane?' Ruth asked.

'She gets Elie. I find it positively stupid. Except Layton, of course.'

'Who'd give Layton a nickname?' Arthur inquired, and Ruth thought for a moment he was being facetious and was about to laugh when she realised there had been no laughter in the whole conversation.

Looking up, she saw Barbara and Henrietta walking towards her, ahead of Mim Shorman, surrounded by all the Amber family.

Arthur stepped forward. 'Welcome home,' he said. 'Was it pleasant over there?'

'Beautiful,' Mim said. 'I could have stayed for months, Arthur,'

'But you didn't?'

'I couldn't.'

'One day you will.'

'Perhaps.'

A strange conversation, tensely to the point and off it again, to some other distant point, equally tense.

'Hello Olwyn. George tells me you are all coming to dinner with us, which will be nice.'

'If you are not too tired, Linda,' Olwyn protested.

'Of course not, I had a good trip. The distance won't catch up with me until tomorrow. Then I'll be sleepy all day, I suppose.'

How serious they were, Ruth thought. Like actors walking onto a stage, not one of the three smiling. Mrs Shorman wasn't smiling and Arthur and Olwyn seemed to have taken the cue from her. So what was she herself to do? Not smile either.

'Hello, Mrs Shorman,' Ruth said evenly. 'Welcome home.' She was immediately shaken from the strange detachment of general observation to the reality of Mim Shorman's eyes.

They were dark eyes, of the sort that change from hazel to violet, from grey to black. They rested on Ruth's face with the pupils distended in sudden deep compassion as if they were bathed in a terrible shine of tears that could never be shed. Almost immediately, she dropped her eyelids.

'Hello Ruth,' she said softly. 'How is Rollo?'

Ruth felt frozen. She could only say 'He's well,' and let Olwyn take over.

'He's adorable, Linda. We really should have brought him. He's walking now; you know how they are at that stage – two steps and then down. I bought him a big red ball – well, not too big, he can pick it up and throw it. You know the little court we have especially to catch all the sun – we can take him out there for a play, even in the winter, it's so healthy for him...'

She's talking about my child, Ruth thought. Talking like a gramophone.

'Shall we get moving?' Layton Shorman said, taking his wife's arm. 'I could never discover a reason for standing around an airport unnecessarily.'

'Molly will have afternoon tea ready,' Maddy said.

'She should have come with us,' Aunt Harriet complained. 'No doubt Thomas is behind her refusal. I can't abide inconsiderate old men. Thomas is most objectionable. Not that Molly couldn't have left him if she'd had a mind to. She pampers him altogether too much. It's ridiculous.'

'Auntie Molly didn't mind,' Barbi said. 'Come on, dear, I'll give you a lean.'

Harriet sniffed. 'A lean indeed! Where do you pick up such expressions Barbara?' But she leaned heavily on Barbi's arm all the way to the car. She could hardly expect Layton's assistance on an occasion like this.

CHAPTER TWO

The lounge room of the Shorman house in Kew was soft with a massed arrangement of early rose-tinted camellias from the garden, which gathered up the muted shades of carpet under polished brass and delicately striped brocade. The winter sun of late afternoon filtered through the wall of window, floor-lengthened with sheer drapes to spot gold patches on the mahogany of the inconspicuous grand piano. Maddy loved the old piano, which invited her fingers by its very silence within the many voices the spacious room absorbed.

The strongest voice was the defiant boom of old Thomas who had risen to his feet with the intention to depart. Barbi's voice replied to dissuade him, but Molly was also on her feet so Maddy ignored the piano and wheeled the tea wagon down the hall into the kitchen. Molly did not hang around. Mim was home and Molly's job was done. Afternoon tea was over and dinner was next on the welcome home agenda. Nobody followed Maddy to the kitchen, not even George, who doubtless thought she was checking the children playing in the old playhouse in the backyard.

Maddy still felt apprehensive though her mother was safely on the ground. She had never felt like this before but her mother's last vague and pointed letter had disturbed her, and no letter at all from Eliane had increased an undefinable uneasiness. George had been no help to her in this; in fact had been difficult, with no comprehension at all of the underlying reason for what he termed her unnecessary frenzy of preparation and fuss. George relegated kitchen activities to the day time and objected in principle when such chores overflowed into his occupation of home in the evening. Blast it! Maddy was his wife and because her mother was coming back from a trip overseas was no reason for Maddy to tire herself beyond the necessary point. George believed in the necessary point – well of course he did. 'It makes sense, stands to reason, doesn't it, darling?'

Maddy, unlike George, was never quite sure where the necessary point lay for herself, although she knew where it was for George and tried to put the brakes on her activities when an overlap seemed inevitable. Usually Maddy accepted each day with a balance of good nature and worry. She tried to be a good cook, housekeeper, laundress, gardener, committee member, hostess, neighbour, wife and mother, varying the order to suit contingencies and George. When the combination from time to time flattened Maddy's spirit, she convinced herself that George supported her with the comfort and attitudes of safe security he provided along with his love. So far she had enjoyed what she needed – a comfortable modern house in a pleasant suburb of young families, where the two boys went to a good school and socially she moved gracefully within the bounds of lesser academic society. One day George would be a professor. There was little doubt that he would handle his cards well in this direction and Maddy was grooming to be a professor's wife because she would never let George down. George was ten years older than Maddy and his dignity still impressed her, even after nine years of marriage, which was why, she supposed, she had surprised herself more than George with her rebellious announcement that her mother's return was more than worth the baking of cakes, even if she had tired herself past his precious endurance in the effort. She might have created the classic in-law situation with such a statement except that George had never shown the slightest objection to her mother. His reply had therefore placated her rising temper. 'Don't be such a little girl, Maddy. Your mother won't even notice whether the cakes are made or bought. The rest of the outfit will merely gobble them up without even saying "Good old Maddy." '

'She will notice – I know she'll notice. It's the sort of thing she does herself and she hates cooking.'

'Then she's a fool to do it.'

'She is not a fool.'

'No, Mim's not a fool, you're quite right – just soft,' George said.

She had let the argument go then, in so far as it was George's classic remark about her mother. His considered opinion was that all members of her family walked over Mim. Maddy didn't agree because she knew the rest of the family considered she herself the worst offender because of the children. Even her father seemed unable to understand the importance of the grandchildren's relationship as she and Mim understood it. If Eliane had married and had children, the situation would be different. Well, there was one thing anyway – she was grateful George had unexpectedly elected to come to the airport. That had been a blessing when you considered the traffic and the boys squabbling in the back seat, and the fact that all the family except Molly and Uncle Thomas had decided to come to the airport, even George's uncle and aunt and Ruth. Unloading the cups into the sink, she mused a little about Paul and Barbi. Probably nothing in it. It was impossible to imagine Barbi settled down, even though she herself was married at Barbi's age. They would all be curious, of course, about Eliane not coming home at the last minute. Elie was different, admittedly. As a professional woman of twenty-five, she could change her mind and stay abroad if she felt like it. Mim must have agreed. Elie never crossed Mim. The funny thing about Mim and Elie was that they seemed almost like sisters, but not the same kind of sisters as herself and Elie, close and all as they were. Mim had always called herself and Eliane 'my two littlies', as if they were the twins in the family. She reflected how she had always felt so much older and protective of Eliane, far older than she really was. She supposed growing up straight into marriage and motherhood had made the difference. Or perhaps it was her father's protection of Eliane and his idea that the twins were still children at nineteen, to be treated much as he treated her own three as nuisances that would dominate the household for a few more years. George's idea about the house in Parkville followed the same line of reasoning towards the children. Maddy was perturbed to find George so obstinate, so persistent in his fifteen-years-ahead point of view, so determined she should ask Mim to further his aim.

Maddy knew she would have to speak to Mim because George had all the points on his side. His arguments were unassailable since chance had placed the proposition squarely in his line of promotion.

She could see it was a once in a lifetime opportunity. Listlessly, Maddy noted that fourteen of the exquisitely iced small cakes were left on the plates. She had made thirty-six and as George had predicted, the family had gobbled them up without comment.

Even Mim had not noticed. George was right, you had to set your sail to catch the big wind, even if you needed an overdraft to purchase a bigger sail. George had offered Maddy what he termed a concrete example to focus her mind, which he teasingly assumed was inclined to wander from the main point in an argument.

Recollecting his words, Maddy thought of the piano again. It was only when she came over to Mim with the children that she played the piano. She had always imagined that one day she would move to a house like this, where the piano was part of the setting.

She put the fourteen cakes together on one plate and began to wash the teacups.

Mim accompanied Molly into the back den, which was the chosen guest room. Except that Molly's suitcase stood in the centre of the carpet, every part of the room was exactly the same as the day of her departure. It was a large room which had gradually filled the space left by Madeleine with the essence of Mim.

'I do hope you were comfortable here, Molly.'

'Of course I was – the room smells like you, so I like it. You needn't have taken the trouble to store away your paints and drawings. I wish you would do something with your paintings. They are better than you think.'

'Funny you should say that. I did some while I was away and an artist saw them and said the same thing. However, I guess I'll spread them all out again and then not touch them for weeks. You'll see, the paint will take over the room, but not me.'

'It's a damn shame,' Molly said. 'You should use your talents like the Bible says, Mim. Observe me – I've got the time but not the talent.'

'Molly – the time, then why do you insist on going home now, not even staying for dinner?'

'Thomas wants to get home, Mim. He only came because of me. He wants to see you of course, but not surrounded; family gatherings wear him out faster than his heart, he says. He prefers coming for lunch. He's old now, Mim – he was eighty while you were away.'

'Elie and I, we bought him a pipe in Regent Street. It's in my case.'

'How nice! He'll be delighted.'

'But not enough to stay for dinner.'

'It's Harriet, Mim. She informed him she took the trouble to come to see whether Layton and the girls were being properly looked after during your absence. He was furious.'

'Oh Molly, no!'

'She did too. She dropped in by taxi one night, just as Layton was leaving for a meeting and waited for him to come back to take her home again. The evening was hilarious. Barbara came home early for my sake, accompanied by Paul Carlister and a friend called Sims. Would that be the name, a Svengali type of young man who put me in a trance in no time as a goggle-eyed listener? I didn't dare open my mouth but I was fascinated.'

'Actually, he's a very clever boy, Molly. He seems off-beat, but he's good for Paul and Barbara. Just the same, I never heard of him having his own way with conversation if the other two were around. Usually it's an all-in go.'

'You forget Harriet!'

'She wasn't rude to him, Molly?'

'No, just ignored him like the shadow of Mephistopheles and concentrated on quizzing Barbara.'

'And Paul?'

'Lay on the carpet and went to sleep over a maths book until I got up to make the coffee.'

'Why didn't Barbara make it?'

'Because Harriet assumed my purpose in the house was to provide refreshments. I was glad to oblige and leave the quiz answers to Barbara. Paul helped me. I think he was as pleased to get out to the kitchen as I was. That's when he told me Ruth was planning to join Mark overseas but didn't want to go – prefers to stay put where she is. She hadn't told me herself.'

Mim lifted one hand to her cheek. 'Doesn't want to go – did you say she doesn't want to go, Molly?'

'That's right. I didn't take Paul's word for it – not that I think he'd lie to me, but he does exaggerate in his efforts to shock. I asked Ruth; she called in a couple of times to see me with Rollo. He really is a beautiful little boy, Mim, in spite of the spoiling he gets.'

'And Ruth said she doesn't want to join Mark?' Mim persisted.

'Well, not just like that. She says she wants to join Mark but isn't a bit keen to like overseas; prefers to stay where she is, right in Australia. Maybe it's true, as Thomas always says, that Ruth is a little girl who doesn't live in Mark's world at all, doesn't understand what he does any more than Olwyn. But I can't believe it, somehow. There is a depth in Ruth that she covers up with inanities, because she's reserved.'

'How do you mean?'

'Well, she's the same age as the twins – you would never think so, would you, from her conversation and theirs?'

'Don't be taken in by the twins, Molly. Their "with-it" sophistication is mostly pseudo; they put it on and off like a wig. Ruth can't do that, she's not a student. She's married, with a child and a home to look after.'

'If Beryl hadn't been such a silly, ambitious, mother-type, Ruth might have gone to the university. I think she should have.'

'Arthur told me she never wanted to, Molly. Actually, if she had any interest she could go right now, part- or full-time. She took a good matriculation and she can afford any help she needs apart altogether from Arthur. He told me he suggested she do something while Mark was away, but she just laughed and said her house and Rollo were quite enough. It's interesting you should think it's not enough, Molly – you know her better than I do. I like her – I always have, but not exactly because I'm encouraged with confidences. Since her marriage to Mark, her conversation is as casual as Olwyn's, as far as I'm concerned.'

'Mim, dear, you don't have to prove anything. I know you like Ruth and she likes you.'

'But you love her, Molly. She's your favourite niece. She's special to you.'

Molly noticed an agitation in Mim's unexpected persistence, but ignored it. 'She's my only real niece, Mim, I suppose I do love her in some extra way.'

'So does Arthur.'

'I should hope so. She is Mark's wife,' Molly said with a hint of sarcasm, then paused and laughed. 'That, of course, is far from a realistic reason, but I guess it proves I love Ruth. I realise suddenly I have come a long way. I have at last arrived at a point of agreement with Arthur and Olwyn. Uncle Thomas will laugh – next to Harriet, Thomas can't stomach Arthur and Olwyn.'

'I have often wondered why he can't stand Arthur.'

'Because Arthur puts money ahead of everything else.'

'He doesn't, you know, Molly.'

'Put Arthur to the test and you'll see.'

'I don't think so.'

'No, darling, you wouldn't. If you did you wouldn't be you. But life has made me another Thomas: rude, ribald and realistic, at least in private.'

'Like Paul is in public.'

Molly picked up her herringbone coat and swung her long arms into the sleeves. The black and white tailored collar gave elegance to her narrow, white face and the neat, close style of her black and grey hair. Her eyebrows, clearly defined as brush strokes, met momentarily to frown above her dark eyes. 'There is always the joker in a pack of cards.'

'Do you still play poker with Thomas?'

'Once a week and once a week chess. He won't allow himself to be a bore. He beats himself at Patience the other nights.'

'Does he still beat you?'

'Of course he does. He taught me.'

'Rude, ribald and realistic, did you say?'

'Until Uncle Thomas rescued me I didn't know one card from another, let alone the moves on a chess board.'

'Thank you for rescuing me, Molly. I couldn't have made the conference without you. Layton didn't want me to go. He hates me away when he's busy.'

'He managed – men always do. But they prefer the usual slave. You do too much for your family, Mim.'

'It made all the difference you being here for the girls. They didn't want to go to Maddy's.'

'As I said – you do too much. I scarcely saw your family, Mim, except flying in and out.'

'Oh, Molly, was it as bad as that?'

'I didn't mind. I told you, Thomas came once a week for chess at midday, bless his heart.'

'All the way on the train. I hope he didn't mind.'

'I don't cook for him, Mim. The pantry in his flat is quite independent. He likes it that way. We never interfere with each other. I wanted to come and I came.'

'Will you both come for lunch next week then, Molly?'

'No, Mim, not next week. Tom and Elsa will come and Judy and the two kids. I'll be busy and so will you – it doesn't take a genius to see your family can scarcely wait to pounce with private problems.'

'Pounce! You make me sound like a mouse. But you're right, of course. Henrietta's love affair, Barbara's degree versus acting, George's career and Harriet's eccentricities have been intimated as possible topics of the week. But not tonight, Molly. I wish you were staying for dinner.'

'You won't miss two; you have all the Carlisters.'

'But you prepared it all.'

'No, dear – Maddy did. Casseroles and cakes, she brought the lot in baskets in the boot of her car. Maddy amazes me, Mim. She must be unbelievably efficient, or else she works eighteen hours a day. The children are always beautifully turned out and she left everybody standing at the airport in that outfit she tells me she ran up herself. She looked gorgeous.'

'I thought so, Molly. I always tend to think my girls look gorgeous, although it's a failing mothers are supposed to restrain. The twins, of course, will look much more elegant when they stop fluttering. It's poise, you know, that promotes Madeleine.'

'Well, all I can say is that George certainly landed on his feet the day he married Maddy. So saying, I really must move or Thomas will track us down.'

But it wasn't Uncle Thomas who was waiting when Molly preceded Mim through the door. Paul, his face painfully bored, removed his shoulder from the wall and took Molly's case.

'Chauffeur ready and waiting, ladies. Uncle Thomas has decided to depart.'

'Did he call a taxi?' Molly inquired.

'No, Thomas told Barbi, who passed the information on to me with the suggestion I have to go home to change anyway. No pity, please, I jumped at the chance to be of service. I can't resist flattery. Old Thomas is willing to take a chance on my driving.'

Thomas was waiting in the hall with his hat and coat on and his lips drawn thin in a stubborn effort to be patient. A tiny bead of sweat forced to the surface of his skin by a combination of oil-heating and aggravation had run down the deepest of the lines that furrowed his chin, and he was further annoyed because he sensed the beginning of a film on his glasses and had forgotten to take his handkerchief from his suit pocket. It was bad enough to be old and forgetful without being plagued by oil-heating. He detested central heating as an American fad, pampering the growing softness of Australian life. All you heard these days was heating – even the young ones had to have it.

Now, after two months in Layton's house, Molly would miss it, no doubt. They hadn't really needed Molly; a lot of ruddy nonsense having her in the house, but they were a spoiled lot. Mim probably wouldn't have got away at all if Molly hadn't offered. Good friends, Mim and Molly. Funny thing, considering how Molly kept well away from the rest of the mob; used her good sense in that direction, Molly did. That Harriet – selfish old galah if ever there was one, and telling him she hadn't got oil-heating either, after asking him if Molly had it yet, pretending to be tough, the old hypocrite. And spending more on gas and electricity in a week than he and Molly did in three months. Well, if Molly wanted it, she could have it and he'd pay for it, put it in before Harriet got it. As the force of still another intolerance of Harriet rose in him, it suddenly wiped out his resistance to the oil-heating.

He was a bloody old fool, he thought. He shouldn't have put his coat on so soon, should have known they'd have a talk, the two of them, Molly and Mim, once they got away from the others – should've expected it. That Harriet had forced him out sitting up like Jackie, expecting to hold court until dinner, when any fool could see the girls wanted to get Mim to themselves. Even young Paul was a wake-up to taking his leave. Unexpectedly gallant, his offer of a drive home, and his insistence. Not the sort of thing he would have expected from Arthur's boy, except that he was rebellious; good on him, not that you could always tell these days – they all dressed rebellious. Funny thing, he'd been quite a lad himself in his day, quite a lad, but he had overdressed. He'd been slick instead of scruffy in his youth, unlike Arthur, who had been the casual, just-right movie star type of his generation. In greys and a reefer-jacket, he remembered, supercilious coot Arthur, smooth as an ad for a hat and careful never to say too much. What a trial for Arthur, this boy Paul must be, especially after Mark, who was the dead spit of himself, except for his profession. Paul had gone to look for Mim and Molly – cheeky as you like. Imagine Arthur or Mark going off on an old man's behalf to look for Mim and Molly.

By cripes, he'd got them too! Thomas sniffed and took his hat off again. Despite the grumpiness of his intentions, the manners instilled by the masters at Geelong remained impeccable.

Besides, he liked Mim. Molly would not let her come out of the warm house to the verandah. It was evident Molly was satisfied now her private welcome to Mim was accomplished. The girls surrounded Mim in the doorway.

'Bye Molly. Bye Uncle Thomas, see you later, Paul.'

The door shut quickly on the oil heat and Paul stood waiting with his car door open.

'It's a bit of a long way down, watch your hat,' he advised Thomas.

'I'll get in the back,' Molly said.

'Let me,' Thomas grumbled, but did not persist.

Paul tucked the overcoat in around the old man's legs and felt resistance kindle, only to falter like it did in old Sarge. He closed the car door smartly and flipped around to the driver's side to fold himself under the wheel with the swoop of a bird returning to its nest.

His voice was laconic, almost bored as he inclined his head slightly towards Molly beside her case on the back seat.

'I think I'll go up to Burke Road to Whitehorse Road and around the Boulevard. You guide me after that, okay?'

'It's good of you, Paul,' Molly began.

'Skip it,' he said. 'I don't even pay for the petrol and I got the car with the licence.'

Thomas was startled into speaking his mind. 'I sometimes wonder if you young blokes appreciate cars.'

'The poor little rich-boy glamour you used to have is gone, if that's what you mean,' Paul said.

'Into aeroplanes I suppose, for your generation.'

'Gawd no, not for me. I'd rather ride a horse.'

Molly laughed. 'I can't imagine you riding a horse to the University, Paul.'

'I'd have too much respect for the horse.'

'Did you ever have a horse?'

'No. I begged, cajoled, barricaded, stormed and bellowed for one from the age of ten to fourteen, but Olwyn was sure I would be thrown and break my neck.'

'So you never learned to ride?'

'Sure, I learned to ride.' I've had lessons for every bloody thing, riding, swimming, tennis, dancing, skiing – the works. Even lessons on the piano. But I never owned my own horse, that's something else.'

He slowed down for a yellow light and a car passed on the inside to cross the intersection on the red. Thomas pulled in his breath.

'Bloody fool,' Paul shrugged and switched on the radio. 'Hm – Peter, Paul and Mary; like them?'

'Love them,' Molly said.

Smooth, this car, Thomas mused. Smooth. Never had a horse, this boy, never had a horse. Thomas himself was eighty years old and he'd had a horse when he was Paul's age. Then he got a ride in a train and then he wanted a car. Couldn't wait to get a car. Paul, he concluded, treated his car like dirt because he never had a horse. Arthur's boy. All that money, the boy didn't look like he wanted a horse – didn't look like he wanted a car either. Didn't look like he knew what he wanted. Thomas had a horse when he was his age, and he didn't want the horse – a horse wasn't fast enough for him when he was young, no sir, not fast enough.

A relaxed feeling settled over Thomas. He liked driving, he should have insisted that Molly learned to drive. She would have driven well. She had the same long fingers this boy had, and wide useful hands. But she probably wouldn't enjoy driving any more than the boy did. Not like he. Thomas enjoyed driving, feeling the power of the engine responding to foot and hand and brain. Man-controlled, that's what a car was, man-controlled. They were travelling faster now, steady and smooth, fifty miles an hour maybe, and scarcely feeling it, then slower again – slower, red, yellow, green lights, two streams of traffic. Peter, Paul and Mary – a hundred miles, a hundred miles.

They braked and then turned. Lower Heidelberg Road! Realising he was on the home stretch, Thomas shunted further down in the seat and a sigh like a little whistle escaped through his dentures.

'Like her?' Paul inquired.

Thomas jerked, ruffled his neck and shoulders inside his overcoat like a turkey and turned his head. 'Speaking to me, son?' he demanded tartly.

'Yeah – it struck me you liked her.'

'Like who?' He sounded withdrawn and peevish, even to himself.

Paul raised his voice, 'The M.G. – this car.'

Thomas grunted, but pleasantly. 'What. M.G. is it?' How fast does she go, boy?'

Paul grinned. 'You don't think that way any more, Uncle Thomas. If you do, you're dead in a week. I had her to a hundred on the straight once for a few miles on the Hume highway, just after I got her.'

Thomas chuckled in his throat. 'Did you say your father was afraid a horse would throw you?'

'No, I said my mother, not Arthur,' Paul snapped, and Thomas fancied the long hand tightened on the wheel and spoke hastily.

'I didn't realise it was an M.G. because of the back seat.'

'I chose this model because the advantage a car holds over a horse is the people you can get on board. Ruth had a sports model – a Porsche. Have you seen it?'

'That must be something – I didn't know Mark was interested in cars.'

'He isn't. Arthur gave Ruth the Porsche to run herself around in.'

'You don't say. A Porsche, eh, must be fast.'

'Too fast for Ruth, that's for sure. She'd be safer in a Mini. Some types take it out on Porsches.'

Molly was shocked. 'Good heavens, does Ruth know that, Paul?'

'I dunno, I don't suppose Mark or Arthur knew to tell her. It's no use me opening my trap – nobody takes any notice of me.'

Molly persisted. 'I'm sure Ruth would take notice of you, Paul. Please tell her – tell her tonight at dinner.'

'Okay,' he said. 'I'll tell Barbi to tell Mim to tell Arthur. That'll do it. I'd hate to see it go, though, it's a beaut job, that Porsche.'

'Seems to me,' Thomas announced, making an effort not to mention Arthur's name, 'Seems to me, boy, it would have been better to give Ruth this and you the Porsche.'

'I can drive the Porsche if I want to – any time, according to Ruth. She can always use Mark's car while he's abroad anyway. Didn't you know little brothers are pampered with anything they desire? I only have to ask.'

'But you don't ask, obviously,' Molly said.

'Sure, I ask. I'm always asking. I'm a bloody parasite, but not for the Porsche, that's all. I haven't descended low enough yet to ask for the Porsche.' He slowed again for another turn and appeared to have a second thought. 'I could, though, it's an idea! Up this road, isn't it?'

'Yes,' Molly said briefly.

Paul turned his head and yelled at Uncle Thomas, 'Would you like a ride in the Porsche?'

'Paul!' Molly exclaimed. 'He's an old man!'

'Sure,' Paul countered. 'That's why he'd like a ride in the Porsche. Uncle Thomas, would you like a ride in the Porsche?'

'Bit fast for an old boy like me, isn't it?' Thomas beamed.

'I'll fix it with Ruth. I'll come and get you one day, okay? Ruth can have an hour with Molly – they admire each other, did you know? Here you are, home in one piece.'

'Thanks a lot. Coming in, boy?'

'Gawd no – I gotta put on my best red shirt for the welcome home dinner. Barbi bought a new dress on tick, on the chance her mother will like it. It's a midi gown in deep green velvet, with lace and pearl buttons. We'll be quite a pair – like Christmas candles.'

Neither Molly nor Thomas rose to the bait as Paul helped them out of the car. Something in the persistence of his mocking insolence frightened Molly and Thomas – elated with the drive – concentrated as the elderly must on the disembarkation process.

Paul literally ran Molly's suitcase to her front verandah and returned, grinning. 'Don't thank me, Molly, it has been a pleasure - although I'm sure none of us has any idea why. Now I'll drive straight home to the Carlister Mansion and let my principles down as far as slicking back my hair. Even I am too weak to let Arthur down in front of the Shormans. Farewell.'

He was under the wheel and away almost before they could wave, the red tail light and the red flicker flashing, the heat switched off and the radio on again, blaring the dance beat of *Zorba the Greek*.

Still bemused and smiling, Thomas remarked to the empty street, 'Fancy a bastard like Arthur producing that boy.'

'I wouldn't repeat that in front of Paul, Thomas.'

'No, Molly, you're right. But what do you make of the boy, Molly? What does Mim think of him?'

'Mim likes him; she likes Arthur too, don't forget.'

'No accounting for tastes,' the old man murmured as they started up the drive.

CHAPTER THREE

On Saturday morning Mim Shorman slept. At lunch time, Layton came out of his study, discovered her still asleep and having made no previous arrangements, decided to ask George, who was always obliging, to join him in a game of golf. The twins, suddenly hovering in the hall, demanded to know if Mim would be getting up soon and were reprimanded sharply.

'Let your mother alone,' Layton snapped. 'Haven't you got anything to do with your time? Let your mother sleep.'

So Barbi phoned Paul that she had changed her mind about going to the football and Henrietta persuaded Greg to take her to a live matinee.

'That was your father on the phone,' George explained to Maddy. 'He suggested a game at his Club. I couldn't very well refuse. He'll pick me up in an hour.'

'Did he say if the girls were out?'

'No, he didn't, just that your mother is still asleep and will probably sleep all day.'

'Poor Mim must be tired out. The girls won't wake her. They'll take themselves off somewhere.'

'You'd better go over, then. You might get a chance to talk to Mim. You won't have a hope with your Aunt Harriet haunting the place tomorrow.'

'Do you think I should, George?'

'Yes, I do, darling. You needn't be long. Send the boys in next door, then Mim can rest while you talk to her. Actually, it seems like a good idea.'

'I'm not sure, George, but I'll get your lunch on anyway.'

'Anything'll do, anything at all – even a T.V. dinner,' George said magnanimously. 'I'm not fussy.'

But Maddy was nervous. 'If Dad's going out, it means he doesn't want Mim disturbed.'

'We needn't tell him,' George said.

'You won't say anything to him, George, about the house, I mean?'

'God no. Why should I? You're dead right about that, Maddy. He won't help. That's why I'm counting on you with your mother, darling.'

'I still can't quite see why you can't ask Uncle Arthur yourself. You could have asked him last night. Why should Mim have to?'

'I don't know why exactly, darling. I've told you that. I'll speak to Arthur later. I know that if he thinks Mim approves, we're set. I've told you it's our best chance, in that it's our only chance.'

'I'm not sure, George. I don't feel sure about it, not even about wanting the house.'

His face grew remote, not from exasperation but from hurt. 'I've explained, Maddy. Do I have to explain all over again? Do I have to spell it out for you?'

'No, George.'

'You know it's for your sake and the children's as well as mine.'

'Yes, dear,' she said. 'I'll go.'

When Mim woke up at half past three, Maddy was standing beside her bed with a cup of coffee and a plate of the little iced cakes.

'Why, Maddy, how nice,' she said. 'Where's the family?'

'All out, darling, except for Mimi and me. And Mimi is delighted to have the doll's house all to herself. Sit up and have your coffee. I – well, I have to talk to you.'

'You're very serious, in spite of your gay little cakes. Molly told me you made them and the casseroles last night. I hadn't the chance to thank you. By dinner time I was absolutely hazy. It suddenly hit me. I can scarcely remember the rest of the evening. Where's George?'

'Dad took him to play golf – phoned up out of the blue and asked him at lunch time.'

Mim wriggled into comfort and sipped her coffee. 'It's nice to be spoiled,' she murmured, but Maddy noticed the rings under her eyes and felt guilty.

'You're still tired,' she said. 'I shouldn't have come.'

'You're tired yourself,' Mim replied. 'So that makes two of us. What's on your mind, darling?'

'George wants to move to a house in Parkville.'

'Why on earth?'

'Oh, it's terribly complicated, Mim. Dr Flair-Jones, who's going to put George's name up for a professorship next year is selling his house in Parkville and he's offered George first chance for it.'

'But Maddy, you are already buying the house you are in, and you've just added two more rooms you haven't finished paying for.'

'But Parkville, Mim – you can't miss a chance to move to Parkville. University people are all trying to get there.'

'Even so, darling, you have to have the money. Do you want to sell the house you're in?'

'We'd have to – for cash.'

'Would you get enough?'

'No.'

'Then how can George consider it, Maddy?'

'He'd have to get a loan – he knows that.'

'Not from your father again, Maddy.'

'No, Mim, we wouldn't ask Dad. George thought Arthur Carlister. Would you ask him for us, Mim? I don't really know him well enough and he's such an old friend of yours. And it's not as if George is his nephew, really – only Auntie Olwyn's.'

'Then George should ask Olwyn.'

'That would be quite useless, and George knows it.'

'Maddy, have you thought about living in Parkville with the children? What kind of house is it?'

Maddy winced a little. 'Two-storied with lace balconies. The rooms are quite big, really. We'd have to redecorate, of course, and put in a new kitchen and bathroom.'

'Why is Doctor Flair-Jones leaving the house?'

'He's old, Mim, he must be sixty. His wife has arthritis and can't manage the stairs. They are going into one of those Georgian ground-level villas.'

'I had no idea you were interested in doing up a bit of Victoriana, Maddy. You have everything modern that opens and shuts in your house.'

'It's important for George's work, Mim. I tell you it's for George. He has a thing about it.'

'You and two little boys and a little girl will have to live in it.' Mim's voice was very tired, almost distant, and broke something in Maddy so that her own voice grew shrill in spite of her intention.

'It's not for ever and ever. People have to move, you know. It isn't much to ask you to do.'

Her mother recognised the tension that would override her judgement and immediately back-pedalled. 'I'll think about it, Maddy. I'm too tired today to promise more. Give me a week to think about it.'

At the back of her mind Maddy could hear George saying, 'Good old Mim,' and relaxed.

'You haven't told me a thing about Elie yet,' she said.

'She's just the same. She was sweet.'

'But why didn't she come home with you?'

'She had her reasons. She'll tell you herself when she writes.'

'Whenever that will be, as George always says.' Maddy's voice held a quiver of satisfaction. What went on within the walls of her own house always seemed to her a natural part of the affairs of her mother, except for the intimacies of her life with George, which she connected with loyalty. Mim was Maddy's confidant. There had been a time before her engagement to George when it seemed a necessity to discuss the simplicities and complications of life with Eliane. But after the advent of George, discussion with Eliane had proved unsatisfying since Eliane refrained from asking the expected questions and yet appeared to demand answers to queries hinted at, but never spoken. There was an unexpected cynicism in Elie that could not accept falling in love followed naturally by marriage as normal, beyond qualification. Mim had explained to Eliane that life for most girls followed a similar smooth succession of foreseen events such as love, an engagement party with a diamond ring and then a whirl of home preparation, shopping, followed by a church wedding. Mim had called it the nesting instinct, which was stronger in some women than in others, so Maddy had known at the time that Mim was sanctioning her marriage to George even after presenting good reasons for the long engagement George was against. Mim had always considered various basic conditions of life as more important than her own opinions. She had wanted Maddy to finish her studies at the Conservatorium of Music, but left the decision to Maddy herself, who had chosen immediate marriage to George.

Eliane had come round to Mim's way of thought, all the way supporting Maddy as chief bridesmaid, but without emotion beyond acceptance of Maddy's desire for marriage with George. She had understood only that the vital element of Maddy's life was being in love with George. The wedding itself and the setting up of the new house was to Eliane like choosing the buttons to fasten a coat, merely a practical trimming. Without saying a word, Eliane assumed Maddy had to have George, which was true, yet to Maddy almost an obscene suggestion, although she could not understand why marriage and George went together in Maddy's mind like marriage and a home and children, which was something only her mother understood. It was this Maddy wanted and this Maddy had.

George, of course, was a main part of it, but not by any means all, any more than her father seemed to be in the family set-up. You loved your husband and your children and you put everything you had and could get into making the best possible home for them. Maddy talked over every problem with Mim because from the very beginning, Mim had understood that when you take on a husband and family, time is no longer your personal possession. Elie had seemed to think you had to love a man to a point that demanded the annihilation of everything else before you gave up your time for him.

Apparently she was unable to understand love and marriage with all the trimmings as a way of life substitute for personal time. It was a paradox in Eliane that she should think as she did and still adore everything about Mim. But then there were many paradoxical complexes in Elie. Time, for example, which she considered so particularly her own but donated with unselfish abandon to any family member who had the slightest need.

Quite suddenly, Maddy realised that it was Eliane who had complete possession of her mother's mind. She felt her sister's presence so strongly she knew immediately why thoughts of Eliane had blacked out herself and George. Resentment flared in her. Mim was holding something back and she felt threatened by the same uneasiness that dominated, yet remained unstated in the last letter from London.

From the bed Mim sighed into the charged atmosphere. 'You said yesterday, Maddy, that you thought Michael will have to have his tonsils out. I think perhaps you had better take him to a specialist as soon as you can, next week perhaps. There's a lot of controversy about the removal of tonsils and you need good advice.'

'Yes, I know,' Maddy said, feeling defeated, beaten back to home ground without hope of counter-attack as she added, 'I'll go look at Mimi.'

'Bring her back,' Mim said. 'I'd love to see her, now I'm awake.'

Both Henrietta and Barbara sidestepped dinner invitations and within half an hour of each other, sent bemused escorts to occupy three hours' time with a meal before returning to Kew for the evening date. Greg complained, 'Well, I must say, Henny, you don't make it with sense. Your mother's probably asleep anyway and mine's out.'

He was only partly compensated by Henrietta's pacification technique of one long, lingering kiss in broad daylight. Barbara offered no more than a cheek or a peck during daylight hours, which scarcely bothered Paul on any occasion, let alone after football with Sims in tow. Admittedly, Paul would have preferred Barbi's company for dinner in some South Yarra bistro since her vivaciousness always proved an antidote that wiped out the memory of the human race en masse, as illustrated with example by Sims at the game.

As he drove towards Barker's Road, Paul was wondering morosely how the hell Sims always found them in such a mob. He had specifically told Sims he wouldn't be taking Barbi to the footy, since she had turned him down on account of the return of her mother. It wasn't his fault she had changed her mind. Yet they hadn't been in the grounds ten minutes before Sims discovered and confronted them with his mournful Spanish phase fully turned on like a pickup without a switch. Sims was too diabolically clever about people's motives and his words had begun to hypnotise Paul into an acceptance of them as fact, even though Sims himself regarded the tirades as no more than an opened safety valve. Barbi always laughed, apparently in complete sympathy with Sims' method of letting off steam.

'He has to be mad sometimes,' she told Paul, and when he demanded why always at the football – he's okay everywhere else – Barbi dismissed that too. 'Because the footy's mad. What better place?'

Damn Sims! Why did he have to think about Sims all the time? What's the matter with him? Why didn't he get ahead with Barbi? What had gummed that up? Sims? Yes, Sims, for all his big talk and big brain looking at Barbi like a bull calf. Is that how Paul looked at her? He took her out but that's as far as he ever got. Why doesn't Sims make a pass at her then? He might make out better than Paul did. She laughed with him and at him all the time. Like this afternoon, when he said, 'Behold mankind swirling round and round in the sink, faster and faster with no idea the plug's been knocked out.' What was so bloody funny about that? But Barbi laughed, laughed at funny old Sims saying something else clever that she understood perfectly as his way of blowing off steam. So he blew and she laughed and Paul remembered every bloody word like the doomsday book.

Well, he'd go home. The dinner would be better than the Bistro and Arthur and Olwyn wouldn't talk about Sims or Barbi or anything else that might possibly remind them that his slovenly appearance was connected with the present day deterioration of university students. Perhaps Ruth might be in Toorak for a meal. She would agreeably divide the concentration, not that Ruth said much. She occupied her own world with a certain finesse that included her in-laws without intrusion either way. He felt himself included without a specialised persuasion to overlook his faults if she noticed them. Even when she didn't speak at the dinner table, which was the only place he saw her, her presence took the pressure off him. Sometimes he wished he knew her better, but when his mind turned in this direction, some sort of pity connected with Mark swung him back to an appreciation of the status quo. They were a handsome couple, Ruth and Mark, and he knew Arthur and Olwyn were proud of them. Arthur had a way of handling Ruth like a piece of fine porcelain and of course Olwyn seemed to consider Ruth had produced young Rollo especially to put her into the exclusive society of well-turned-out grandmothers. He supposed he was also grateful to Ruth, one way and another. But gratitude seemed a mean term for a silky blonde girl of perfect proportions like Ruth, even if she was his sister-in-law whom he didn't happen to know very well.

The Shorman twins were stripped to similar housecoats in paisley shades of orange.

'Maddy came over and woke Mim up and tired her out. That's what it amounts to. What else?' Henny flung at Barbi from a draped position barely inside the kitchen door – any further incursion on to the linoleum might involve her slender, freshly pearled fingernails in an engagement with an omelette, which Barbi was preparing for the evening meal.

'I'll take a tray in anyway,' Barbi said. 'But we won't have time for a decent talk now.'

'What gets me is the cool of our Maddy – gets Pops out with George and then comes right over. Pops only asked George for golf to let Mim sleep it off. And why didn't George go to the footy as usual, may I ask?'

Barbi put two plates on the table and a third on the tray. 'Look, Henny, I don't know what you're dramatising about. It'd be more useful if you got out the butter.'

'My nails, darling!' Henny wailed. 'Still tacky. It's this new stuff, takes ages to dry.'

'It's always something. Not that I mind making an omelette, but I'm going out too and you've had the bathroom first even though it won't be Greg but Paul who's first on the doorbell.'

'You needn't get snaky. You know I had to wash my hair. Greg's fussy, but really fussy about my hair. He goes for elegance in a big way. And you must admit he's worth the effort. His new pale blue dinner jacket is a perfect foil.'

'Crumbs,' Barbi sniffed. 'Who wants to go out with a perfect foil?'

Henny straightened and threw back her head with regal disdain, then she slumped again. 'God, you're awful when you're upset.' She beamed. 'No cool at all. You don't need to fuss about the tray. Mim's probably dreaming away the dinner hour.'

'I came back especially,' Barbi muttered. 'I'm worried about Elie. Mim has hardly mentioned Elie.'

'She's hardly mentioned anything, except perhaps to Maddy. Why else did Maddy come over? What happened to Pops, by the way?'

'Gone to Maddy's. He and George came in while you were under the shower and George said, 'Barbi's home, you might as well come and have a meal with us, sir!' Sir, mind you! Pops took one look at the kitchen, another at Mim and went. He said he'd be back by nine. I'm taking this tray in now. Are you coming?'

When Mim opened her eyes, the twins hovered like flowers.

'You are darlings,' she murmured and sat up to balance the tray. 'Bring your plates in and tell me where you're going tonight. I'll have to catch up with both of you. I take it the ground's the same as when I left?'

Henny threw her arms wide and let Barbi go for the omelettes. 'Romance is divine,' she told her mother. 'And the next step looms. I'm going to change my religion. Greg is getting anxious for an answer.'

Mim laughed. 'Take your time,' she said easily.

Henny grew serious. 'It's true, but I'll wait to tell you. I've scarcely time to get dressed for tonight as it is. Barbi and I want to know about Elie.'

'Yes, we do,' Barbi said, settling like an elf cross-legged on the floor to balance her plate. 'You haven't told us why Elie didn't come home.'

'Next week, when I'm not so tired, I'll tell you where Elie and I went in London. We stayed at the old Cumberland at Hyde Park Corner for old time's sake. It was fun.'

'But why didn't Elie come home with you?' Henny was eating her snack outlined with double grace in front of the full-length mirror.

'At the moment, Elie prefers Europe. I don't blame her. I prefer it myself at this time of year. Who wouldn't? Come back and show yourselves before you go. And get home at a reasonable hour. I'm all mixed up. I may have to indulge in a midnight breakfast.' She yawned as openly as a child. 'Off you go now, and make yourselves pretty.'

Later that evening, Layton was not so easily put off the subject of Eliane.

'I didn't wish to say so yesterday, in front of the family,' he announced in the privacy of the bedroom. 'Nevertheless, I'm more than provoked that Eliane did not return with you as I was led to expect. To a certain extent, Linda, it was my reason for arranging that you attend the conference.'

'I was invited to be part of the delegation, Layton.'

'Certainly, and with my approval. However, I was led to believe you would convince Eliane it was time for her to take advantage of her opportunities here. I made a point of speaking to the Dean of the Faculty on her behalf. Just at present it is most inconvenient and not politic that I am now forced to make an explanation to him.'

'I'm sure it was not Elie's intention to put you in an awkward position. She hadn't asked you to speak for her, had she?'

'No, she had not. Nor did I write to her, naturally enough, when you were going to see her.'

'It might have been wiser to write to her before you spoke to the Dean, don't you think?'

'It did not cross my mind that you would not persuade her to return with you. As I understand it, you broke your journey back to spend the week in London for that purpose.'

'My purpose was to see Eliane. I hadn't seen her for two years, dear. We were longing to see each other.'

'Exactly, and you said you were sure she would come home with you. Why didn't she?'

'At the last minute, she changed her mind.'

'So you said in your telegram. You did not say why.'

'She didn't want to come home, Layton. She's an adult and she didn't want to. She'll write with her future plans as soon as she knows them herself.'

'Really, Linda, you amaze me. What makes you think I'm to be satisfied with that explanation? What plans do you refer to?'

'Eliane's plans, dear. Eliane's plans, which are not mine but her own to make and break as she sees fit.'

'What utter nonsense! She is a member of this family and I am her father.'

'She is nearly as old as Maddy and you haven't expected Maddy to consult you for years.'

'The situation is in no way the same. Maddy is married.'

'You are out of touch with women's liberation, dear. There will be no more Aunt Harriets in the world of the future. Professional women no longer consult their fathers and brothers and nephews unless it suits them.'

'Are you telling me Eliane has joined this women's lib thing?'

Mim laughed. 'Don't look so horrified, dear. All modern girls are part of women's lib, even if they don't know it. It's a movement that started with the suffragettes and then got side-tracked by two world wars and affluence. The present variety is noisier, that's all. More vocal because of the power of the Pill.'

She settled down comfortably into her bed and switched off the electric blanket with a quick snap. 'Turn off the main light, will you, dear? I'm so tired. I feel as if I could sleep forever.'

'No doubt you'll wake up about four A.M. and disturb the whole household getting yourself a meal,' he grumbled.

'Well, you got me up to get you one after your last trip,' she murmured.

He sat on the edge of his own bed and informed her with forced resignation, 'I had hoped to tell you some news of particular importance to you.'

'Hm, I'm still awake.'

'It may be necessary for us to influence Aunt Harriet. If I can raise a good donation towards the new wing at the hospital, I'm in line for the birthday honours.'

'How nice for you, Layton.'

'What did you say?'

'I said how nice for you – and for Harriet, of course. Does she know?'

'What?'

'Does Harriet know?'

'Linda! Of course Harriet doesn't know, nor will she know. The matter must not be mentioned, not under any circumstances.'

'Very well, Layton. I won't say anything.'

'I simply wished you to know because of the considerable importance such an honour will bring to the family, and to you in particular.'

'Thank you, dear,' she sighed and he knew that in spite of herself she had fallen asleep.

CHAPTER FOUR

Driving in to the university on Monday morning, Layton Shorman noted that even after her weekend of rest, his wife was still too tired to offer more than token concentration to his deliberations, which were aimed, of course, at phasing her in again after absence. Sunday conversation had been impossible with Maddy and her entourage, Harriet milling around and the twins edgy, not to mention the incessant jangling of the telephone. He had found the midday roast dinner particularly trying and afterwards had insisted that Mim rest. Then he had taken George to the Club again, a move to which the girls had agreed but over which Harriet had taken umbrage. She had demanded he take her home immediately, since she had expressly come to 'talk to Linda about my illness'. Behind Aunt Harriet's head, Henrietta had been extraordinarily insolent with her hands, before she bounced out of the room leaving Maddy and Barbi to the dishes.

Layton had been explaining his position as they understood it in this decade. As a successful man in his chosen profession, he had up to now seen himself retiring in a following decade, within the aura of his present success. However, the ground of the last decade had shifted constantly and recently his dignity had been offended when he had been forced to hop about professionally. He was finding it necessary to maintain fixed attitudes against suspected change, although with his intellectual capacity he had always prided himself on maintaining an open mind that increased in size with increased knowledge.

'You know I still think the human brain is all important,' he said. 'With emotion and any form of sentimentality purely secondary functions. I have always felt the university is an educational institution to absorb the knowledge required for professional community standing. No other institution in our society has similar importance. It is right that the university take the cream of society distilled from the milk, the best brains, that is, and my experience has shown the cream to be a product of the best families.'

'Oh, Layton,' Mim interjected – but, he noticed, with little enthusiasm for argument. Still, he granted her point.

'Well, I know there are exceptions,' he conceded. 'But for us there is a necessity to take a stand somewhere. The university as presently constituted is a better hill to stand on than any other. It will see us through, dear.'

'But I doubt if it will see out the family,' Mim suggested.

'That hardly matters since we have girls.'

Unexpectedly, Mim sat up within the confines of her seat belt and he felt her bristle in a direction he could only collate with the detested development of women's liberation. He commented quickly, 'Girls marry, and considering the number of boys that haunt our dinner table there is no doubt ours will. You do your job well there, dear.' He was driving, of course, so did not remove his eyes from the road, but sensed her settling again with small, nervous movements of her limbs. He admitted to himself a sudden apprehension, followed by the hope that after he was dropped off at the Faculty she would get the car to the garage without mishap. He really should have had the brakes overhauled, but he hadn't got around to it. Mim's answer, however, surprised him with an anecdote that knocked his planned complacency.

'You remember that party for Professor Brooke we went to before I left? Becky Forman staggered me by saying she was horrified that Mary was graduating without a suitor in sight, let alone a decent catch.'

'So?' he queried lightly. Privately, compared to her husband, he found Becky Forman light but amusing.

'So that's why I didn't invite the Formans to our last cocktail party.'

He was astounded. Lucky for Linda he was 'at the wheel', as he put it, and had to contain his irritation until he was safely turned into Wellington Parade. Otherwise, his temper would have taken control. As it was, he waited a good five minutes before remarking with contemplated sarcasm, 'If you find your personal opinions and the politics of university life incompatible, Linda, you would be well advised to smother your opinions from time to time. Naturally, I assumed Forman and his wife had a previous engagement the night of that party. I had no idea you had given him a reason to be uncooperative.'

'Have you ever found him cooperative, Layton?' she inquired mildly. 'He's hardly your type and I've heard you call him an ambitious upstart.'

'Which is all the more reason for tact. I have always left the social side of our life to your discretion. I hardly expected you to let me down at this stage, particularly for some ridiculous female fancy of no importance.'

'But I am female, Layton, so are my daughters and so is Becky Forman and her daughter.'

He waited until he had pulled the car up and turned off the ignition. 'I would have thought Becky Forman would warrant the sympathy you so readily accord to most women with difficult husbands and offspring.'

She smiled. 'In this case my sympathy rests with the daughter.'

He decided to make a joke of it. 'Your thought patterns never cease to amaze me, dear. However, as Henrietta says, have it your way. Will you be able to pick me up tonight, round about five?'

'I doubt it, Layton.'

'Surely your battery will be recharged when you take this in. Stupid business that was. Naturally I assumed you'd tell Molly or Maddy even if you didn't want the twins taking your car out.'

'I had no objections whatsoever to the twins driving my car. They both drive very well. You objected, dear – don't you remember? They got touchy and said they had all the lifts they needed anyway.'

He recalled, as he got out of the car, that Henrietta had added that Mim's car was a bloody disgrace and had to be driven by charisma, after which remark he had told her to keep her hands off it then and promised to rev it up himself every day or so. Molly should have reminded him or Maddy. He wasn't a fuss about cars like Arthur Carlister and George. Cars were a tool for his use, and no more.

'Oh well,' he said, letting his wife slide into the driver's side. 'Do your best, dear.'

'I'll phone,' she said and drove off. He had refrained from reminding her to phone Harriet back in order to keep the old girl sweet.

His secretary waiting for his arrival in his outer office informed him there would be a meeting of the Steering Committee at five o'clock.

'I'll have to phone my wife,' he said.

'I'll get her on the line right away, Doctor Shorman.'

He regarded the woman with distaste. He preferred a secretary to be young and pretty or old and devoted. This one, like the last two from the pool, was in her thirties and married. She had a husband, a boy and a girl in primary school, and a new home in a housing estate at Bulleen. It annoyed him that her sort swarmed in and out of the university buildings like migratory birds, and often turned up at official social gatherings as the spouse of a staff member. You never knew where you stood with them, in or out of working hours, since they were educated beyond secretarial duties, past the point of easy correction.

'Mrs Shorman is not at home,' he was forced to say. 'If she phones, be sure to put her through. I wish to speak to her personally.'

'Would you like me to remind you to call her about the meeting, if she doesn't phone, Doctor Shorman?' Impersonally efficient, she beamed the question at him above the Chinese neckline that stiffened the simple elegance of her dark green pants suit. He felt he could not say yes without loss of face or no with decency. So he walked towards the sanctuary of his own office, where politeness forbade her to follow without his invitation.

'Thank you,' he said, with his hand on the doorknob. 'I'll remember.'

On his desk his appointment book was open and his correspondence tray arranged for his convenience. When this secretary departed because his work load increased, or one of her children went down with the after effects of measles, he would miss her.

He wrote 'Linda' on the white face of his scratch pad. After Mim phoned, he would crumple the sheet and put it in his pocket.

Mim's car was not ready at the local garage. 'Sorry, Missus Shorman, two o'clock at the earliest. Beaut to see you back,' so she shopped for as much food as she could carry and then walked home past the facades of familiar houses with deadened winter trees. The wind from a grey sky chilled her face but did not increase the speed of her feet. At her own gate, she gathered the post from the box to scan it with eagerness and regret before entering the house with a relief that shrugged off a shiver.

Layton liked his mail put on his desk, so after sorting it there, she left two letters, probably invitations for the girls, on the hall tray and went straight to the kitchen to drop her basket, light the gas under the kettle and, still wearing her coat, go out the back door to set up a first load in the washing machine in the laundry.

Back in the kitchen, unloading the groceries, she noted that the food shelves were neat, thanks to Molly, but deplenished. She would have to make a list. Turning to make herself coffee, the tension of pressure overtook her, although she had resolutely pushed it back walking home.

Another list – her list was too long as it was, she thought. And ineffectual, banal, stupid, unworthy of her time. Did nobody have ten minutes to take heels to the shoemaker while she was away, or think of the dry cleaners? Why should she have to pick up the seedlings and the two registered letters from the post office, pay an instalment on Henrietta's record album and the final lay-by payment on the white turtleneck Barbara wanted to wear to the rehearsal tonight? Why was Barbi absolutely certain a beautiful fresh white wool at her throat would accentuate the throw of her voice by some coziness against her chin? Did she feel she must be a kind of polar bear to charm the director? Would it never be any use to explain to her that dramatic gesture read in a book on the Method would have less effect than re-reading the part a hundred times until she felt she was in the character. Oh, she knew *she* was not a future actress in this day and age, and therefore mustn't tell Barbi that understatement had its own importance, particularly when everyone else was living on emotional overstress. She was not supposed to know, though it often seemed to her she was acting the role constantly herself. Surely she was the understatement as opposed to the Method.

Then, over coffee, she laughed at herself for dramatising. Poor old Barbi! Henrietta had out-acted her at every step of the growing-up process. Perhaps it wasn't so strange that she should try to preserve her individuality by this medium; character development was so complex in the inexperienced. The twins were young, and needed help; very young in a difficult world and she loved them.

Suddenly the warmth of the house settled over Mim like the healing of a great sun and her head slipped down to rest on her hands, elbowed on the kitchen table. Was it only two weeks ago she told the story of the three bears to the refugee children? Was the moment no more than two weeks past when she saw the face of the child that haunted her still, even beyond the happiness of times spent with Eliane? Maybe the child was Elie, or Elie the child!

Her mind murmured as she rested. *The eyes of those children, first on my sketchbook, and then on me – enormous liquid wells of hope. Shades of brown getting darker inwards to that one distant, golden spot. The problem was to get inside those layers and layers of mirrors to light up that shiny gold. I looked at them and they looked at me while the teacher explained in Arabic I would tell them a story in English and all the gold was remote until I told her to say I would tell them The Three Bears, and they knew it! They knew it, so I could smile at them, say – 'there were three bears; Father Bear...' and pause and stare back with them into the little house in the woods with awe for its potential in my face, and when I said Mother Bear and then paused again, there was silence so deep the trees around the little compound breathed on the gold spots down in their eyes. Until I said Baby Bear and paused for the third time and the children themselves sighed the name after me. As for Goldilocks, by the time she came into the picture, we were all telling the story together in Arabic and English, slowly, with tremendous agreed pauses for effect but not one of us moving a finger, lest we break the spell of absorption that would take us away from the beautiful place, back to the reality of where we were – ten minutes, then 'Who's been eating my porridge?' but all the time we knew they were nice bears; big, furry, gentle bears like the great bulk of our loving mothers when we were tiny babies, like the teddy-bears and rag-dolls we hugged ourselves to sleep with in substitution, all dangers were our dangers but we knew we would escape them, 'and Goldilocks ran and ran and ran all the way home.' Funny, I can't remember the school bell rang then, but all the children gathered round me and took me in a great baffle of moving arms and legs and shining eyes and high voices, to another shed where I was to be given coffee – where did they go then? But I don't remember the school bell.*

Mim stirred, shifted on her chair so that one arm slipped the support of her head to thump it forward. 'What school bell?' she wondered, straightening up in her chair. Coffee dripped from her upset cup to a brown puddle spreading across the floor. As she stood up, she heard the bell again and, startled, recognised its source.

'Heavens, it's the telephone. I must have fallen asleep. Good thing I didn't do that driving to the garage. Where's that towel? I'm sure there was a towel here. If it's Harriet I just can't call in or do another errand. I just can't, there just isn't time. Don't answer, let it ring. But it might not be Harriet, she already phoned once before we left this morning and I said I'd ring her back. Anyway, if it is, I must be charitable; she has never held a child of her own under her breast nor had the sense to pick up a good substitute, thousands of substitutes for the taking – millions, all the eyes in those faces. The phone has stopped ringing, but if it is Harriet she will ring again immediately. I better get as far as I can with the dinner because of the meeting this afternoon starting at three; it's bound to go until five and then the traffic will be fierce. I can't walk out earlier. Mary said they didn't have a quorum at the last meeting and we've got to get the resolution through for Save the Children. I have to go, family notwithstanding.

'If I get the car at two I'll have time to get the registered letters and the shoes. Then I'll try to get that sweater for Barbara. I suppose it will give her confidence. But her confidence is too built-up as it is. What a thought – she's a darling. It's crazy, but she wants so much to be an actress though that's not the point, which is that it's Barbara's life. All I can do really is get her the pullover and forget all the pullovers and slacks in the drawer. I seem so tired and irritable, perhaps I will make up the extra sleep I need tonight.'

She was already in the laundry when the phone rang again and she had to run to answer it. 'Hello; yes, darling, did you ring a little while ago? I was in the laundry getting some washing done - uh-huh, I remembered, it's on my list. Don't worry about it, yes I think the black tights will be fine – uh-huh, no I can't meet you this afternoon, no it's the annual meeting of the Auxiliary, uh-huh, no I couldn't, dear, we have to have a quorum and I promised. Could I what? No, dear, not without going to the bank - uh-huh, sure the black ones will be fine with the new pullover, well, dear, it's hardly worth missing the lecture just to come home to wash your hair. I know Paul's always a willing chauffeur, but it's hardly fair is it? Oh,

I see – uh-huh, no I don't suppose one more makes much difference for dinner – five-thirty? No, darling, I can't do that – your father won't be home until six at the earliest, particularly if I have to pick him up, because I put his car in to have the brakes checked. Yes, I know, but he likes to sit down to a proper meal. Well I don't know yet, I was going for the messages first and then go to the meeting – but, Barbara, your father can't stand spaghetti and besides, it's not enough nourishment for you and Paul – if that's all you want, you could get a bite at the cafeteria. Oh, I see, what do you do with your allowance, dear? I see, uh-huh, well I really must go – uh-huh, I'll see what I can do, dear – if I don't go now, I haven't a hope – No, I don't like you borrowing from Paul or anybody else – what about Henrietta? Oh, I see – uh-huh; darling, I really must go – uh-huh; see you then, when I get home from the meeting – uh-huh, it's nice to be home too, darling – Bye.'

Mim got back to the kitchen to be greeted by Maddy coming in the door with Mimi in her arms. 'I didn't hear the station wagon,' Mim said.

'I've taken it into the garage and walked up,' Maddy said. 'The door on the driver's side doesn't shut properly and George is such a fuss. He absolutely insisted I take it in – it will take about an hour and a half. I've got the shopping to do and Mimi is impossible this morning. Can I leave her with you? I'll bring something back with me for lunch. I'll make some coffee before I go. Who was on the phone?'

Mim laughed. 'Just Barbi. The kettle is on the boil. I made some coffee for myself and spilled it on the floor.' She took Mimi in her arms to be smothered in squiggles and kisses and put her down again with the pretty little mouth protesting. 'Mimi wants a pway in doll's house; don't wanna do shopping.'

'She's in one of her moods.' Maddy grimaced. 'Showing off like a little tyrant. She's very difficult and so determined.'

'Go and play in the doll's house, darling,' Mim said, and when the little feet scuttled off, 'You talk too much in front of her, Maddy.'

'You're still tired, Mim. You're white as a sheet.' It was Maddy's way of changing the subject. 'I had to walk up with the groceries,' Mim told her. 'Sometimes I think people are the servants of cars instead of the other way round. Both of our cars are at the garage. I have to get mine at two o'clock, so I'll have to leave here at a quarter to. I can't leave it any later, dear. I've got too much to do.'

'It's only your first day home really, not counting the weekend with everybody milling around. I didn't think you'd have all that to do today. It's not fair – both cars in the garage! Why?'

'My battery was flat and I dropped the Ford to have the brakes look at after I drove your father in this morning.'

'Look, Dad drove George to golf in the Ford yesterday; didn't he know? George would have had a fit! I had no idea or I wouldn't have come, or I would have come and not put ours in until tomorrow and taken you shopping. Why didn't Dad say yesterday?'

Mim calmed her. 'We'll have two out of three cars back by two, Maddy, with a bit of luck and I'll manage. These things happen. Make your coffee and off you go. Mimi can play around with me. I'm just washing.'

'Washing – you ought to send out the heavy stuff to the laundry.'

'With a brand new washing machine?'

'Well, Molly did, and in the most matter of fact manner presented Dad with the bill, which he paid like a lamb. After all, you didn't want the new one, did you?'

'It was a birthday present, darling, you know that. Your father surprised me with it.'

'After the twins had been on to him. Henny, I'll bet! Anyway, don't do too much. I'll go now, I guess. I won't be long. There's the phone again, will I take it?'

'If it's Harriet don't put her off, Maddy. I'll have to talk to her sooner or later. She phoned at breakfast time.'

'She would. There's no doubt about her. She had all day yesterday, which she wasted moaning around like a prima donna with a lolly stuck in her throat,' Maddy mumbled going down the hall.

'Hello – no it's her daughter Maddy Amber here. Yes, yes she is. Just a moment please, I'll get her. No, it's quite all right – yes, I know, but she's been home since Friday; Oh, yes quite recovered, thank you. I'll get her.'

Mim was pulling out tomatoes and onions from the refrigerator towards the evening meal. 'It's a man for you, Mim, calls himself Alan Grosvenor, I think he said. Who is he? I never heard of him – must be somebody for Dad.'

She noticed her mother's eyes light up like a spark in a smouldering fire as she answered. 'Thanks, dear, it's for me. Alan runs an Art Gallery in South Yarra. I met him overseas. Let yourself out, Mimi will be okay. I'll keep my eye on her.'

As if in face of another dimension, Maddy felt herself dismissed. 'For heaven's sake,' she thought as Mim left her and she found herself like a little girl tempted to listen. Going down the side path, she reminded herself that she really must remember to ask Mim about her trip. Mim had been six weeks in the Middle East and Europe before she even met Eliane. She had been very busy at the conferences and her letters very thin and the postcards, though regular, had said nothing at all. Now there was this remoteness about everything she said, a kind of mental distraction that provoked a sense of unexpected distance into her normal conversation. A remark of Molly's began to itch the back of Maddy's mind. 'You're a lucky family, your mother is always a mother before she's a person. There aren't so many around.'

Mim was on the phone again when Maddy returned, and this time there was no doubt she was copping it from Aunt Harriet. Maddy looked down the hall to discover Mimi at Mim's feet, absorbed with a carved wooden doll and a small replica of a Nile felucca. Above Mimi's head Mim raised her eyes to Maddy and grimaced in the direction of the watch on her wrist as she talked. 'Well, dear, try for the appointment for Thursday if you can't get it for tomorrow, otherwise next Monday... Maddy's back... Didn't I tell you she came with Mimi? No, dear, we couldn't get you we don't have a car between us, both in the garage... Had to have the battery recharged.... Nobody ran it while I was away... No, it wasn't Molly's fault. Layton promised to do it... Yes, Auntie, I know he's very busy. Anyway, I have to go now. Maddy has to go for her car and she's putting the lunch on for a bite first... No, Auntie, it won't make any difference if I phone, the nurse makes the appointments...'

Maddy went to the kitchen and Mimi jumped up to follow. 'Mummy, Mummy,' her high voice trilled. 'I dot dis booful boat to hold in my hands for feeling, it's nice smell see.'

Lifting the carved sandalwood to her nose, Maddy sniffed. 'Did Mim lend these to you? Aren't you lucky?'

'Yeah.'

'Yes.'

'Ye-es see did. Mimi's a dood girl, Mummy.'

'Did you help Mim hang out the washing?'

'Nope.'

'No—'

'Un-o. I didn't cause we couldn't cause the tel-phone ringed.'

'Rang,' Maddy said, giving up. 'We'll have lunch, dear, get your cushion and I'll sit you up.' She looked with anxiety at the Egyptian felucca she had set for safety on a shelf. It was new from this last trip. She sighed as she speculated. Two months away from home could be too long a time or not long enough.

Henrietta and Greg made a handsome pair; so handsome, in fact, the similarity of their individual appearances was striking. It began with a walk of natural, uncalculated arrogance and followed through with long legs, long wrists and fingers, to be crowned by blonde heads of shining hair. Both of them flashed faultless white smiles of melting sweetness in the direction of expected assistance, particularly from the meek and humble members of the opposite sex. Even their dress was similar: pencil-line pants, broader psychedelic tops of secretive and tantalising proportion. They wore without intention the bored air of young and therefore uncommitted gods.

To Mim, this six-month liaison of like to like was puzzling since she suspected the inner projection to be in direct contrast to the outer. Their personalities bit at each other, perhaps as mutual escape from the inanities of surface adoration.

Neither Greg nor Henrietta seemed at ease in the kitchen where they fidgeted a little to charm away the purpose of their arrival as a double instead of a single to partake of the dinner she was hurriedly preparing. They had discovered themselves with nothing else to do.

'If I cause any inconvenience, Mrs Shorman,' Greg said, 'I'll take off. I realise you are just home and may not be organised. I admit Mother would be in a flurry of agitation but Henny says not you, and I believe her every word.' He beamed at Mim.

'When it suits you.' Henny smiled. 'And me.'

'Now what could she possibly mean by that?' Greg asked Mim. 'Do you find your beauty a strange child?'

'I don't even find her a beauty every day, Greg,' Mim said, wishing them out of her kitchen and Barbi there instead. 'But of course you are welcome to stay if you like chops.'

'Not chops, darling,' Henrietta moaned.

'Chops, mashed potatoes, and tomato and onion sauce with soup before and pie to follow. I might even say, Henny,' Mim added tartly, 'You are lucky to get that. I'm just in.'

Henrietta threw two long arms around Mim's shoulders and squeezed tight. 'You poor dear,' she squealed affectionately. 'And I told Greg you were home quietly recuperating all day after the weekend invasion.'

Extricating herself, Mim laughed. 'Did you forget about your shoes then, and the bit about the payment on your record album?'

Henny stood back, exquisitely crestfallen. 'Did I ever?' she breathed. Sympathetically, Greg entangled her chagrined languor in equally long arms and mingled his pageboy mop with her flowing crown of similar gold. Something about them reminded Mim of a cigarette commercial.

'Oh, get out, the two of you,' she said. 'And let me get on with the dinner.'

They made it as far as the door. Then Henrietta turned. 'There's a car,' she said. 'It's Paul's M.G. Mim, don't tell me Barbi's bringing Paul. Well, that really is the end!' Then she shrugged and added, 'If she wants me we'll be playing Greg's record. It's heaven. That's why we came, really, to listen to it again without a mob around.'

'I'll tell her,' Mim said. But she didn't, because Barbi threw her coat over a kitchen chair and demanded, 'Did you get it?'

'It's on your bed. Do you like it? Uh-huh.'

'Then I love you, that's for sure. But I'm not going to look at it yet. I'll set the table first.'

'If Paul doesn't mind, I'd rather you went to get your father for me. I don't see how I can go. Greg's just come in with Henrietta.'

'Sure,' Paul said. 'We'll go.'

'What's the matter with Dad's car?' Barbi sounded peevish.

'In the garage.'

'But you put yours in today.'

'I got mine back and put his in. Would you rather do the dinner, Barbi? Somebody has to go for your father. He'll be ready by six-thirty after a meeting. He phoned.'

'But Mim, I've got to be back by eight. I told you on the phone. I've got to get dressed as well.'

Paul said, 'Come on, Barbi, we can get back. I'll get you there in time, like I said. Your mother is probably too bloody tired to drive anyway. I'd be after that trip.'

Barbara looked at Mim with her eyes half closed and acquiesced. 'Okay, we'll be right back as fast as Dad'll let Paul drive,' she said. 'See you. But I just have to be there by eight.'

Paul's placating contribution going out the door— 'That bird won't be there by eight anyway, Barbi, if he turns up at all' —was no comfort, as Mim realised. Barbi felt her future as an actress threatened, yet her acceptance to undertake the ... demanded extra was automatic. She grumbled but her good nature was such that in the family her willingness could be presumed.

Mim sighed. She knew she would have been wiser to send Henrietta for Layton. Henny would have driven up in Greg's car with the flourish of granting an unexpected and extraordinary favour and Layton would have succumbed to the ridiculous blandishment of a conversation studded with 'Pops' and 'Sirs'. Why then had she deliberately waited for Paul and Barbi? Layton was suspicious of the intentions of Paul Carlister, yet did not appear to notice that Henny and Greg could scarcely keep their hands off one another and were playing themselves into every aspect of passion like puppets trying to buy a dream.

Fatigue flared up in Mim again as she filled the electric fry-pan with fifteen small curled chops. Reaching for the last two tins of small garden peas, she felt her head swim and wondered if she could escape to bed right after dinner. Greg would probably stay until midnight because Henny had nothing else to do and would rather die than be seen lounging around during the casting of the play at the Union. After ten, Layton would say privately that he considered Greg's presence an imposition and accept with resentment his wife's need for sleep. It was important, in Layton's view, that a mother saw teenage suitors off the premises. Besides, there would be Barbi's return with or without the coveted role. In either case there would be the usual tap on the door. 'Mim, are you awake?'

Placing the wine glasses she remembered Layton's weekend remark about a list for the 'Cellar'. She'd remind him tonight. And in the morning she had better phone and make the appointment for Harriet herself and be sure of it, otherwise Harriet was sure to demand to be taken on the day Maddy was taking Michael about his tonsils. That was Wednesday and meant minding Mimi and picking up Tim after school. She must not think about Maddy and that house in Carlton, not until after Thursday, which was the day of the welcome home luncheon and the formal dinner for Sir Alex Smith at the university. Surely she would have had enough rest by then? Better to take each day as it comes, she told herself; tomorrow first. So towards tomorrow, which would begin in the small hours of tonight, she went into her room and swallowed two aspirin and a multivitamin pill.

Layton rang the doorbell before he put his key into the front door lock. Barbi flew past him down the hall into the bathroom, calling, 'Henny, Paul's here. I'm washing my hair – it'll dry! I'll wear it straight.'

Paul said, 'Excuse me, sir,' and followed his ears towards a recommencement of muffled music. Mim mashing potatoes in the kitchen was relieved to greet Layton by himself.

'Nice of Paul,' he said. 'Barbi says you're knocked. She laid it on rather thick. Are you all right?'

'Yes, dear. I'm just tired.'

'Why did you let them bring boys in tonight? This isn't a motel, although you'd think so the way people mill around. Did you see Harriet?'

'No, just talked to her on the phone.'

'I thought she said she was sick this morning.'

'She's not really sick. I'll see her tomorrow.'

Layton poured himself a generous whisky. 'God, what a day, and then I had to walk out of the meeting tonight because I told you six-thirty. Did I tell you Sir Alex is bringing his wife?'

'No.'

'It'll mean we have to put up a wives program. Naturally, I told them you'd be in on it.'

'Call the children, will you, dear?' Mim said. 'I'm serving the dinner now. Barbi has to be out again in half an hour.'

'Surely I can relax a minute over my drink.'

'If we don't eat now, Layton, Barbi won't eat at all – or Paul – and they did go to get you.'

'Who's with Henrietta?'

'Greg.'

'That beautiful boy! I'll call them. But I'm not having that hair dryer contraption at the table no matter how late Barbi is.'

'You tell her, dear.'

She began to ladle out the soup into six flat bowls.

CHAPTER FIVE

Ruth tucked Rollo into his white cot with loving but no-nonsense efficiency and he knew in his baby way that the games were over and Mummy meant sleep. Under the button eyes of a black and white plush panda as large as himself, he snuggled into comfortable inactivity with his hands dimpled pink around his bottle. Ruth touched his forehead lightly before she pulled down the Mickey Mouse blinds, replaced a velvet elephant to a space on the toy shelf and let herself out the padded nursery door. She was in a hurry to get Rollo down because on Fridays her daily help was always anxious to get away dead on twelve-thirty for marketing on the way home. Ruth had to smile, collecting her handbag from the unit-wall wardrobe in her bedroom. Mrs Jenkins was so precise and regulated that her presence in the flat was like the ticking of a clock. Everything domestic in Ruth's life was done to time from nine-thirty to twelve-thirty in the morning and then with Mrs Jenkins gone she could relax into being the happy mother of Rollo.

She knew, of course, that Mrs Jenkins would return via the Prahran Market to a husband on worker's compensation and four children. But this did not increase the hours Mrs Jenkins was willing to work for Ruth. She was fond of Rollo, but not interested in baby-sitting. Nor would she re-appear for a dinner party. Sometimes Ruth wondered about Mrs Jenkins' ménage, but her interest was not encouraged. It took Mrs Jenkins three hours five mornings a week to keep Missus Carlister's South Yarra flat in perfect order, down to the last polished teaspoon. In two years, Mrs Jenkins had not so

much as laid eyes on Doctor Mark Carlister, although she had tidied his desk and den with daily patience. She had eyed the young
scientist's father and his mother and his brother, but not once had
she served them. Ruth made her own trays of coffee for morning
visitors. Mrs Jenkins prided herself on being as impersonal and efficient as the Dutch Cleaners. She had her tweed all-weather coat
already buttoned up to her scarf when Ruth arrived to pay her. The
electric clock above the sink showed a minute past the half-hour.

'Thank you,' Mrs Jenkins said to Ruth, placing the money in her
open purse. 'While I was waiting I brought up your post. I'll be off
now. See you Monday – God willing, as I always say.'

Ruth wanted to ask her how her husband was, but as usual,
Mrs Jenkins was out the door before she found the words. Olwyn
had more than once insisted that Mrs Jenkins had too much pride
for her station. Remembering this, Ruth once again shrugged her
shoulders to smile as she picked up the mail. A letter from Mark.
She held it in her hand and then put it down.

She would make herself coffee first, since Rollo was asleep. And
a sandwich – a nice ham and chutney sandwich, and enjoy the letter
with lunch on a tray in the big armchair by the balcony French
windows overlooking the park. Before she split open the letter, it
seemed to her thin, considering it was the first since his arrival in
London. Then she noticed the date stamp was French and, alerted,
realised everything must be changed. His itinerary had not included
France. There was one thin sheet of blue airmail paper and the message was brief.

Dear Ruth,

*Hold your breath like a good girl because this is going to hurt. I'm sorry,
but I can't help it. I tried the other kind of letter but it was no good. I
thought of writing to Dad but that would have been a feeble way out and
even more rotten.*

*I'm not sending for you. I don't know what I'm going to do as far as my
appointment is concerned, but that doesn't matter. Financially I'll always
do my best to look after you and Rollo, for what that's worth. What does*

matter is that I ran into Eliane Shorman in London and this time never in-tend to let her out of my sight again. You won't understand like the others, and I know now that I should never have married you – certainly not with-out telling you – but excuses can't help. Naturally, the next move is up to you. You will have to decide what you think best and let me know care of my London Bank. Take time if you want it. I don't expect consideration, but you must realise this is real and final.

I'm glad you are young and pretty. You'll get over me, I think, although I don't deserve the hope, and you'll never be sorry you had Rollo.

With sincerity,

Mark

Ruth did not know how long she sat clutching Mark's letter. From some great distance of shock she found herself reading it again and then for a third time. Finally, the words blurred out on the paper and she sank back on the chair, exhausted. She sat up straight again then, thinking suddenly that she would need all her strength because of Rollo. Immediately, her baby came into her mind and she felt affronted on his behalf, and also frightened. He would be protected; he was so small; so soft. A battle would have to be fought to protect Rollo who could not fight for himself.

After that, she realised that she was also affronted, had been cast aside, rejected along with Rollo. Mark no longer wanted her and was also willing to give up Rollo. For Eliane Shorman. All this was for Eliane and for some reason connected with Eliane that she, Ruth, the legal wife and mother of Rollo, did not know.

She read the letter for the last time. She was expected to un-derstand, it seemed, because this time the relationship with Eliane, whatever it was, had come to final consummation, the proper and expected event had ultimately taken place. It was as if she and Rollo did not exist at all, or were merely bystanders. Yet it was assumed that everybody else knew. Could it be possible that only she, Mark's wife, had not been told the secret? Well, then, that was the first thing. There was something she had to find out, a well-kept secret she had to know.

Ruth stood up. A shiver, ever so slight, ran down her spine so that she squared her shoulders a little. There was one thing she had learned from Mummy and that was the subtle and undermining means by which it was possible to counteract unnecessary involvement by sizing up the opposition and standing up to it only at a level similar in size or less than yourself. In this way it was possible to side-step that which might prove too big to handle. Mummy, as a pretty widow, had applied the principle socially and Ruth subconsciously on the playing field. In both cases the issues were rarely important past personal satisfaction. For all that, the principle had proved itself worthy of practice and had made Ruth the best sportsgirl of her years at school. She could always size up the opposing team and allot her teammates and herself positions where their chances of using ability were at least equal. As captain she had played her own game with dignity and the ease of experience.

One by one, she considered the people who might know the past importance of Eliane Shorman to Mark. There was, of course, Arthur – but she could not go to Arthur because his kindness towards her would weaken her defence. He might evade the issue or camouflage the truth. Paul's tactics would be rough and uncertain out of embarrassment for her even if he knew, and besides, his relationship with Barbara was a disadvantage. Barbara herself would be safer but she was a Shorman. Also, the age of the Shorman twins might have protected them from knowing the necessary truth. George and Maddy were the nearest to being Mark's contemporaries, but she could not separate them in her mind and knew they would see themselves as the protectors of married life, or at least George would and Maddy, of course, loved Eliane. There was Doctor Shorman, of course, but she would be tongue-tied because he frightened her with his sharp intelligence.

She was left with the choice of only two people, Elian's mother and Mark's mother. For a long time she thought about Linda Shorman and was startled to discover that all her conversations with her were casual and kind, with Arthur's brand of affectionate escapism which was natural with Arthur but not in character with Mim Shorman. As her mind played with going to the Shormans she suddenly remembered waiting in anger for a final game with a team that never turned up. You couldn't make a team turn up. If they forfeited the game, you got it by default and that was all there was to it. She knew then quite definitely that she could not make Mim Shorman turn up if she did not want to. Mim would know more than all the rest put together, but she might not play, so it was no use to go to her.

Anger rose in Ruth as she made her decision. She remembered Mim Shorman at the airport and the strange look of pity in her eyes. Oh yes, Ruth thought, Mim Shorman was the one, but she must go to Olwyn. Poor Olwyn had no chance of escape.

She went straight to the telephone.

'Oh, hello dear,' Olwyn's voice answered. 'Yes, I'm alone, but I'm going to have my hair done in half an hour. Oh, but you know how they are, dear, if I cancel at this late moment I'll never get Andre again. You'll phone? Oh, I see, and say I'm sick. But why, dear? Ruth, it's not Rolly, is it? Oh, I see, just me, a surprise, you want me to see it before your mother. And Arthur too. Terribly important! Oh, well, I suppose so, Ruth, if you don't mind phoning Andre. But when will you say I'll come? Oh... yes, I see. Maybe it is better to leave it. Do hurry, Ruth. I'll be dying of curiosity. Oh, isn't he awake yet? I'm so looking forward to the little darling. Can you both stay the night? Oh, good. Bye now.'

It did not occur to Ruth to study the letter further or allow herself even one night's contemplation. She had to act because of the danger that threatened Rollo and to act she needed certain information.

The Carlister home in Toorak had a great circular two-way driveway that disgorged guests under a pillared portico at the crescent of the arc. The rounded stair levels were marked with enormous urns of Italian marble for the display of pastel azaleas surrounded with the deep marine blue of lobelia.

As Ruth swung the Porsche beyond the steps to the parking court, she noticed Arthur coming down the steps. So as well as everything else, Arthur was home! Had Olwyn told him, called him home? No, it would be coincidence, chance, the horrible malevolence of this day working against her like the bump she'd given the car backing out of the garage.

Arthur was beside her, lifting Rollo out of his little seat before she was out of her seat belt. The thought struck her with irony that he was handsome like Mark in all the superficial ways: tall, slim-hipped, tailored and perfectly shod.

'Come on, old man, come on,' he was saying to his grandson and she felt soiled with disloyalty as she replied – 'He went to sleep driving along. He usually doesn't, but today I went into his room and woke him up too soon.'

With a still-recumbent Rollo settled in his arms, Arthur glanced at Ruth. 'Olwyn said you were coming over specially – had something to tell us. You look a bit white on it, Ruthie. Traffic bad?'

'No, but it's not my day. I backed into the stone wall coming out of the garage.'

Arthur surveyed the damage. 'Two dints. Tell you what, Olwyn says you're staying the night. I'll run it round to the panel-beaters, or Paul will. My outfit will do it for us by tomorrow morning.'

'No, Arthur, it doesn't matter. Next week will do. Don't bother.'

His laugh, she thought, was also sharply reminiscent of his eldest son. 'No time like the present, Ruth.' She did not agree with him, but let it go, knowing that determination was another characteristic Arthur shared with Mark.

Olwyn received them at the top of the steps in the picture curve of the entrance hall. She took Rollo from Arthur and eyed Ruth apprehensively above the child's fair head. 'His playpen is all ready for him. Come along, darling. We'll put him in, shall we?'

'Okay, Olwyn,' Arthur said. He looked at Ruth, raising his eyebrows in semi-humorous concern and noticed her half-blink both her eyes and sway towards Olwyn. 'Please, Olwyn, let's put Rollo in his cot. Now, right away. I think I need a drink. Do you mind, Arthur? A gin and tonic, please, long.'

Olwyn said, 'Why, Ruth—' but Ruth picked up the baby bag she had put on the floor and went down the hall towards the bedroom wing in long-legged strides as if the bedding down of the child was suddenly a matter of life and death. At the door of the room she waited and took Rollo from Olwyn's arms, and put him stirring into the waiting cot, tucked him firmly into it and pushed his protesting grandmother back to the door. 'Let's not wake him,' she said. 'I'm glad he's tired. I'd rather he sleeps.'

It was then that Olwyn noticed that Ruth's face was white at the nostrils and twitching at the corner of the lips, so she bustled ahead of her daughter-in-law to a place in the hall beyond the hearing of the child.

'I can see you are upset. I really am sorry, Ruth,' she burst into apologies outside the door of Paul's room. 'I had no idea Arthur would be home early today, let alone Paul. Are you ill?'

The door beside them opened and Paul was physically present. 'Hello Ruth,' he said and looked into her face and said, 'What's up?'

She couldn't answer and hurried down the hall ahead of them into the moss velvet of the circular lounge where Arthur had opened the bar. She took her drink from his hands and held it in both her own and stared and breathed into it as if its iciness held her salvation.

Olwyn came up to Arthur with baffled exasperation and behind her, Paul thought, 'Some bloody thing's collapsed for Ruth, and Arthur suspects but doesn't know,' so he said, 'Thanks, Dad, I'll have the same as yours with soda.'

Olwyn objected. 'You know I don't like you drinking whisky, Paul. It's not good for you. You shouldn't allow it, Arthur, should he, Ruth?'

Ruth did not answer and Paul, taking his drink, said evenly, 'Mother dear, I may not have sired a son but I have my majority.'

'Paul, I do wish you wouldn't talk like that. It's so unnatural. I've told you before I just can't bear it. It upsets me even more than those terrible clothes you insist on wearing.'

'We're only family, Olwyn,' Arthur began, unsure of the atmosphere because he sensed the tension in Ruth. His voice tailed off uncertainly. 'It's nice to have a family drink together.'

With a sudden, spasmodic movement, Ruth lifted her glass and swallowed. The iciness trickled down to the very pit of her stomach and then she said, still staring into the glass, in a voice of deliberate detachment, 'There is something I want to ask the family, since we are together. I planned just to ask you, Olwyn, but as everybody is here, what's the difference?' She paused, but did not lift her head to savour the mixed anticipation in the faces turned towards her. 'I would like to know about Mark's affair with Eliane Shorman.'

'For heaven's sake!' Olwyn cried. 'Is that all it is? Wherever did you hear about that? Why, it was ages ago, long before Madeline and George were married. You could scarcely call it an affair. Mark was just a boy, really; he hadn't even finished his education.'

'How long did it last?'

'Last?' Olwyn's voice grew sharper. 'Last? Why, no time at all really. It was just one of those shipboard attractions... You know the kind of thing... Two or three weeks at the most... All off when the voyage ends. Fancy you hearing about that, darling.' Her tone demanded dismissal, which Ruth ignored.

'I thought there was more to it than that,' she suggested softly. Arthur's voice cut across Olwyn's gasp with gentle precision. 'There was,' he said distinctly.'

'Thank you, Arthur,' Ruth said. 'I thought so.'

Into a charged silence, Olwyn spoke with suppressed fury, 'Really, Arthur, what a thing to say to Ruth. As if it makes any difference. As if—'

'Stop it, Olwyn,' Arthur said. 'Ruth deserves the truth. It's a long time ago now, certainly, and Mark got over it, but it's true, Ruth, that he was in love with Eliane Shorman. They wanted to marry at the time.'

'Tell me about it,' Ruth said flatly. 'All about it.'

'I've just told you,' Olwyn reiterated shrilly. 'There's no more to tell. Arthur and I with Mark met Linda Shorman and later Eliane travelling on the same ship, that's all, and the young people went around together.'

'I understand that, Olwyn. But what happened then?' Momentarily, Ruth's eyes swept Arthur's face, but finding it stiff and withdrawn, returned again to Olwyn to force the demanded secret from the easiest source.

'Nothing, Ruth, just nothing.' Olwyn's voice dropped, 'Mark went on to Cambridge and Eliane returned to the university here, as her father had wished her to from the very beginning.'

'The very beginning of what? Ruth asked, still firm in the role of detached interrogation so that Olwyn fluttered for escape from her unsuspected stronger will. Ruth was usually so amiable, had hitherto adapted with grace, but now was probing like Paul where there was no defence. Olwyn felt cornered and backed away from Ruth's hard eyes seeking a support unattainable in Arthur and Paul, neither of whom moved or spoke. She thought of Mark on that dreadful voyage; Mark with the blank look coming down like blinds over his eyes so that it was useless to reason with him. Up until that voyage, there had always been moments when he seemed young and unprotected and turned to her for comfort, absorbing from her some vital need so that she had been strangely satisfied, even with very little affection, in return for the love and pride she lived on through him. Self-pity overwhelmed her again in thoughts of that miserable voyage and she was close to tears as she cried out in bitter anger against Ruth who would not release her from memory. 'The beginning of that wretched affair, of course!' she snapped. 'It was a despicable business. Arthur introduced me to Linda. He'd met her once years before and recognised her on the boat, so naturally when her daughter got on we were all together and I couldn't do a thing, not a thing, Ruth. Can you understand the terrible position I was in? It was even my fault we were on the trip. I persuaded Arthur into a first-class cruise to take Mark to Europe by way of America. Arthur did not want a sea trip. He hates Hawaii, you know, and Mark wanted to fly straight to Cambridge, but I insisted and Arthur knew how much I would enjoy the trip because I was going to miss Mark terribly while he was abroad. I had such pride in him, Ruth. You've got Rollo, you know what I mean. And Mark was so clever. I don't think my pride was exorbitant. I considered pride in my son an honourable thing. I put Mark's advancement first in my life. I couldn't let him ruin his future with a girl like that.' Her voice began to tremble towards hysteria. 'I didn't expect Mark would take a notion to a girl whose appearance was such a shock to us all. There we were, all waiting for Linda's daughter to get on in Honolulu, everybody adoring Linda as usual, even Mark. It was just as if the setting was all prepared by the mother to put in the hands of the daughter. And then when the girl got on, she was an adopted daughter, she was coloured. She looked as if she belonged in the islands and all the eyes of all the passengers followed her everywhere she went on the ship with Mark like a shadow. It was a nightmare, Ruth, can you understand? A nightmare. I nearly went crazy but there was nothing I could do, nothing at all. Not even Arthur would help me.'

'Oh my Gawd!' Paul said. 'Excuse me!' and made for the door. Arthur's voice stopped him in ringing command, 'Paul, you will stay and let Ruth finish what she has to say.'

Ruth stared into her drink to escape looking at Olwyn. 'I have to know, that's all. I just have to know what happened. Mark didn't even tell me.'

Arthur moved towards Ruth and, ignoring Olwyn's attempts to speak again, kept his words precise and measured. 'Mark didn't tell anybody much, Ruth. He just got over it and it wasn't as dramatic as Olwyn makes out. When we arrived in San Francisco, Layton Shorman came on board and took his family off the ship for an excursion to New Mexico. Mark expected Eliane and her mother to return to Australia via England. Instead, he had a letter from her calling the whole thing off. That's all there was to it. Olwyn exaggerates her own part in the affair just like she tells everybody how she introduced you to Mark the very week of his return. What was it, three years later? A long time, Ruthie.'

Ruth could not look at Arthur. She knew if he touched her she would be undone, so she lifted her eyes and fixed them on the face of Paul as if to hang on to the deep hurt behind his darkened glance. Her response was a series of jerky phrases. 'Olwyn does not exaggerate. She did introduce me to... Mark. The very first week of his return... and she does not exaggerate his interest in Eliane Shorman... they have just gone to Paris together... this time... he says... he will never give her up.' She took the letter from her bag and waved it like a flag.

Olwyn shrieked. 'You can't give him a divorce for that girl. You can't, you can't. It's not right. It will ruin him...'

Paul shifted his eyes from Ruth's white face to watch the last trace of his mother's dignity dissolve in hysterical tears. He sensed Ruth move imperceptibly to avoid his father's sustaining arm, which was kinder-intentioned but for all that like the arm of his brother Mark and he propelled himself forward like a robot into battle. 'Ruth's okay, Dad,' he heard himself say. 'I'll get her another drink while you take Mother. She'd better have a pill and lie down for a bit. We'll wait here.'

'Don't touch me, don't touch me!' Olwyn screamed. 'I can't stand any more. I'll die.'

Arthur looked at Paul and then at Ruth, shut his eyes and opened them under a new skin to look at Olwyn. Paul was surprised and then terribly embarrassed by this film of pity that fell as habitually as a shadow across his father's face. Olwyn ran from the room. Arthur followed quietly after.

But Ruth watched them go with pity only for herself. Stiff with shock and shame, she felt withdrawn from herself as Mrs Mark Carlister. Inside, in some distant part of her psyche, a little girl called Ruth was moving forward, wailing the injustice of physical chastisement received for no known cause. She pulled her lips tight with bitter contempt as she took the second drink from Paul and handed him her empty glass.

'I'll take it to my room, thanks, Paul,' she said, and walked like a mannequin across the carpet to the door. Then she turned and Paul thought her head was magnificent, held like that. It was as if he were looking at the landing of a water bird.

'When Rollo wakes,' Ruth said, 'they can take him out and look after him. It might help them. I don't want to be disturbed. I'll see you in the morning.'

CHAPTER SIX

Ruth, surmising that Arthur and Olwyn would have taken Rollo to the sunny garden away from the wind, braced her shoulders and opened the door to the hall to go out to them. Paul was reclining on a full-length wait-in-the-hall seat, one leg flung out and the other doubled under him Roman style. He scowled, lionlike in a tan turtleneck pullover under his black mane.

'Oh, Paul,' she got out and no more while her hand flew like a fluttering bird to her cheekbone spotted red like the painted doll in Petroucha where the heavy circles underlined her eyes. She felt washed-out and haggard, looking at the youth who was Paul; now on his feet filling the hall space so that, arms extended, he could have touched both walls or even the ceiling.

'I've been waiting for you to come out. Thought you might come to the footy with me.'

'But I... don't... follow... the... footy.'

'Oh, don't give me that. I've seen you putting your transistor off and on. I've got two passes in.'

'I've never been to the footy, Paul. You see, I—'

'Time you went then. I'm not offering any glam seats, you know, only the bloody hill. I'll get the car. You needn't get dressed up. I'm going like I am with the old duffle in case the wind gets up. You got one?'

'Not here.' She swayed a little. 'My clothes are...' She couldn't make herself call her apartment home.

'I'll lend you that padded car coat Mum presented me with last Christmas. It's a bloody gorgeous grosgrain, even got a hood towards persuading me to pay some ruddy rogue of a barber every week. It'll suit you.'

'I'll be drowned in it.'

'Why not? All the females are swamped up top and cold below.'

He stopped as he so often did with Barbi, shocked at the prospect of shocking. Ruth merely regarded him with wide empty eyes. The poor kid's face had shrunk, he thought. All eyes and hair – some hair too. Her hair fell to her shoulders, a flat shining crown, wheat-coloured and undressed. 'Come on, you'll go fine just as you are.'

'Is Barbi coming?'

'God no. Nobody but a guy called Sims Flavin who'll seek me out and roar away my eardrums like all the morons on the benches, only for other reasons.'

'Why? Why will he seek you out?'

'He's my friend. The thing is not to take any notice. He just likes to talk. It's his way of coping with the human condition.'

'He's lucky. I haven't got a way.'

'Oh, I dunno,' Paul said. 'You haven't met Sims yet. Actually, you don't see much of the variety types in your own generation. Do you good to have the cobwebs blown out of your lungs. The thing about the footy is that you can yell as loud as you bloody well want to.'

She giggled self-consciously out of unexpected embarrassment because she was touched. 'You know, Paul, every second word you use is bloody.'

'Sorry,' he said and laughed.

She sobered again. 'I can't leave Rollo.'

'Don't be a bloo—' He halted and finished lamely, 'Don't be a fool, Ruth. What are his grandparents for, sitting there watching his every step, hanging on his words? He's at the age they understand.'

'I'll give him his lunch first then.'

He grunted. 'The technological age provides hygienically balanced baby diets. Don't deprive poor Mum of the pleasure of wielding her automatic can-opener. Actually, Ruth, it would be a good idea to leave Rollo with them this afternoon. They need him.'

'Maybe they do,' she said. 'It was awful, Paul, what she had to tell me.'

'She's only what she is, Ruth.'

'All I could feel at the end was shame. It was shame for Arthur too. He cried; his eyes were full of tears. I never saw a man cry.'

Paul put his huge, bony hand on her shoulder roughly as if by mistake and quickly swung it back to his hip again.

'You haven't seen much yet, Ruthie. Men cry. The whole bloody human race cries. Get that into your head, see. Even the rottenest old reprobate cries. What the hell do you think they all yell at the footy for? So they won't cry. Look.' He led her through the dining room door and across to the window. In the centre of the velvet back lawn, a tartan rug shouted the colours of Cameron to the sky. Olwyn was sitting on the rug and so was Arthur and between them Rollo was making up his mind in which direction to throw the big red plastic ball he held in his pink, dimpled fingers. Already, he knew that both his grandparents were holding out anxious hands.

'See,' Paul said. 'He's your son and my nephew – sure, but for them at this moment, he's all they've got. They don't want to cry any more either.' He flung up the window and roared out, 'I'm taking Ruth to the footy. We'll pick up some grub on the way. Maybe we'll eat out too. Okay?'

Olwyn sat stiff, staring across Rollo's head at Arthur. Arthur raised his hand. 'Okay, son. Take the car if you want it.'

Neither of them moved. Little Rollo stood up, dropped the ball and clapped his hands in happy excitement. 'Pau, Pau, see me, Paul...' He didn't see his mother, who would have brought tears.

'Hi, punk,' Paul called out at him. 'See you later,' and slammed down the window. He hoped Ruth wasn't going to blubber, although she had a right to. 'I'll get the coat,' he said.

'And I'll get my... I'll get my bag.'

He thought he'd better not let her out of his sight.

'Look, it's my date. I'm paying.'

'I know, I'll only be a minute.'

He heard her run into the bathroom and close the door and went to grab the coat and take up his stance again, blocking the hall. His mother would be standing up by now, arguing with Arthur, her sense of propriety beginning to dominate her pride.

Ruth came out of the bathroom and dived into the spare room, to emerge again with a patent leather handbag clutched in her hand. The bloody letter was in her handbag, he thought. The bloody letter had to go with her. 'Hurry up,' he urged her. 'Hurry up, for God's sake. They'll be in in a minute.' He steered her ahead of him out the front door where his father's car was parked in the driveway. He didn't have to go around to the garage. Then he remembered Arthur had gone earlier for cigarettes. Arthur had left the car with the key dangling. He had never done that before and Paul hadn't mentioned the footy to Arthur, hadn't spoken to either of his parents; in fact hadn't opened his big mouth since last night; had even waited to eat until they took Rollo outside. He pushed Ruth into the car and slid under the steering wheel. That Mim Shorman must have known it before she went to London... Sure, the bloody witch must have known it would happen before Mark even married Ruth. Longer than that – God!

At the wheel he heard the front door click open again after he had closed it. His mother! He switched on the car radio and started the car. Ruth was staring straight ahead, her eyes as blank as the windscreen. She wasn't looking back. He revved the engine, stepped on the accelerator, switched the radio dial, all in one swift movement, and moved out of the driveway.

Olwyn watched the car drive out and shuddered at the wild tune drowning the smooth Mercedes engine. Why couldn't Paul take his own car? Where was his own car? Why should the Mercedes radio be subjected to that tune, 'Hitchhiker, hitchhiker?'

Inside the car Ruth said, 'Turn it off, Paul, turn it off. I don't want to be reminded.'

'Sure. Okay.' He switched it off.

'That's what I did, baled him up at a red light and got in.'

'I wouldn't let that worry you, Ruth. We're all hitchhikers, hitching lifts off somebody. Look at me in this—'

'Where's your own car Paul?'

'Repairs. I underestimated a parked car yesterday. She had to be towed in.'

'Does your father know?'

'I guess so. He left the key dangling in this one. I was too lousy to tell him yet... You know... waiting for the psychologically right moment. I've hitched off him all my life you see, Ruth, ever since I discovered both of them were all wrapped up in Mark.'

'Oh, Paul.'

'Well, hell, they had me. It wasn't my fault Mark had all the bloody brains. I was a mistake, I guess. Mum only had space for one son, really. Still, here I am.'

'You've got Arthur, Paul. I'm sure you've got Arthur.'

'Well, that's what Barbi says. Got it from her mother, of course.' He was still raw about Mim Shorman, as let down, somehow, as if he'd brought her a slashed hand and she'd told him to wrap it up himself. 'Anyway, it's too late. I tell you I've hitchhiked off him too long. It's a habit now.'

'Paul, where were you when they took that... That trip to England?'

'Following my brilliant brother's footsteps in my father's school, where else? *Really, Paul, I can't understand your attitude to study. We had no trouble in this school with Mark,*' he mimicked.

'You hated Mark?'

'God no, the reverse. I idolised him... Big brother stuff and all that.'

'But I don't understand.'

'I was so far behind him, the distance was always too great. I got to know I wouldn't catch up until I was grown. That was okay with me. He'd see me when I grew up. But it didn't work out that way.

He got his degree, then the scholarship to Cambridge. That's when they took that trip... Mum had to go with him, of course, to see if Cambridge was good enough for him. I don't think he wanted them to go. I went in as a Boarder to school. He asked me straight out if I wanted to. I can remember how he looked at me, or through me, I should say.'

'Like you were a little baby,' she said softly.

'Yeah, that's right. So hell, I lied like a trouper of course... Cliché! Barbi's always jumping at me for cliché's. I was a hell of a little liar, but I thought when he gets back I'll be grown and I'll look him straight back and tell him the truth. Whatever the truth happens to be, without distinction. That's what I thought.'

Ruth smiled. 'That's when he came back and married me.'

'That's right. He never even saw me.'

'He never saw me either, Paul... Not really. What's she like? Eliane... Inside, I mean. I've seen her picture at the Shormans'. You can't really tell from a photograph... About her colour, I mean. Anything else? I remember once thinking that she had a beautiful face, but not more so than other people's photos I've seen. You see, I want to hate her, Paul. I want to hate her, but how can you hate anybody you've never even seen? That you don't know?'

'You can hate her, Ruth! You're the only one who has the right to hate her.'

'Then you can't tell me anything?'

'Nobody hates Eliane, not even Mum. It's Mim Shorman Mum hates for adopting Eliane. I guess nobody really hates anybody for what they can't help. If Mark had fallen for Maddy, Mum would have got over losing him quick smart.'

'You can't tell me anything then, about her, I mean...?'

God, he thought, she's persistent. She'd only come to pump him about Eliane. He couldn't escape the bloody Shormans. They were like a maze the rest of them had got stuck in. 'Well,' he said. 'You asked for it. Elie's brown, sort of blue-veined, pale brown with dark eyes and black hair. She doesn't walk like Australian girls, she just moves – sort of glides smooth like a pony. She went to the university here for three years and ate the lectures up as easy as Mark, only in Arts, not Science; got some sort of a post-grad scholarship to the University of Hawaii and went to Singapore with Mim for a holiday before she took it up. That was the year Mark came back because Barbi's mother was in Singapore when he got back. I know that. Then Eliane took a job in Hong Kong. The twins were horribly disappointed when she took it. They adore her, you can't put a word out of place there. That's all I know, Ruth, honest to God it is, except of course that she was to meet her mother in London and come home with her for leave, which she didn't'

'Paris' Ruth said. 'Mark's letter was from Paris.'

Well sure, he thought, but he would have met her here if she had come home. Ruth obviously didn't bloody well believe it yet. He supposed she would begin to cry if he didn't keep her talking until she could yell...

'My God, the bloody traffic's awful. I'll have to concentrate... Can't afford to wreck this buggy. I reckon we'll park soon as I see a spot and then walk. We can pick up some sandwiches on our way...and chips. I go for chips.' She wasn't listening and then he thought he'd gotta park bloody quick.

'She can speak perfect French, I suppose?' Ruth said.

'Hell, Ruth, I don't know. I was only a kid. I only saw her two or three times. I never began to hang around with Barbi's crowd until I got to the shop. She never came to our house except for the party when Maddy married George. I guess she had to come for that... She was the bridesmaid.'

'But you remembered when she walks she glides.'

He shrugged and gave up trying to evade Eliane. 'Yeah, she does. That's when I noticed...at Maddy's wedding. I wasn't all that taken in by the wedding fuss, but I did notice that much, and Barbi. Barbi fell over...she would.' He began to chuckle. 'Best part of the whole show that was. Elie picked her up and brushed her down while everybody giggled. Elie did a lot for the twins, but mostly she hung around Mrs Shorman. According to Barbi it was Elie who called her Mim, when she was little, and it stuck. Before Elie and her mother went to Singapore, the Shormans gave a party for Elie. I was dragged to that too, as George's young cousin. Boy, was she a knock-out that night. The stags fell over their feet trying to cut in. She wasn't anybody's doll and she sure could dance.'

'Mark doesn't go for dancing much.'

His quick eyes spotted a place large enough for the Mercedes. It was miles from the game. Still, she couldn't very well keep at him on the tram. He pulled in. It was a good safe spot and he parked carefully dead centre of it, just in case some fool cramped him fore or aft. They got out. Paul faced his sister-in-law in the street and handed her his car coat.

'Look, Ruth, I really wouldn't know but it looks as if this thing bit Elie and Mark when they were our age. That's a long time. It's rotten for you, but it's rotten for Elie too. Mark's a heel as far as I'm concerned. Can we let it go at that and enjoy the footy?'

'You do yourself well, as usual,' Sims remarked.

Paul never knew how Sims found him so quickly in the crowd.

'Hi Sims... This is Ruth.'

Sims said 'Hi' to Ruth, surveying her keenly with a deep brown bear stare, finding her blonde and one of the beautiful people... Enigmatic, since she didn't bother to smile; looked as if she went in for a bit of nightlife with those heavy, ringed, unmade-up eyes so gorgeously vague they fell before his own. Paul's breed sure packed them in as far as looks were concerned. He noticed she moved closer to Paul, the clinging vine type, perhaps, which was interesting; a contrast to Barbara who was independent and astute considering her youth, throttling what she wasn't prepared to hear.

'The spectacle is about to begin,' said Sims. 'Behold the fanfare... Soon, the teams will appear to the screams of the blood-hungry crowd on the one side and the quadrilla, toreros, banderilleres and pecadoes, our popular heroes; on the other the challengers, the bulls and the horses. Finally we shall see the poor matador running from side to side playing up the blood-lust with his shrill whistle.'

'Oh, shut up Sims,' Paul interrupted, irritable. 'It's Ruth's first game. Give her a go.'

'My dear lady, I had no idea. I assumed, but naturally, that you were a regular, minus only the white mantilla. My apologies, dear lady. Receive them graciously.' He stared down like a grotesque sculpture into her face, his height between her eyes and her view of the arena. She was forced to speak.

'Why do you come if you hate it so much?'

'Ah, that is the question. Why do I come?' His face shrank back into the hood of his worn duffle-coat like a monk retiring to religious reverie in the midst of the rabble. 'I come because it is here I detect the speed of development of my country. It is here I see the largest majority of my kind together in one place and without their masks on. It is here I am enlightened.'

'Not at the protests?' Paul put in with laconic tolerance.

'As the required balance, el Cid.'

'He's learning Spanish,' Paul explained to Ruth with the same almost indifferent toleration. 'Because he's allergic to Spain. It gives him a rash.'

'It is the fascination of similar opposites, you realise, dear lady. We go forward after a history of subjection to the freedom of football while the Spanish go backwards to keep the Inquisition alive by means of the bullfights. There will be the same release to drunken debauchery after this game in Melbourne as there is after similar games in London and New York and the bullfights in Madrid.'

'And you do not approve?' Ruth suggested, forced to assume a stiff, unfelt politeness by Paul's unexpected tolerance.

'Approve, dear lady, you ask me if I do not approve? Who am I to disapprove? I am here as you are in this place. You have not been before. Surely it is you who do not approve.'

'Mark, my husband, is not interested.'

Sims smiled and was suddenly natural and young. 'You are that Ruth. But of course, married to our brilliant Mark the physicist.'

'It's not necessary to go that far, Sims,' Paul said with noticeable distaste.

'But it is true, Paul,' Sims insisted seriously. 'Your brother is at the height of his brilliance. He must be twenty-nine or thirty – the peak, I understand, for physicists. Biologists, for example, must wait until the age of at least fifty for such distinction. What Mark is now, at this moment, is the ultimate manifestation of the component parts of his superior brain construction. Why bother with football? Ruth is absolutely right.'

Paul put his hand in his pocket, extracted a ten dollar note and flourished it in Sims' face. 'Do us a favour, will you, Sims? Get us some chips and stuff. I don't want to shove Ruth through the mob.'

'Sure,' Sims said. 'Glad to be of definite service. The usual?' He took the money and stored it safely.

'The usual, and spend it all. The queue will get worse later on.'

Sims slithered off like a snake into the crowd. Ruth did not speak. She didn't trust herself to move her lips. Besides, she sensed what she thought must be the fierce anger of embarrassment in Paul. In a minute she might think of something to say.

'Don't worry, Ruth, he won't be back. He's hungry and if he can't find us again in half an hour, he'll start to eat what's in his hands for want of something better to do with the stuff.'

'He won't forget where we are – he's too clever,' she said in a small, bitter voice. She was used to cleverness. Paul shrugged and his action dismissed Sims.

'I'm not supposed to know, being affluent,' he said. 'But I've noticed when he's hungry he doesn't come back. He's always hungry. He's big and he hasn't much money.'

'How did he get in, then?'

'Somebody gave him a pass. He knows where to suck around, I suppose. Anyway, he always gets in.'

She thought he was another hitchhiker, but she didn't say it, though the word began to beat in her head. Paul's voice droned on like a crooner at the drums.

'If he did have the money he wouldn't pay. He'd still use his wits and other people's stupidity to get in.'

'And get money from you to eat with when he is in?'

'That's chicken feed, Ruth. He's putting himself through, God knows how. Dad helped him last year, although he doesn't know it.'

'Paul!'

'Oh, nothing serious, only to the tune of half my allowance – loaned, of course. He has a job as a Saturday night waiter and dish-walloper and leaves it at that until he's professional.'

'Where does he live?'

'In a room owned by a pensioner in Richmond.'

'What a way to exist!'

'Oh, I don't know. He has his own den, he does what he likes; nobody's on his back.'

'Except the landlord.'

'The landlord likes him. The old man's a veteran on a pension. He's an agnostic and they talk about religion all the time. They argue with Barbara.'

'Barbara! Does she go there?'

'Well, sure, why not. We all do. Barbi delivers the Shorman cakes and leaves enough over for a week.'

'Does her mother know?'

'Yeah, Ruthie, her mother knows – as far as I can make out, her mother bakes the cakes and fixes the Christmas hamper.'

'You can't blame me for being surprised, Paul.'

'Don't be surprised, Ruth, don't be surprised at anything – especially anything the Shormans do. Barbi might end up marrying Sims.'

'What!'

'Maybe not, but she might, and if she wants to, that'll be it. Sims worships her. I'm sorry for him but he does.'

'He's got a nerve,' Ruth snapped.

'He's human,' Paul snapped back, 'And he's clever and Barbi is more than pretty.'

'But she's your girl.'

'I don't know, neither of us knows. I can't let her go and I can't keep her either. She never lets me get past first base. Barbi plays it safe.'

'You know, Paul, maybe if you—'

'No, Ruth, don't say it and for God's sake, give up thinking it. Our generation just won't hide any more under a suit of respectable clothes or a set of respectable rules either for that matter. What I wear doesn't mean a damn thing to Barbi.'

'Just the same, people might think you are something you're not Paul.'

'What people?'

'The professors for instance.'

'They don't know one student from another until your last year and then they want you in any clothes if you've got brains to give them honours material, at which stage Sims' moth-eaten pullover will be more important than any Saville Row outfit my old man can provide. Look Ruthie, get it into your head. Anybody, including the garbage collector, can go out and buy himself a high-class business suit any time he feels like it – that's the way it is nowadays. There's no class distinction on the sales front. You don't even have to pass over the money, you can get anything you want on tick – all you need is a job to mortgage yourself with. Sims could mortgage himself if he wanted to. He could be bonded to some outfit but he won't. He could get a living allowance but he won't. He's going through independently as Sims. When he graduates, he'll still be Sims belonging to himself, not the Education Department or the State Electricity Commission, and he'll make it!'

'Then he'll try to take away your girl.'

'He might. I introduced her to him and he's carrying a torch. Unusual men often get beautiful girls. So far Barbi can't see it, but Sims is a better bet than I am.'

'I can't see how.'

'I'm an in-betweener, Ruth, without Mark's brains or Dad's business instincts. I'm only making a stab at Engineering; I don't know how I'll go. Right now the pressure's almost killing me but I've got started and I know it's now or never. I used to think Mark would be around to help if I got stuck, but even if he was, he couldn't – nobody can. I'm giving it a go. If I fail, I'm going bush – fine future for a girl in that.'

'You mean you'll go on the land?'

'Yeah, if I'd had the brains before I would have done Ag-Science or tried to be a vet, but I didn't have what it takes so if I can't build roads either, I'll start as a rouse-about. They'll be disappointed at home, prefer to set me up in a nice P.R. job, but I won't be having any.'

Her voice answered him with unexpected emotion. 'I know, I know what you mean, Paul. There's something wonderful about the land. I had a holiday once with a school-friend who lived in Northern New South Wales. The sky was so close I couldn't get over it. I felt so free. I kept feeling I could fly!'

He looked at her with a wondering expression on his face like a child seeing the emergence of a butterfly for the first time. Then, beyond her head, he noticed a tout closing in on them and came alive again to the roars of the crowd. In one quick movement he put his arm around Ruth's shoulder and swung himself between her and the leering face she had not even sensed. Simultaneously he shoved his elbow hard into the man's chest.

'Take it easy, mate,' the man hissed and moved off.

So, Paul thought, she is a liability like a wallet full of cash would be a liability, only worse, much worse. Barbi wasn't a liability to Paul but to poor old Sims. Sims would have been back already, to stand on the other side of Barbi to set up his conversation flowing non-stop between the crowd and her mantilla as he called it. Funny, because Barbara didn't need protection; she could look after herself but Sims always acted as if every beast in the jungle threatened Barbi at the footy.

He began to walk, taking Ruth unprotesting under the shelter of his arm, pushing a way for them both with the force of his free shoulder, away from the direction of Sims' departure. He didn't want the words of Sims to batter at Ruth's raw sensibility. It was bad enough to have brought her. Alerted, his eyes and ears registered the arrival of the teams on the oval, the whistle, the great wailing scream from the stands. No, he shouldn't have brought Ruth. But at least he could keep her away from Sims; she needn't hear what Sims had to say about the spectacle. He would take her a way up the hill where the stand would hide them from those clever, probing eyes, beyond the place that was the farthest they ever took Barbi. Sims would sit in that place and give up trying to find them and begin to eat the chips.

Ruth did not speak, not once, not even when he finally spread out the rug. Even then she only smiled, sat down and turned her eyes on the game. He had intended to explain it to her point by point, but he sat silent, every nerve acute, seeing every movement of the players and the crowd with Sims' mind. It was as if Sims stood whispering in his ear, 'Look at them! Footy offers the possibility of press and T.V. fame and a good salary like a bull-fighter, like a matador gets in Spain. Education and social background is unimportant – only prowess matters. No other sport offers the same personal risks before so many spectators at one time. There are hero possibilities. The crowd loves the spectacle of a little blood – an accident to a player is conversation for a week, like a bull-goring. The game is the excuse for gambling and carousing, getting drunk and home late, off the hook of respectability. An excuse for driving a car like a lunatic – egged on by mad passengers with similar suicidal urges towards personal distinction through fearlessness, even though it leads to annihilation. It is the re-enaction of the charge principle in all wars from primitive expeditions in pre-historical times to equally primitive, mechanised expeditions today. The fundamentals are the same – old men round up ignorant young men, teach them to believe the power generating the mysterious male life force must be stimulated by violence. Indoctrinated, the young men charge and the old men, having lined up the women and children, scream encouragement. It is the war cry of the Indians, blood-curdling, life-destroying. It is fire, pillage and power, and has made the human condition a quagmire instead of a possible paradise – it is clothed over in a blind fanaticism – the fighting instinct, cruel, jeering at everything decent, and it must be stronger in man than in any other species because it never ceases – always rises to rousing.

'Blood sports have always been a spectacle. The exciting spectacle of torture and death – still needing an escape value. Is going back to barbarian pleasure a disease of the male? Does indulging brutality raise some mysterious facet of male ego? Is the unhealthy but persistent craving for violence stronger in some than others, passed on from generation to generation? That great roar of applause and awe always goes up when some player really gets rough and puts the boot in. It's like a release for all the spectators – what some deep, throw-back instinct urges them to do. At a football game you don't have to act revolted. It is the release of the blood spectacle – the outlet needed for men of ambition!'

A long sigh escaped Paul and was echoed by Ruth, but his mind did not escape Sims spitting out the bitterness.

'The moon and space travel temporarily roused interest in the majority. It is too scientific and cold. It is white vs. red. Warm, red blood vs. cold, white nerve. The enemy must be human or animal – able to bleed and suffer – don't tell me it's different now because it's not. It is only tempered at last by education and particularly by education of women, who previously have contributed nothing but screams and tears.'

And that other Sims pronouncement that made Barbi laugh, 'Look at the world set-up! Look at it. All the top politicians are old bull males, hardly one under fifty and most over sixty. Look at the young soldiers, all conscripted, can't get enough volunteers any more, must be caught between 18 and 25. Look at the political fear of the educators of scientists and philosophers whose opinions are put into reports and shelved; of women kept safely on the home base, bullied for not wanting to conform.

'Look at the elderly male control of television, the people's mass media, pushing out a daily diet of violence in half-hour stretches. Look at advertising and the newspapers, and scream-it-out-of-your-system. Saturday spectator sport – even Sunday spectator sport and what can we expect of ourselves; how can we demand sanity and security and beauty to balance our lives when we force our women and children to watch and read about war violence and crime all week and then drag them to a spectacle like this for week-end recreation. At least we ought to keep women away from it...'

'Oh, shut up, Sims,' Paul muttered. 'Shut up and leave me alone.'

Ruth turned sharply, gazed round and then focused her eyes on Paul. 'Paul?' she questioned, then sighed. 'I... I thought I heard you speaking to Sims. I... I was thinking about Sims, Paul. Were you?'

'Yes,' he said simply.

'He's right, of course,' she said. 'About all this, I mean.'

'Sure,' he said. 'He's right.'

'After a while they aren't going to be able to crowd any more in. There will be more and more who don't go – like me.'

'There'll be more and more old men to fill up the stands and pay young players for their fun.'

'What did you say, Paul?'

'Nothing Ruth, nothing. I quoted Sims. Forget it.'

'I wasn't thinking of old men, Paul. I was thinking of young men – like you and Sims. What's going to happen to all the young men when they can't get in? What are they going to do?'

'Barbi says they will batter the gates down and let the bulls go free.' He laughed.

'Barbi said that?'

'Sure, she says a lot of things that she and Sims understand, but I'll have to let my nephew Rollo figure out for me someday. Shall we go?'

'You don't mind?'

'Mind? Gawd no. I don't know why I thought of it.'

'You thought it would take my mind off the letter. It was the kindest thing anybody could have done for me today.'

'It didn't work.'

'Yes,' she said. 'It worked, just like you said.'

'You haven't yelled once.'

'I didn't need to. They all yell for me! That is what is so terrifying about it, Paul, they are all yelling for me.'

'They're all bloody well yelling for themselves!'

'Each for himself and altogether for the combined calamity – all for love lost. Oh yes, they are yelling for me, Paul.'

He stood and helped her to her feet in the same way Sims helped Barbi before she could help herself. Once again he put his arm across her shoulder to protect her passage past the stands to the gates. 'You'll have to forgive me, Ruth,' he said lightly. 'I'm not deep like Sims and Barbi – or Mark for that matter. I'm just hungry. We'll go somewhere and eat.'

But by the time they reached the car again she said, 'Paul, would you mind running me out to see Auntie Molly? That's what I'd like more than anything – to see Molly now, while Rollo is with Olwyn and Arthur.'

'Okay, if that's what you want,' he said. 'I'll drop you for an hour or two and come back.' He didn't want her out of his reach.

'Where will you go – to see Barbi?'

'Gawd no – I'm due there for the family lunch tomorrow.'

'No date tonight?'

'Sure I got a date. I'm taking you to dinner, eight o'clock Ma'am and then home to Rollo.'

CHAPTER SEVEN

Molly opened her door and said, 'Hello Ruth,' and to hide her obvious surprise added, 'How nice to see you. Come in,' because she sensed some urgency in her niece, perhaps from her clothes or stance or even her face.

Both women turned as Paul's car revved and took off and Ruth said, 'Paul brought me. We've been to the football. He'll be back by eight to take me back to Arthur and Olwyn...they've got Rollo.'

Following Molly inside, Ruth noticed that the broadcast of the football from Thomas's flat at the back of Molly's house took precedence over the neighbour's motor-mower. Thomas was getting disgustingly deaf by his own definition. Molly opened the door into her own room. 'Let's sit here,' she said. 'Make yourself comfy. I'll be right back. I just made myself some coffee. I never disturb Thomas while the game is on, or after either if his side loses.'

When Molly returned, Ruth was still standing where she had left her. Yet for all her stillness Ruth felt forced because of some time pressure inside herself to speak even before Molly had time to lay her tray on the table.

'Mark has left me,' she cried bitterly. 'Mark has left and gone to Paris with Eliane Shorman. I had a letter yesterday... Left me for Eliane Shorman and Mim Shorman must have known when she came home and didn't tell me.'

Molly was very gentle. 'Well, if it had been Judy – that is to say, if Eliane had been my daughter, I would have done exactly the same thing as Mim. I would have waited. I could not have precipitated the situation in case I was wrong or in case things did not develop as I expected.'

'But if you knew for sure?'

'Even if I knew I had every reason to be sure.'

'But why? What I can't understand is why.'

'Look at it this way, Ruth. Would you have been better off if Mim had told you? Would you have believed her or would you have waited in agony for confirmation from Mark?'

'I would not have believed her. I couldn't have believed anybody but Mark or – well, maybe Arthur.'

'Well, if she had tried to warn Arthur and Olwyn first, or told her own family, would you have preferred that?'

'No.'

'Mim had no choice, Ruth. She came home with either suspicion or certainties, one or the other which she couldn't speak. If it was only suspicion, then the daughter she was so close to hasn't told her the truth. If she was sure, she had to trust Eliane to make an honest decision about their affair. You realise, don't you, Ruth, that Mark and Eliane could have become lovers and deceived you for years. Mim could not have stopped them.'

Suddenly, a hard, clean spark of amber rode across Ruth's sombre eyes. 'Yes she could,' she cried out. 'That's it. I'm sure she could have stopped them. I believe that when she saw how it was between them after all that time she didn't want to stop them. She only wanted Eliane to have what she would always long for which was Mark. I don't think I even exist for anyone of the three of them.'

'Not even Mark? Nobody else matters to you, Ruth.'

'It's true – you are shocked, Molly. I never really existed for Mark. Sometimes I have consoled myself that nobody existed for Mark. But I thought it was because he was a physicist. I didn't mind. You see, I had more of him than the others had. I had all of his personal life and the distinction of his career and his son. I don't think he wanted any more on the personal side.'

'But Ruth, what about yourself? What do you want?'

'I don't know, Molly, I don't know. I built up everything else. I built up his career, I suppose, I'm like Olwyn and Mother in that. I've built up his career.'

'You think his career is all that important?'

'I don't know. I tell you, I just don't know, Molly. But Arthur and Olwyn feel a scandal will ruin his career. Because of it they are against a divorce.'

'But that's stupid, Ruth. He's not in politics or the church. If you'll excuse my saying so, any other career outlives a divorce and nowadays outlives it easily.'

'Then Mark and the Shormans won't care, will they? They will want Eliane married to Mark and not the other kind of scandal. Do you see now what I mean about Mim Shorman not considering me? Do you? But I don't have to give Mark a divorce, do I? I have Rollo to think about, haven't I? He needs a father, doesn't he? It's not fair.'

Molly reached for another cigarette, lit it and smoked it halfway through in silence. 'No, it's not fair,' she said at last. 'These things never are. God knows I wish it hadn't happened to you. I don't know why it should have, except that there's a kind of innocence about you. There always has been. Perhaps that's why your mother was able to get you safely married without the pangs the rest of us have to endure. No, I take that back. It isn't true. I was as innocent as you were when I married. Only I was different. I wasn't so pretty or so poised. I was awkward when I left school and I was ignorant.'

Ruth began to cry, gently at first, as if her eyes were pools slowly over-flowing with continuous soft rain. Then she caught her breath and the sobs came from somewhere deep inside so that she could have screamed with the pain and buried her face in the nearest cushion.

Molly said, 'Cry it out, Ruth. Let it come. I'll make some fresh coffee,' and went out to the kitchen.

'I never cry,' Ruth said when Molly came back to find her sitting upright again in her chair. 'I always despised the girls at school that cried when they didn't win.'

'You don't despise anybody, Ruth, once you've hit rock bottom yourself.'

'Don't you?'

'No, you don't. But sometimes when it happens to someone you love, you hope they'll stay there long enough to take a good look at their own essential nature and put it first for once.'

'You think I haven't done that?'

'Not like you have to do it now.'

'I know that and I know you know it. Did you realise when I was a little girl how I fought to spend those weekends with you?'

'I suppose I suspected. Anyway, I wondered how you managed.'

'It was because of your divorce. That's why I came tonight – because of your divorce.'

'Thank you for telling me.'

'You are the only person I know well enough to talk to who's had a divorce. I'm sorry, Molly.'

'You needn't be,' Molly said, and waited.

The silence of the moment went a long way back to awkward weekends when Judy and Tom had plans spoiled by a telephone call from their rich little cousin who decided periodically to visit.

'What's she want to come here for? She's got everything and her mother thinks she's perfect... She's too superior for our crowd... Gee, I just can't take her again, everything about her just shrieks her posh school and she's always right...' Molly remembered how sweet Ruth would be when she came, how she would help with the dishes, prefer to go to the local with Auntie than the barbecue with her cousins. How she never argued, never fought. How she sat for hours on end stroking the dog behind the ears. How she weeded the tomatoes. More than anything else, Molly remembered how she could never bring herself to put Ruth off by suggesting another weekend without a sense of humiliation.

'You never let me down,' Ruth said flatly, now in a voice of the little girl on the telephone. 'Can't you tell me, Auntie Molly, can't you tell me? What to expect? Can't you tell me what to do?'

'I can't tell you what to do, Ruth,' Molly began, continuing urgently, emphasising every word. 'And don't let anybody else tell you either – not anybody, particularly not your mother, or Olwyn. You must find your own answer – and abide by it.'

'But I don't know where to start. I... I just feel as if I have been whipped. That's why I thought you could help... Because you... Because you have been whipped too...'

'No, Ruth... It wasn't the same for me. Not the same at all. I will tell you, but it isn't a pretty story. It is what most people would call sordid. That's why I haven't been able to share it. I'm not what you'd call a sentimental type. I don't read penny dreadfuls; they bore me. I hate marriage advice columns; I make a joke of them. I did when I was a girl and still do with Thomas. Life pays back! In a certain sense, nobody should make jokes. I suppose the kind of girl I turned out to be in our family was a joke in itself. I didn't fit. Oh, I had dates, but I wasn't popular with boys like your mother. I was tactlessly outspoken and I held you couldn't judge a man by the cut of his jacket or his tie. When I met Les, I was already on the shelf according to Mother, and of course I had escaped any real experience because I knew all the answers.

'I loved Les – there was no doubt of that; for me it was the grand passion, the full abandonment to the overflow that somehow purifies and shines life to a point that justifies and gives meaning to everything. It was my first experience of the sexual urge and sanctified by marriage I was as absorbed in it as a willing slave-girl in the Arabian nights. I had never been so alive to sensation and dead to everything else connected with it. I discovered the lure of the flesh that illuminates nature, the driving force that stimulates evolutionary reproduction. I didn't care about anything else but the physical gratification of myself and my beloved. It took me two years to even suspect that his experienced sexual wisdom overlaid my similar innocence. Of course, I knew the so-called facts of life, but you can't know passion in the full sense until you fall into it. When you do fall in, you have all the sensations of temporarily drowning but yet are so buoyant you can't really sink as you so often wish to. I didn't love him long, Ruth; I couldn't once I realised that what for me was love in the full sense was for him only physical. Once I had to face reality I knew that what he wanted was my body more than full-time or he would have had to have somebody else's part-time as well. At first I tried to save him, as I thought, from himself, from the seed of his own destruction, his driving necessity for sexual over-indulgence. I thought the expected baby would do it, thinking his unexpected reaction to the natural result of our passion was another jealousy of love. Then I thought that the love a man has for a son would swing into a normal welcome upon our return from the hospital. When the baby was ten months old, I discovered he had substituted for me even when I was in hospital, though not from love, he assured me, but from need. I tried again with him, but well before the birth of my little girl, he was away again. On the dark, lonely nights I knew myself to be learning a strange kind of physical gratitude. I had come out at the end of passion to the fullness of a woman's need; the balanced love of husband and children, but Les was still as infantile as the babies, there was no end to his means, with me there never would be.'

'So you divorced him?'

'Oh no, not immediately – not for four years. I just carried on. But I didn't have any more children, that was easy. He didn't want any children, really, but as he didn't know what else to do, he supported those he had. He gave me half what he earned and we had this war-savings home as you see it now in this room, only new then and without the extensions of course and cheaply built as they all were in the immediate post-war period. Les stuck to the same firm in the office for another year after I had Judy and then to make more money, went out as a salesman on the road. I never saw the extra commission money, but he agreed to have the firm pay the same, regular amount into my savings bank every two weeks in case he wasn't home on pay-day. It was a poor living, better when he was away than when he was home, but I managed. I made the children and the garden my life. The fact that I was disappointed and ashamed didn't matter. I had cut so many contacts anyway, in the wild flight of our first two married years.'

'But you did divorce him?' Ruth persisted.

'Yes, I was lucky.'

'Lucky – you call it lucky?'

'Oh, I had evidence enough, Ruth, more than enough. But I couldn't bring myself to a point of decision. When I thought about it, my mind went around in circles. I was so financially dependent I wouldn't have known where to start. I had to balance a home and food for the children against divorce and I had a kind of personal routine of housework, taking and going for Tommy at kinder, with Judy in the pram, shopping for bargains on the way home, gardening until tea-time, radio programs and free library books until I went to bed. Any dealings with a lawyer would have jeopardised this regime which was my only known security. I deliberately balanced this against the time Les was at home, which had become the difficult period of my life, for he still demanded his full measure. His urge was insatiable and I had grown what is now called frigid.'

'You had nobody to help – nobody at all?'

'No, not really. You know I'm reserved by nature and the way I saw it, I was undermined by circumstances of my own making. I shared no confidences.'

'But what happened – you did get a divorce.' Divorce was still Ruth's statement of need.

'A girl came, a girl from Portland – a blonde, well-developed girl of about nineteen, in a flowered dress. She rang my doorbell at eight o'clock one night and said she had come to see me about Les. He was in town at the time and I never quite knew when to expect his key in the lock. He had one of the firm's Ford cars that summer and I remember I looked out beyond the girl into the street to see if it was parked on our nature strip. But the girl seemed to be alone so I let her in. I had no doubt as to why she had come to see me, and was only conscious, really, of the hard, thumping knock that began in the pit of my stomach.

'Maybe you can imagine us in this living room, my deliverer and I. It was a soft room then, with one pale green, magnolia pattern linen armchair I had covered myself to match the curtains. Everything else was neutral beige, the carpet square, the chesterfield, the walls, even the tiles of the open fireplace. The one small table had a bowl of pink geraniums. That young woman came into the quiet room like a flame and sat belligerently in her bright dress of orange and yellow and brown, on the edge of the magnolia chair. Her eyes swept briefly the room with myself sitting tentatively on the corner of the neutral chesterfield. She wasted no time with preliminaries. "I'm Olive Bent from Portland," she announced, as if that explained everything, which it did – although I had never seen or heard of her before in my life. "Les and I have been in love for months and my family has just found out. Something must be done about a divorce for Les so we can get married."

'"Are you pregnant?" I managed to whisper, incapable of loud speech.

'"No, I'm not pregnant!" she snapped, "And have no intention to be. But I'm living with Les and want to marry him. He's got everything I want."

'"Are you sure?" I asked.

'I think she saw me then, for the first time. But she was not taken aback and her attitude was in no way altered.

'"Of course I'm sure – why do you think I came? Les and I love each other."

'"Les is a man who is often in love."

'"So what? I've been in love too – but not like this. It's too bad he's married, but he's no good to you wanting me, is he?"

'"No."

'"You'll give him a divorce then?"

'"Does he want a divorce?"

'"You know perfectly well he does. He's told you often enough."

'"How do you know?"

'"Because he's told me of course – how else? I know it's lousy for you, but after all, this isn't the eighteenth century."

'"I'm not concerned about the century. I have two children."

'"I know. But children are no reason to hang on to a man these days. Naturally you'll get an allowance for the children." '

'You know, Ruth, there are some things you never forget. A scene fixes and sets colour, sound and atmosphere, down to the finest detail. I participated in this scene and yet I was on the outside of it, as if viewing a film. I saw with surprise my own mind snapping down like a trap on a mouse and I heard my own voice as soft as the room we sat in.'

'"The children must have a house to live in," I told Olive Bent.

'"Well, who said anything about them moving out? I'm sure I don't want your house. It wouldn't suit me. Les will make over the house to you if that's what you want. Anything else?"

'Anything else! I looked at her, expecting to sigh and producing no more than a cow-like stare. She was a phenomenon, like I must have been eight years before. She was in a cocoon of passion. To sigh for her would be as useless as a warning. I started and the scene flicked. There was a little light tapping on the door.

'"That will be Les," she said and stood up. Les, of course, had his own key. But she walked straight to my door and his, to let him in. All planned. The whole thing all planned on a basis of Les's lies. The very night before Les had been home with me and sneaked out later, doubtless to go to her. She must have embraced him during the moment of silence, during which my stomach turned over and the door was shut. I didn't move. Devoid of love and hate equally, I simply sat and waited. It was my house, my garden, and my children slept behind the closed door facing across the hall to the open door displaying the double bedroom suite Les and I had bought the day before we married. But I seemed to be at the cinema, waiting for the play to unfold – a mere spectator.

'The voice of Olive Bent was smug as she came back to the room with Les behind her. Les had a lean face with the beautiful eyes and sensuous lips that give charm to the face of a young boy. He always looked a little abashed, a little hurt. His wide-eyed golden glance fell tentatively upon me, with his usual bland, calculating expression. I always remember Les as he stood in the door while Olive took over his life. She made her pronouncement with flat glee: "So everything is good-o, darling, as long as she can have the house and the allowance for the kids, we can have the divorce. We only have to make the arrangements."

'"Arrangements?" Les muttered, mustering the grace to look at his feet instead of at me, instead of at Olive.

'"Arrangements with the lawyer. She can go to Mr Cohen. I've told him you wanted the divorce, Les." She turned to me, her eyes glittering like the wings of a Christmas beetle. "When will you go?"

'"Tomorrow, if you like," I said. "I'll get a pencil and write down the address."

'"Tomorrow!" Les seemed surprised. In fact, he looked almost let down.

'"There's no point in waiting, darling, and Mr Cohen's as good as any other lawyer."

'"But he's your lawyer, not Molly's." It was as near as Les ever came to argument.

'I said tentatively, "I don't have a lawyer, Les, nor any money to get one. It's you wanting the divorce."

'Immediately, Olive turned apologetic for Les, for his hedging. She apologised to me for Les and at the same time bullied me on his behalf. "It's hard for Les, you know," she said. "He doesn't want to be mean or anything. Naturally, he wants to avoid a row at all costs – all men do."

'"It's hard for me too," I said. "I'm..."

'She snapped at me before I finished. "I've admitted that, haven't I, and agreed to the house and the children's allowance and to pay for the divorce? All you have to do is go to Mr Cohen in the morning."

'Once again, she dismissed me and turned to Les, glowing like a shining torch. "I suppose, darling, you have a few things around you'd like to collect. Will you get them now, while I write Mr Cohen's address?"

'He was trapped – so trapped he couldn't even "collect" as she put it his latest dressing gown or the shirts I'd just washed for him.

'"Oh, let it go, Ollie, there's nothing much," he said.

'"If there is anything, I'll put it in a parcel and send it to the office for you," I said. "Will that do?"

'"Oh sure, sure," he said. "Anything at all – cripes, don't mind me!"'

'That's how I got my divorce, Ruth. A woman gave it to me on behalf of a husband I no longer wanted. When Harriet heard of the divorce later, she came out you know, and made a great fuss about me being a fool to let Les go – other woman or no other woman! She didn't know, of course, that I sat up all that first night with the lights blazing and next morning, first thing, got all my locks changed on the pretext of a burglar scare before I went to Mr Cohen at noon.'

'Was it awful, the divorce?' Ruth asked. 'You know, the court and everything?'

'No. At first, I couldn't believe in it, you see. I was unprepared for the speed of the whole development and I didn't trust Mr Cohen, who could be described as a middle-aged race track type of lawyer. You know what I mean. He talked about 'my client' all the time, meaning Ollie, whom he'd known since she was a little girl, he told me. I never felt he was working for me in any sense, yet when the time came, he put the case through smoothly, on infidelity with proven adultery, which was necessary at that time.

'Perhaps Cohen was better than any lawyer I could have chosen. He never once tried to mend the marriage. He asked no awkward questions. After I had been to see him, I was still so unsure, I decided to at least live in my house as I liked while I had it. I advertised and sold the bedroom suite which was both elaborate and expensive, and re-arranged the children in my bedroom, which was larger than theirs, and moved myself with a divan bed into their room, which had the pretty bay window looking into the garden. I put that oval table from an auction into the window and bought another wardrobe at the same time. It was a good change and gave me as big a dose of confidence as changing the locks. I think after that I began to count on at least a legal separation. I was in a strange state of mind, you will realise, when I tell you it took me a month to think up the idea of selling the bedroom suite, during which time I slept on a spare stretcher dragged into the children's rooms and kept the radio turned down low in case I heard a key tried in the new lock.

'I think I felt as if Les had been let out of jail and was blaming me for giving him away to the police. I never let the children out of my sight, for what reasons I don't know until this day. Les was not a violent man, nor had he ever shown the paternal qualities that inspire the bitterness that leads to kidnapping. Actually, he scarcely knew the children and to them was rather like a teenaged relation who simply stopped visiting them. He had insisted on them calling him Les, as might the casual lover of a widow or a divorcee. Only I didn't know that at the time – hadn't reasoned on the situation. If I had, surely I would have realised I had nothing serious to fear from Les.'

'Then he never tried to see the children?'

'No, nor me. The divorce went through in about ten months from the time Olive Bent came to the house. The same money came through with the same regularity paid into my bank by the firm. I guarded every penny like a miser, buying no more than immediate necessities. I wasted no food. Except to go to see Mr Cohen, I spent no tram fare, I used my garden and my half dozen chickens all to the purpose of saving towards the rates and the bills. Finally, two months before the divorce, I took money I saved from my payment bank and opened another savings account in another bank. All the time I was terribly apprehensive from lack of sleep, and yet I was better off than I had been for years.

'In the September, little Judy was accepted into kinder. Alone during school hours, I scrubbed and cleaned and gardened, off-setting with work strange, unmanageable fits of lethargy and depression. I had only one activity outside of home – a turn each Wednesday at the little church over the lunch period. A capable, middle-aged widow named Mrs Jones ran the kinder lunches and the young mothers gave voluntary help. During September, I offered extra services when Mrs Jones went down with arthritis. In October, I was offered her job. I happened to be present when the emergency arose and she couldn't turn up one Wednesday. The principal asked if I would take over until the end of the year. It was a small job, but I seized upon it greedily, like a life-line attached to my children on the safe raft of school. At the end of November, the divorce came up in court. I simply changed my day off with one of the other mothers and went to the court. Mr Cohen took care of everything. I didn't even have to speak to Les and Olive Bent, who sat on the other side of the court-room as defacto man and wife. It was the last time I ever saw Les.'

'The last time. What about Olive?'

'Over the years I've seen Olive once or twice.'

'And yet Les never wanted to see his children – I suppose she wouldn't let him.'

'She didn't marry him. She married Mr Cohen.'

'Mr Cohen?'

'It's a funny story, isn't it? Les walked out on her. After the divorce, I had two payments, one at the end of November and one in the middle of December. Because of the job at the kinder and the divorce, I let my head go a little for Christmas. The ladies' committee gave me a gift when school broke up and the Head invited me to take over Mrs Jones's job on a permanent basis in the New Year. It broke the strain in me and I felt I could celebrate – that I owed it to the children. We had a special dinner and a Christmas tree. Tommy made a remark I remember after the dinner, that it was funny Les hadn't turned up for such a good feed.'

'Where did Les go – what happened?' Ruth demanded. She was seeing Molly, feeling Molly, and had momentarily forgotten herself.

'He went interstate somewhere. I waited until the end of January, thinking perhaps Les and Olive had married and would make good the payments after the holidays. Then I phoned the firm and the manager told me Les had left the firm before Christmas; no, he didn't know where he was working. Finally, he suggested I contact a solicitor. I phoned Mr Cohen who told me my husband had proved to be a scoundrel. Did I have any means of support? If not, I had better apply to the Social Services Board. He was too busy to take another case, but he was sure the Social Services Board would investigate the possibility of a matrimonial payments investigation order. He would forward to me all papers in connection with the divorce and the house in case the government officials required them. I could almost feel him washing his hands across the telephone. So that was Mr Cohen.'

'Whatever did you do? Molly, whatever could you do?'

'Like so many other women in a similar fix, I did nothing and somehow with the part-time job, the child endowment for my second child, a few more chickens and the garden, I managed. I paid the rates and the bills and lived on the rest. I found a friend at the school who was a war widow with three children and problems like mine, whose youngest was a little boy in Tommy's class. The part-time job proved harder than I expected, requiring reserves of tact and persistence. It was a small, church school and I was required to do several jobs as well, for which I had no training. I slept the sleep of the justly exhausted. A busy year. At the end of it I happened to read in the marriage column: Mr Ignacious Cohen – Miss Olive Bent.'

'You never heard from Les?' Now Ruth was truly shocked, hating Les with fierce, young hate. Molly looked up at her ceiling before she answered.

'Yes, twice before he died. Both times he sent fifty pounds at Christmas time, postal orders with post office addresses. The first time I opened a bank account for Tommy and Judy and let the interest build up. I never spent it.'

'And you stayed in the same job? I remember I thought you were a kindergarten teacher.'

'For four years. I felt safe there. It took all that time to feel secure enough to move. Yet, you know, I fought to maintain that job even when I knew I wasn't wanted. But Tommy wasn't happy at the school. He got too big and bouncy and I couldn't afford to send him to the big-brother school. So I glassed in the back verandah with a room at the end for Tommy and his dog, took Judy in with me and let the other room as a bedsitter. It worked very well and had taken the ache out of the budget by the time I gave up the job at the end of the year. Once I was free inside again, I knew I could manage. I put Tommy and Judy into the State school and would you believe it, was invited during that year to take over the tuck shop there. I found my kind of willing, part-time slave was in demand.'

'And you never took legal action against Les?'

'No, and yet he paid off the house in the end. He died from injuries received in a car accident between Kalgoorlie and Perth. It seemed he had lived for two years in Kalgoorlie, of all places. He had a job and a savings account. A girl was with him in the car and another car driven by a woman ran into him, but at the hospital he gave my name as beneficiary and the children as his heirs. So not even another Olive Bent had made him marry again. It was ten years, almost to the day, since I had last seen him, sitting beside Olive Bent in the Melbourne Divorce Court. He was forty-two years old when he died, but the age he gave which was on the death certificate was thirty-nine. I knew the significance for him of that last year before forty. Age is cruel to a Don Juan.'

'But why didn't the family help you, Molly? What went wrong with the family?'

'I didn't ask for help. As Aunt Harriet reminded me, none of my family thought Les was good enough for them when I married him, but since I had, the least I could do was stick to him. I told her nothing. I had my pride. Mother was overseas, giving your mother the grand tour when I got the divorce. Father was dead and Uncle Thomas at sea. I had cut myself off.'

'What about the Shormans? Dr Shorman is your cousin, isn't he?'

'Yes, but if he hadn't married Mim I don't suppose I would have ever seen him again. It was Mim who gathered me back into the family fold.'

'You were never close to Mother, were you – not really?'

'She's younger, Ruth, and very different. She was Mother's favourite when we were little and I suppose I felt shut out. Then she got married in London and when she came back with you to Mother in South Yarra, they both seemed to find me too forward as a working woman to be quite nice, rather as if I were a revolutionary, although they never mentioned my divorce. I didn't mind, really. I couldn't have kept up with their style of living.'

'Yet you came from time to time. You always came until Grandma died.'

Quite suddenly, Molly laughed and changed the subject. 'And after that, if I didn't, you phoned up and came to me. Thomas says the Shormans can't keep away from each other out of sheer curiosity. He says there's a lot of Shorman in me. Maybe it's in you as well.'

Ruth managed only the semblance of a laugh in response. 'Maybe that's why you have told me what you have, Molly. Nobody on the other side of the family would have, that's for sure. Thank you.'

Molly sighed. 'It hasn't helped, has it? It's too distant from you... Too remote from your experience, too long ago, although sometimes it seems like yesterday to me.'

'I don't know yet, Molly. I think I'm shocked. I know I'm shocked! I shouldn't have asked!'

'You wanted to know about divorce, Ruth – so you might as well know it is always shocking… Is always particularly personal. Why do you think it causes more fear than war and makes better newspaper headlines? Will you please sleep on mine, for what good it can do you, and then forget it?'

'Oh, Auntie Molly, how can you ask me that?'

'You're young,' Molly said. 'And I'm not. It makes a difference. Why don't you have dinner with me and stay the night.'

'No,' Ruth said. 'I've got to get back to Rollo.'

'But he'll be asleep.'

'I want to be there when he wakes up.'

'You're sure Paul will be back for you then?'

'Yes, Paul will be back, I'm sure…' That was the one thing Ruth was sure of. Paul would be back

CHAPTER EIGHT

Number seventeen faced the curve of a tree-lined avenue in the suburb of Kew. On the listings the house would be called a 'gentleman's residence': spacious, fully modernised, with beautiful grounds. The words 'backing on to the Yarra,' or 'river view' would be modestly present by implication. Overstatement was not expected concerning the better parts of Kew, where simple suggestion could suffice for a detailed list of architect-designed amenities.

Atmosphere, Paul conceded to be the descriptive word. There would always be plenty like himself willing to partake of a meal in a house with atmosphere, he decided as he braked his car two doors up. Then he told his ironic mind to shut up. A Kew address was better than an address in Toorak anyway. An address in Toorak was a helluva thing to overcome. His foot burned on the brake; there must be a hole in the sole of his suede desert boots... no the uppers had come away on one side. He might have known the hard plastic sole would never wear out. He would have to start wearing one of the other pairs lining his wardrobe floor. He wished he could give a pair of that lot to Sims. Gawd, his own feet were big enough but Sims wore a size larger, and had thinner feet as well. Besides, he couldn't fool Sims; one try at buying a larger fitting to pass off as useless had nearly finished him with Sims.

Well, Barbi had asked him to Sunday lunch; only family, she said, so he hadn't thought about shoes, hadn't thought about his dear cousin George being there either, so of course he was, as his this-year's Holden station wagon was parked out front of number seventeen. Good old George, he'd sure learned how to play it smooth, never missed a trick since he married Maddy Shorman. And how poor Olwyn had fallen for it... Nowadays, George could do no wrong. However, dear George for his part did nothing to assist any but his own relationship with the Shorman family. It was certain he didn't want to see his cousin Paul around and made it plain even to poor old Arthur, who obviously thought Barbi Shorman might be what parents called 'a good influence'.

Under the shade of a tree on the avenue and warm in the heat of his car, Paul felt another of those inexplicable twangs of regret about Arthur. The old man had come up tops with Ruth, with more decency actually to both himself and Ruth than might be expected of him anyway you looked at the bloody mess. Paul sighed, knowing how soon he, Paul the wrecker, the family misfit, would be the one to let them all down. Probably before this day was out he would be the one who could not navigate the hole. God knew how anxious he was to skirt around the edge of it, if only for the sake of Arthur. And Ruth. Both of them meant more to him than he had realised before.

Last night, after he'd got Ruth home with no more food inside than Molly had made her eat with the coffee, and no more words than a wax model, he had stood in the hall waiting while she sneaked in to look at Rollo asleep. Just as she came out of the baby's room they heard the voices of his parents and suddenly, as if they were conspirators in the night, Ruth had reached up to kiss him lightly on the cheek and whisper 'Thanks' before she ran into her own room. He had faced his parents gruffly, telling them briefly that he had taken Ruth to see Molly and now he supposed as she had gone into her room she wanted to go to bed. Arthur had restrained Olwyn.

'Well,' he had said, 'I guess that'll do for us too... It's been a long day.'

So now Paul knew that because of Ruth he was going to tell Barbi. It would not be hard because within half an hour she would pull it out of him with that deadly female instinct that held him off with concerned, affectionate frankness and impaled Sims with its opposite. Sims was another one he understood better now than he had yesterday, now that he knew the hurt he dared not face could force him, even if Barbi did not, to be the one to say what was probably better left unsaid.

He sat ten minutes in his parked car and twice pressed his foot on the starter. He did not have to go in, he could back out and get a meal somewhere and then phone from the nearest phone box before they got to the apple pie. He could say his car had broken down again – after all he had only picked it up from the garage this morning. Barbi knew he hadn't a car last night. Anyway, what the bloody hell did it matter what they thought? George would make sure they realised he was unreliable, nicely of course, but he'd put him in for all that.

But each time he thought of driving away he connected the thought with Ruth and knew that if he did not go in to the Shormans' for lunch he would go around to see Ruth. An hour ago she had insisted on going back to her flat with Rollo and he knew she would not go to her mother who played bridge on Sunday afternoon. She would not go to Molly's again. She would not go anywhere.

Suddenly, Paul began to ache for Ruth as if she sat beside him in the car. With a jerk he pulled the car key from the dashboard and in one swift movement was out of the car and walking towards the Shormans'. He went in the side gate and appeared at the kitchen door. Mim Shorman was alone in the kitchen, concentrating on gravy, and he was enveloped in the aroma of roast beef. An idea fluttered that this was his chance, that he could speak to her about the thing on his mind. But it was a flash thought, gone as she spoke. She was abstracted and for all she saw him he could have been in bathers.

'Hello Paul,' she said. 'Maddy has taken the children in to pay their respects to Layton in the lounge room. Then we are going to feed them in here first. Henrietta is on the telephone and Barbara said she'd study in her room until you came. Go straight in... You can leave your coat in her room or the hall.'

He did exactly as she told him. Somehow, he was relieved to be so easily trapped.

Layton took his place at the head of the dining table in a silence that awaited the conclusion of his statement begun over his second pre-lunch whisky. He seated himself last after the muted scuffling of the family feet on the carpet. 'While you were putting out the soup, Linda,' he continued, 'I was saying I deplored the press comparisons pushed forward at the present time between Australia and Canada. My opinion is that people who enjoy the bounty of this country should show a sense of loyalty.'

Mim picked up her soup spoon and murmured vaguely, 'I'm not sure what you mean, Layton.'

'While you were overseas, Mim, we had a spate of criticism of the federal government – with Labor taking over, of course,' George said smugly.

'About time, too,' Barbi put in suddenly, looking intently across the table at Paul, who failed to respond or even lift his head.

Layton put his spoon back into his soup. 'I will not have disloyalty in my house, Barbara – you know that,' he said. 'I am fed up with it.'

'Who's being disloyal?' Barbara looked surprised and belligerent but her mother, suspecting some strain concerning Paul, overtook her.

'What comparisons were you speaking of, Layton?' she asked mildly.

'The armed services system is an example. It is very new, quite revolutionary in fact, and there is no reason to believe it would work in Australia where we are based on the British system.' Layton paused and glanced around the table, his eyes returning to Mim. 'But perhaps, dear, you wouldn't know about it.'

'If you mean the Canadian unification of all three military services under one head for greater efficiency, then I approve of it as much as I approve of any military system,' Mim said, standing up with her empty soup plate in her hand. She served herself very little soup on Sundays.

'It's a lot better than our system anyway,' Barbi said, jumping up to collect the rest of the soup plates. 'Finish your soup, Dad.'

'There's no need to get emotional or rude, Barbara,' Layton remarked, handing over his plate. 'Why is it that in this family, emotional outburst always takes the place of analytical discussion? Every time I mention loyalty to one's country, one of you girls starts to argue.'

Henrietta trailed a delicate hand across her forehead and down the sweep of her long hair, a gesture guaranteed to attract even more attention than her brief verbal contribution. 'Pay no attention, Pops,' she said. 'You don't have to worry about the military set-up, you haven't even got a son.'

Only Henrietta called Layton 'Pops' and he pretended to hate the term, but when she used it always felt flattered and laughed. He considered her the baby of the family, for all she was Barbara's twin.

This was not a thing he bothered to analyse, so his answer was, 'Perhaps. Nevertheless, as I have said before, the women in this family always get emotional over any aspect of military services.'

Paul lifted his head to say without noticeable feeling, 'It's not a female thing, sir, the males of my generation feel the same.'

'They would,' George laughed and felt Maddy's foot under the table as she rose from the table to check on the children who were outside playing after their early lunch. If they realised Mim and Barbi were serving out in the kitchen they would push in from the garden and hold up the meal, which annoyed her father. She suspected the slowness of the meals in her own house to be the reason her father had dined with her only once during her mother's absence. Layton fancied himself as a disciplinarian and just once or twice lately she had noticed George displaying the same tendency.

Layton surveyed the three empty chairs with distaste before he continued to inform George, Paul and Henrietta on the danger of

Australia following in the footsteps of Canada. Canada, he pointed out, was overpowered by American investments, had Atlantic seaports more important than the Pacific counterparts, and impossible climatic conditions across the great open spaces of the north. George listened, Paul held his peace and Henrietta surveyed the polish on her fingernails until the arrival of the roast dinner. Unlike his father before him, Layton, although capable, did not carve the Sunday roast. Also, he preferred roast beef to the leg of lamb he had been brought up to expect after Sunday morning service. He still expected the roast, although the church service in the local Anglican church was no longer part of his weekend routine.

Mim and the girls placed the sliced roast beef on a platter and the vegetables in the serving dishes on the table. The hot plates and the gravy bowl were put in front of Layton who made a ritual of handing each person present a plate with two slices of gravied meat while Mim and the girls reseated themselves. Once, when George remarked to Madeleine how much he liked this ceremony, she had informed him briskly that her father carried it on only to impress Aunt Harriet. On this occasion, George repeated Layton's opinion of Canada for the benefit of the ladies as Layton passed the plates. George added his agreement to keep the conversation moving. Another thing he liked was intelligent conversation at the family dinner table.

'Thank you, George,' Layton said. 'At any rate, the differences are too marked for Australia to consider a parallel system.'

'Oh, I don't know,' Mim said. 'The conditions you mention for the unification of the armed services would make it harder for Canada than Australia, I would think, but they wouldn't rule out our taking a look at the system. Other countries with very different conditions are studying the Canadian scheme. There was a lot of discussion in England while I was there.'

'Then, my dear, you may be sure our government is aware of it and sizing up the pros and cons without the interference of the press.'

Again, Barbara was belligerent – unusual for her at meals, 'And you may be sure, Daddy, our government will do nothing at all unless something stirs them up. It's just the same with demonstrations. The protesting does stir,' she snapped.

'Whatever the subject under discussion, you bring in demonstration,' Layton said, unperturbed. 'I've warned you to keep out of them, Barbara.'

George looked quickly at Madeleine and asked, 'How are the kids going?'

'They're in the old playhouse at the back,' Maddy replied. 'And with luck they'll be happy there for an hour. We should get our dessert and coffee in peace.' She glanced at Barbi anxiously and jumped when Henrietta suddenly laughed with the trill of running water.

'I thought I took sweet potato and it's pumpkin. I'll say for Aunt Molly, she didn't give us pumpkin.'

'You wouldn't have known if she did,' Mim said. 'From what I gather, you and Barbi were hardly ever home while I was away.'

Barbara pushed away her plate with the food only half consumed and demanded, 'Why do we always have to have pumpkin anyway? I hate it and so did Eliane. What's more, nobody ever made her eat it.'

'It made her sick,' Mim said softly and there was silence.

'That's not true. She was always protected, that's why. And it's going to be hard to protect her now.'

'Barbi!' Paul said and put up his hand.

'Well, Paul, you know and I know it. Why should I get picked on all through lunch while Eliane is being protected for ever and ever, no matter what she does.'

'She is not here to protect herself,' Mim said, her voice even softer.

'What are you talking about?' Layton queried sharply. 'What's the matter with you, Barbara?'

'I just don't think it's fair, that's all. I just don't think it's fair all of us sitting here talking about pumpkin, while Mim knows all about Eliane and she hasn't told us. She's been home all this time and... She hasn't told us, just let us go on as if nothing has happened. It isn't fair.'

Shocked, they realised Barbara was at the point of tears.

Paul stood up and even George noticed his face change colour as Barbara pushed her chair back. Like a flash, Henrietta was also standing to protect her. Maddy felt George stiffen.

'Don't,' Paul pleaded. 'Please don't, Barbi.'

'Yes, I will,' Barbara whispered. 'Can't you see, Paul. I have to. They have to know.'

'No, Barbi, tell your mother first. Not here... Please, Barbi...'

Layton stood up. 'Whatever you have to say, Barbara, say it... Quickly.'

Her voice in defiance of Paul was a hissed, angry whisper only less silent than the clock. 'Eliane has run away to Paris with Mark Carlister.'

Paul sighed, rooted to his place on the carpet, while the rest of them crowded around Mim Shorman sitting silent on her chair.

'This is preposterous,' he heard Layton Shorman say. 'Preposterous!'

So, Dr Shorman hadn't been told either. It wasn't just the girls. He heard them bombard their mother with questions, one after the other, nobody listening for answers. They told each other above her head that of course she knew. They would be personally injured, each and every one. He heard George whine, 'It's a scandal, you should have been told. You of all people, Maddy. It'll make all the difference to us; it makes my position impossible.' Heard Henrietta bleating like a lamb, 'Just when I'm going to get engaged, as if it isn't difficult enough as it is,' heard Barbi demanding over and over, 'Why didn't you tell us, Mummy? Why did you have to let me find out this way? Why didn't you tell us?'

The reality was no more than an extended minute before Layton demanded silence, forcing them all back.

'Is this true, Linda?'

'Is what true?' Still the small voice.

'Has Eliane gone to Paris with Mark Carlister?'

'I think so.'

'You think so! Didn't you ask her?'

'No.'

'In God's name, why not?'

'I could have stopped her.'

'Of course you could have stopped her! It was your duty to stop her! Why didn't you stop her?'

She put her hands against the table and helped herself gain her feet, then she lifted her head and faced her family, her mouth a thin, straight line under misted eyes. 'I wanted to give her time to tell... What she has to tell... Herself.'

Layton Shorman's voice grew cold with sarcasm. 'Then you didn't really know.'

'Yes, I knew.'

Layton opened his mouth to speak, closed it grimly and lifted his eyes to the ceiling. Then he turned to Barbi. 'Would you mind telling me how you found out, Barbara?' he snapped.

Into the sudden silence, Barbara's voice visibly shivered. 'Paul told me before lunch. Ruth had a letter from Mark.'

'I see,' Layton said. 'So you didn't think of that, Linda?'

'I hoped for it,' she said.

'Really, Linda,' he cried, with a terrible exasperation that crowded all of them closer in fear. 'Must you continue to give ridiculous, vague answers to everything I ask?'

Her eyes flickered and in a glance encompassed them all like a sharp diamond, but she spoke to her husband in the same hushed voice that seemed to come from some place behind her. 'Don't excite yourself, Layton,' she said. 'I am entitled to my hopes, whatever they are. You were speaking of loyalty to one's country. I hoped to find it in my family. I also hoped for love and understanding – the kind you give, not the kind that only expects to receive. Excuse me, please.' She walked past Paul out the door and into the room where Molly had been and they heard her close the door and turn the key.

Unexpectedly, Henrietta insisted on making the coffee. 'I don't want any help. You go with Barbi, Paul... I'll bring it into the lounge. Go on.' Her voice was tense and bossy.

Paul was talking fast as Maddy and George came into the room five minutes later, 'What bloody difference do I make? What real difference has anybody else ever made to you all wrapped around like you have been? You've had a built-in head start... Oh, subtle and all that, but fair, see, fair and balanced delicately between the lot of you. I never had it and neither had Mark in spite of his wonderful brains and ability. I had to go looking around to try and find out why the circles some people move around in click. Yours clicked, Barbi, so I hung around trying to shock. I didn't make any difference. You could let me in and let me out again, because you were safe. Well, now you've laid yourselves wide open. You're not safe any more.'

'Oh, do shut up, Paul,' Maddy said. 'Dad will be in for his coffee in a minute.'

'Yes, shut up,' George repeated. 'Actually, you've outstayed your welcome.'

'But you haven't, eh, George? You're married right in tight, aren't you? Good and safe with Maddy's beautiful children.'

'Paul,' Barbi said. 'Please stop.'

He turned and looked at her with great, dark shining eyes. 'Don't let me stop, Barbi, don't let me stop, because I won't start again. I promise you that much. You won't be troubled by my shadow on your window pane any more.'

'What are you trying to say, Paul?'

'Like every other damn fool in this world. I can't say what I'm trying to say; can't get it across, can't communicate. After this I won't try again.'

'Thank God for that,' George murmured.

Maddy looked at Barbara and felt her misery. 'Leave him be, George,' she said softly. 'I'm sorry I butted in, Paul.'

'Go on, Paul,' Barbi said.

'No, I can't, Barb,' he said. 'It's only that you've lost something, Barbi, and I'm sorry but I can't explain. You've lost the very thing Mark is trying to get.'

'I don't understand, Paul, who are you talking about... Mim or Elie?'

'My God,' George said. Maddy put her hand on his arm.

'I'm talking about both, I guess. It just struck me all of a sudden that your mother must love first and criticise after. Maybe that's strange to you. Anyway, that's what she's done for Elie and Mark, the only one of the lot of us, including me.' He was looking at Barbi like a sleep-walker talking out loud. 'All I wanted from you, Barbi, was to get in too. Just like Mark, I wanted to get in too. Cripes! Well, I've succeeded only too well. Today I am in, quite in, in on the outside just like all the rest of you. And I don't like it. I'm not staying.'

'He's drunk, darling,' George whispered to Maddy.

'No, I'm not,' Paul raised his voice, which rasped now. 'You are... Drunk with your own importance... The whole bloody lot of you. Psychological prigs.'

Suddenly they realised Doctor Shorman was standing in the door. 'That will do, Paul,' he said. 'You may be right, but you've said enough.'

Barbara's eyes filled with tears. 'Where's Mim, Daddy?'

'She's in the room where Molly was painting.'

'That'll be it,' Paul said. 'That's it... Painting! Now the painting will get it all – bedrock – she's painting. I wonder what I'll do when I hit bedrock? She was prepared for it. All the time she was prepared for it, ready to swing over.'

He began to smile, then to laugh, and in the end threw back his head and shook the room with ribald gusts of mirth. His magnificent teeth took over his face and shook his long hair into confusion.

The little Buddha on the mantlepiece sparkled copper darts at the lamplight and all the small ivory deer from Sudan danced imperceptibly on their polished shelf. Then the reds in the room picked up the blues and merged into the green copper-tinted chairs. The room rolled upside down as Paul collapsed his long legs like a Yogi to sit on the carpet.

George, aghast, forgot Maddy's restraining hand and Layton's influence and his sister-in-law's tears. Fury that Paul should be his cousin consumed him like a flame. He stood over Paul, ordered him up and then, without giving him even the time for the impulse to disobey, leaned down and seized him by the shoulders and shook until Paul, amazed, threw him off and sprang to his feet like a panther. It was unfortunate for George that the panther was taller, quicker, more supple and cunning, full of potential power. Not that it mattered. Paul merely brushed one shoulder and then the other with a swipe of one large, long-fingered hand, his eyes holding George's eyes like deep slits of exposed explosive oil. His voice was laconic and cold. 'Just keep your hands off me, George. You are my cousin, but you are not responsible for me. You are not responsible for Mark, either. Nothing you will ever do will make the slightest difference to either of us, nor does Mark hold any responsibility for me any longer for what I am or am not, nor does Father or Mother. I am responsible before myself, George, and so are you. So far, that's all I can make out as the first law in this urban hassle we live in... That's why I'm going. Wake up to yourself, George, and concentrate on keeping your own nose clean.'

He turned slightly, half smiling, to the girls and bowed towards Doctor Shorman near the door. 'I'll let myself out, sir,' he said and did.

Outside, a full moon was already rising, although the sky over Melbourne was still hazel with the misty blue of afternoon. The Sunday sounds drifted eerily up and down the street like a distant corroborree of barking horns and clanking trams with transistors and mowers providing the beat of the drums. Over the city a little wind sighed like a flute in and out of the clustered trees and shrubs of the garden. In this pale symphony, Paul's feet on the pavement sounded heavy like the close throb of a didgeridoo.

He was going to Ruth – in a way he had never been away from Ruth.

CHAPTER NINE

Layton announced himself and waited until his wife opened the door and quietly closed it again behind him. Inside the room he glanced at an enormous new canvas stretched on the old easel dominating the end of the room. If he raised his eyebrows he said nothing, ignoring the preparation as no more than a symptom of her present irritability.

'I came to tell you, Mim, that on your behalf young Paul Carlister has just been magnificent, prior to leaving our house forever and banging the door on his way out.' It was Layton's way of assuming himself to be apologising on behalf of them all. Mim, seated in front of the canvas, busied herself mixing a violent and sickly shade of purple. 'Aren't you interested?' Layton asked.

'Yes, very.'

'Barbi was flabbergasted. We all were. George almost had a go at Paul. It was touch and go.'

'But of course George wouldn't.'

'You'll never know how near it was. Then Paul left and Barbi ran to her room in a flood of teenage tears.'

'Are they different from other tears?'

'Henny ran after Barbi and Maddy won't go home as George wishes her to until she has seen you. So she is making tea while George sulks.'

'I daresay.'

'Daresay what? What do you mean?'

'I daresay all you tell me is true.'

'Really, Mim. You make it very difficult to be patient.'

'I wouldn't bother to try, Layton. You don't really have a very patient nature.' She reached out her hand as she spoke and deposited two daubes of white paint like a pair of old-fashioned pearl earrings in the centre of the canvas. Immediately, the mauve colours already placed made nostrils of the earrings and the thing became a macabre head with enough human resemblance to startle him into anger.

'Do you intend to live in this room with that thing, or come back to the rest of the house?' he demanded.

'I think I'll stay here for the present. I'll get more sleep.'

'And what do you mean by that?'

'That when you come in late, you disturb me.'

'Since when? Now just what happened at this conference, Linda?'

'Nothing happened at the conference. I was away eight weeks only; one week pre-conference work, two weeks conference, three weeks post-conference in Europe and two with Eliane. You keep insisting on this repetition as if I went abroad to receive new glands or some fantastic political indoctrination. The situation here is exactly the same as it was before I went away. The twins were pleased to have Molly around for comfort, although they scarcely saw her... Or you, I gather. I have been home a day over one week and until this afternoon, life has gone on in this house in exactly the same manner as it was before I went away or when you flew overseas to Boston for your conference three months ago. I have just taken over where I left off. Would you have preferred me to have stayed away longer?'

'Perhaps you should have,' he snapped. 'Perhaps it's an idea you should think about.' His eyes hardened and narrowed to watch her reaction. She merely smiled thinly and added vermillion to yellow ochre, to play at mixing the result with her brush and her answer was almost a dismissal.

'Don't let today's upheaval go to your head, dear. I haven't felt like a double bed wife for some years now, which is perfectly normal at our age. And you don't want freedom, you want comfort and prestige; your Club, your golf, plus mixed social engagements with your colleagues as relief from your work. These things you are entitled to. You work hard and I have seen my job as the one who provides for you the right atmosphere, the comfortist setting that the affluent society apparently demands of an eminent man of your generation reaching the honours stage.' She pulled her lips tight.

Layton was amazed, but not enough to miss his opportunity. 'But not Mark Carlister's generation, I take it. He can get away with something I couldn't.'

She rubbed the mixture of vermillion streaked ochre down one side of the picture in a hard line, as if in desperation as to where to put it, having gone to the trouble of mixing. His trained eye saw her hand tremble and her mouth involuntarily twitch so that the steel still in her amazed him when she spoke.

'Your big news when I came home, Layton, was that you are in line for a knighthood. It seems Olwyn sees Arthur in the same position and he, of course, is rich enough to cinch it with a hospital wing. George wants an appointment as a professor at the university, Henrietta wants a big society wedding, religious barrier notwithstanding, and Barbara wants to be a star on the stage without the benefit of the hard climb up.'

'All to be jeopardised because Elie wants another woman's husband,' he interjected.

Still she wouldn't be caught and interrupted flatly, 'Let me finish, or, for a change, you might ask what I want...'

'Well, what do you want? What in heaven's name do you want?'

'Until today I wanted all the things just mentioned... Everything everybody else wanted to make them happy. I thought everybody deserved their happiness.'

'For God's sake, Linda, you are not going to bring up your old bogey about the end not justifying the means again.'

'I don't need to bring it up again, Layton. I had my answer to that question over the lunch table. Which reminds me that I had better speak to Maddy or Barbara about food for the evening meal. Do ask Maddy to come in, will you, if she wants to see me?'

'Do you mean to say you're not coming out?'

'That's right.'

'I'm to tell Maddy, then, that you intend to sulk all evening in your room.'

'If I was sulking, I wouldn't speak to you, Layton. Or Maddy. You can say whatever you wish but I'm not coming out.'

'And you don't intend to give us the required information about Eliane?'

'I have said all I intend to say about Elie until I hear from her.'

The wrath she saw in her father's face terrified Maddy where she hovered near the dining room door, with a window eye on George who was pretending to supervise the children in the garden. Layton spoke abruptly in a manner so cold she scarcely recognised him.

'You can go in, Maddy,' he said, 'But your mother won't come out.' He went ahead of her into his study and slammed the door.

Mim looked up and smiled as Maddy slipped into the room.

'We'll have to go, Mim,' Maddy said, her eyes darting about like trapped blue wrens. 'George had a fight with Paul.'

'Your father told me.'

'Dad says you won't come out.'

'That's right, darling.'

Hurt welled up in Maddy along with its emotional concomitant – anger. 'Why?' she cried bitterly. 'You needn't worry. Nobody will say anything more to you about Elie if that's how you want it. There's nothing much worse for us to know anyway, is there? None of us meant to hurt you. We were shocked, that's all, just...unbelievably...shocked about what Elie's done to us all. We were shocked.'

'So was I,' Mim said.

'Just the same, it has to be talked about. We can't ignore it. You know we can't ignore such a thing. It's an appalling thing for Elie to do to us.'

'Is it? Do you really think it is, Maddy?'

Tears were creeping up on Maddy, but she held them with a new force of wonder because Mim wasn't helping. Mim was ignoring each chance to commiserate, was deliberately not being Mim, and Maddy retaliated.

'Well, if that's the attitude you're going to take, I may as well get my family home until you get over it.' Her voice quavered at the end of the sentence, waiting for her mother's reaction. She couldn't remember speaking like this to Mim – not ever. Yet Mim picked up the paint brush she had put down and put it into a pot of turps.

'You're missing the point, Maddy,' she said, unperturbed. 'My attitude doesn't matter at all. Don't worry about the tea, dear. Barbi will put something on for your father. After all, everybody ate well at lunch time. Perhaps it is better if you get your little family and George home now.'

Maddy opened her mouth and shut it again. With her hand on the door, she turned. 'I – I'll see you tomorrow, maybe,' she suggested.

'I'll be here,' Mim said. 'It's always nice to see you.'

'What time will you be home?'

'I won't be out dear. I'll be here.'

'But isn't tomorrow the day you take Harriet to see about the Clinic? I thought that's why she didn't come today, resting up for tomorrow.'

'Harriet will have to take a taxi I suppose.'

For the second time, Maddy opened her mouth and shut it again.

Outside, she leaned against the door, breathing hard. Well, at least she had something else to tell George that would balance his unanswerable questions about Eliane. Perhaps Mim was in a state of nervous shock, which was more important than Eliane, even if Eliane was the cause of it. Why else would Mim consider that her feelings did not count, were secondary to some other inferred family attitude she would not define? Maddy felt threatened into an inexpressible trauma by Mim's silence over Eliane. The telephone rang hard in her ear, but she did not answer it, actually passing it by for the first time in her life, as if it had become infested with germs.

'Telephone, telephone, Dad,' she called out. 'We're off home.'

Her father looked at her intently as he passed her in the hall, but she winced nevertheless, seeing he still maintained the withdrawn expression of lips and eyes that characterised an awkward relationship with his family. He opened Mim's door.

'Harriet is on the phone, Mim. She'd like to speak to you.'

'I'm terribly sorry I can't come just now. I'll phone her in a day or so, after the weekend, perhaps.'

'She's waiting, Mim.' The silence broke him down. 'Mim, Harriet is going to the Sanitarium on Thursday and wants you to take her out.'

'I won't be able to go with her this time, dear. She'll have to get somebody else. You better tell her now so she won't be stuck.'

'Of course you can go with her. You always have. She expects it, after all she's family and you're apparently her favourite. It may interest you to know that I offered to go this time in your place, but she turned me down.'

'That's interesting.'

'It certainly is, considering the time she recuperates, time after time, in my house.'

'That's why she turned you down. She knows who looks after her when she recuperates in your house.'

'This is no time for sarcasm, my dear girl. She's on the phone. She knows you're home – I told her.'

'I shouldn't worry. Just go and hang up. She'll blame the telephone company, wait and try again, several times if necessary. For a sick woman, your Aunt Harriet is extraordinarily persistent.'

Without shutting the door, he went to replace the phone and returned to talk with belligerence at Mim. 'She won't do that too often to me.'

'Of course not. It's not you she wants – it's me.'

'Then it's up to you.'

'No. It's up to you. She's your aunt.'

'So that's how you've been feeling all these years. All this kindness laid on. All one big act.'

'Exactly, in which I play the minor role of the faithful servant, without which it is inferred the whole show would collapse – you know, like the Greek empire minus the slaves... We would never have had the classics. Which is a lot of nonsense and we all know it. Life always goes on. If I died tomorrow, Aunt Harriet would survey the field and failing to find a relative to her satisfaction, hire a housekeeper-nurse, which she can well afford.'

'That's a bit strong, Mim. She has a housekeeper.'

'She has, at present, the Dutch Cleaners once a week, and me. Her help apart from what the solicitor arranges, as I remember telling you, only agreed to stay on while I was away, as a personal favour to me. Harriet is not an easy employer. She is a selfish old lady. When Harriet comes here to recuperate, it is usually to give me time to hire new help for her.'

'She is good to you, Mim. She will probably leave you something.'

'She gives me only the normal seasonal gifts like any relative would and should. As for leaving me something, forget it. It's a wrong reason to help anybody, and therefore obnoxious to me, not to mention being an untruthful supposition. Aunt Harriet belongs to the old school where the male predominates in business affairs. What she has will pass on to the male heir, after the government has taken at least half with death duties. This may or may not be you... I don't know. What I do know is that Harriet refused to give or even lend two hundred dollars to a woman in desperate need who had worked for her for three years.'

'She probably had reasons. After all, Mim, you can't go around lending every Tom, Dick and Harry money. I remember the case, I think she spoke to me about it.'

'It was only part of the multiple hundred dollars the government will take anyway in death duties, and besides, as a personal favour I asked her to give it.'

'That was going a bit far.'

'She thereupon said she would seek advice of her male relative who knew all about business matters, as she told me sweetly. I told her not to bother and lent the money myself.'

'You did?'

'I had every cent back within the year, from Mrs Green.'

'But she left Harriet's service.'

'She was extraordinarily tolerant and good-natured and an efficient hard worker and has to work. She went to a motel and she's there yet. Had your Aunt Harriet seen the light, she would have had her wonderful services still, instead of a series of triers that drive her, according to her own reasoning, in and out of hospital.'

'Has Harriet discussed her will with you?'

'Why of course! She only has herself to think about and therefore it is only reasonable that she discuss the matter with me.'

'She does not discuss the matter with me.'

'Feminine guile. You are a puppet to be kept wondering, being a male. As a simple female, I don't count as more than a pair of ears.'

The telephone clanged again.

'You must have heard the phone in here before.'

'Of course. But I'm not answering it any more.'

'Really Mim, you're being quite impossible – it might be for you.'

'No, all that matters to me at present is in this house.'

'But your friends? Your personal friends?'

'Are personal friends and will try again next week or come around.'

'Do you want the phone switched through to my den? It's closer than the hall.'

'Dear me, no! I don't want to hear family conversations.'

A light knock sounded on the door and Henrietta delivered a message to Layton with more than a measure of vehemence. 'Aunt Harriet's on the phone. She hung up and re-rang. She wants to speak to Mim, and definitely not you, Pops, or any of the rest of us. She told me off before I could get a word over. So she's all yours, familio, take her.' Behind her father, Henrietta sensed the controlled movement of paint squeezing out of a tube to a place on a palette, but she couldn't quite see in.

'Tell your aunt your mother and I have just gone out,' Layton snapped.

'What!' Henny shrieked.

'You heard me, Henrietta,' Layton repeated. 'I refuse to have my home turned into a switchboard. Tell her we're out.'

'You're a genius, Pops.'

'Thanks,' Layton said dryly.

Mim took the opportunity to get up and close her door.

Barbara and Henrietta lay full length on parallel beds, contemplating the ceiling. Both were pale at the corners of deliberately un-lipsticked mouths and a little wild around the eyes, where the eyeshadow had mingled past advertisement level with the mascara.

'Wasn't Mim cool when we took in her dinner?' Henny said in her voice of respect.

'Just as if nothing had happened.' Barbi sighed and added, 'Paul wasn't home when I phoned.'

'Greg was. He was beaut, said of course we wouldn't go.'

'He would! You two might as well have gone.'

'Oh, don't be wet, Barbi. You had no date with Paul walking out like that. Anyway, how could we?'

'You could have gone.'

'I've got feelings. Greg was understanding... He's sweet like heaven.'

'All your dates are...real mum's boys.'

'You are stinking, Barbi. Greg's different. Don't forget I've just about decided to marry Greg.'

'Okay, okay, I'll chicken out.'

Lapsed into silence, Barbi studied the rows of the famous running in layers of even frames the full length of her bed and Henrietta the tiny gold stars studying the pale blue of the bedroom ceiling. There had been a fizz in both cases to achieve these fantasies of décor. But at nineteen, little satisfaction was gained from a study of persistence already two years achieved.

Henrietta shunted and growled, 'I hate George, don't you?'

Barbi jumped. Where was the filmy wedding veil under which Henny let her face merge into Maddy's under the exalted devotion of themselves as flower-girls nine years ago? She felt no surprise at Henrietta thinking of Maddy and automatically George at the same time as she did herself. Though not identical, she and Henny admitted coincidental thought transference as common enough phenomena. However, Maddy's beloved George hated was something radical, for Henrietta only saw George as the necessary groom to Maddy's glamorous bride, the husband to the wife, the father for the mother, the hero to match the heroine.

But Henny persisted. 'He was putrid this afternoon, so important and pompous, a real square with Maddy all fluttery pretending to hold him back and everything.'

'I suppose,' Barbi said, unexpectedly seeing her future self in Maddy's shoes. 'There are times when wives have to restrain their husbands the best way they can, even by being fluttery.'

'Well, I won't flutter, you can bank on that, even when married.'

'No, maybe not.' The bride vision had not quite faded from Barbi. 'Perhaps after all I'm like Maddy and you're like Eliane.'

'Not a chance. I haven't got Elie's looks to start with, let alone her brains, and I haven't got the racial problems either.'

Barbara sprang up and the bed creaked. 'Henny, what a stinking thing to say!'

Henrietta sat up slowly and faced her sister. 'Well, I just thought it,' she said defensively. 'And it's true, isn't it? Actually, that's what all the trauma is about, isn't it?'

They regarded each other wide-eyed, as if trying to communicate across a snake-pit instead of a length of carpet.

'Why did they adopt her, I wonder,' Henrietta breathed. 'They must have known.'

'She's only part.' Barbara, idolising Elie, felt filthy inside.

'Exactly, and that's why we all... That's why Mim loves her so much.'

'Wanting to make up, you mean?'

Henrietta threw wide her arms with the grace of an Indian dancer. 'Kipling, Barbi. Never the twain shall meet and all that blurb.'

Barbara lifted a purple cushion still indented with the round impression of her head and threw it straight into her sister's face.

'Don't you ever use that damned cliché again.' Yet, somehow relieved, she retrieved the cushion and pounded it over and over with her clenched fist like a woman beating dough. Finally, she said, 'Of course that Paul had to see it before I did.' But on that thought she threw the pillow down and buried her face in it.

Henrietta leaned over her, doubly distressed. 'Barbi, sit up. Barbi, we have to talk about it. It's colossal and we have to get it figured. We have to think and then we have to go to Mim. Barbi, do you hear, Barbi?'

Barbara turned over and lay staring at the ceiling stars. 'And after Mim I'll have to go and apologise to Paul. All the refugees in India and Pakistan are brown. We've got nothing against them, Paul keeps saying. He's got a thing about it. I never realised before that Elie has never had anybody else but Mim to talk to really... Nobody at all, nobody else understood. We didn't. We all took her for granted; our beautiful, clever, adopted sister. I guess she couldn't just decide and get married like Maddy. Maybe she hasn't been able to do anything just naturally, like Maddy – not even fall in love. I can't even quite remember what Mim told us that time we asked her about Elie. It didn't seem to matter, did it? We were just talking.'

'We asked why her eyes were different. It's only her eyes,' Henny said. 'You can't miss her eyes. They are so beautiful and sad. And Mim said her mother had those wonderful eyes. Her mother lived with Mim when Maddy was a baby. What was it that made us ask? I wish I could remember what made us ask. I don't think we ever noticed her eyes particularly before that. We always knew she was an adopted sister.'

'How old were we when we asked, can you remember?'

'Nine or ten, maybe. It was after that trip to America. The Carlisters were on the ship and there was all that excitement when they got back because Maddy wanted to get engaged to George who turned out to be Arthur Carlister's nephew.'

'Elie flew that time, didn't she?'

'Don't remember. She flew with Dad as far as Honolulu to stay for Christmas with the Barrets, and then she picked up the ship Mother was on and went on to San Francisco. They flew back because Elie had to start university.'

'University? How old was Elie then?'

'She must have been our age. Maddy was married the next Christmas.'

'Was Mark Carlister on that ship?'

'I don't know.'

'Shall I ask Pops?'

'Henny,' Barbi snapped. 'Stop all the questions. You're not James Bond. Dad? No, don't ask Dad. Don't be so simple.'

'He might know.'

'Of course he'll know. But we can't ask. Can't you see it will make everything worse if what we think is true?'

'But what are we going to do, Barbi? We have to do something.'

'I'll find out. I'll find out from Paul.'

'When?'

'Monday, when we go back to Uni.'

'I wish I didn't have to go, Barbi. I'll never get through.'

'Of course you will. You got your Matric. and got in.'

'Only because of Mim. I haven't got your brains. I worked so hard. I can't do it again... I'll fail.'

'Look, Henny, you're always in the Union with Greg, or sitting on the grass or walking around talking. He'll fail too and I can't see how that'll help.'

'You know his mother's not a bit with it, Barbi. She told Greg again I'd have to change if he's serious. Greg doesn't care... Really, he doesn't, Barbi, even if he is at Newman. He says he thinks I have a perfect right to my own religious views, but it would just make it easier if I change.'

'What did Mim say? You talked long enough to her about it after she got home.'

'I told you. She said wait until after Christmas and not to tackle Dad until Greg is sure he's got his degree, or gets out of Newman. I can't wait that long... I just can't. Anything might happen.'

'Henny, you have to take Mim's advice. There's no choice. It's the least you can do, especially now. All you have to do is wait a few months. After all, Greg eats out of your hand. I'd encourage him to stand on his feet and work instead of mooning around. You'll have to, Henny, if you really want to marry him.'

'Of course I want to marry him. Maddy married at twenty, why shouldn't I?'

'Don't be such a baby, Henny. Because the man she married was ten years older and established. George was thirty and had all the answers, even a house, besides being a good Methodist. And Maddy wasn't a Uni student. She was at the Con.'

'I wish I was doing something else.'

'This time last year you didn't.'

'It was only to keep up with you and please everybody.'

'Not bad reasons.'

'Oh, Barbi – I'm so miserable. Why can't we just be happy any more?'

'Because we want everything, a university education and a boyfriend who wants to marry us. We want dancing and a car and to lie on the beach and surf in the sea and wear with-it clothes and spend money. We want everything and all at once. None of us are willing to wait for anything. It's been like that, I guess, ever since the Atomic Bomb.'

'Is that why you think it is?'

'I don't know any other reason. Look at me. I want a university degree and to be an actress and famous. And I want Paul to like me and Sims to stop acting like a scarecrow following when I don't know he's there. I want Mim to be happy and you and Elie, but I can't help any of you, nor do I really believe I'll be a famous actress or marry Paul – don't even know if I want him anyway, now, some-times I think Sims suits me better.'

'We were awfully happy when we were growing up though, don't you think, Barbi? I guess we just didn't realise. Maybe Mim didn't let us. Maybe she did the same for Elie, the wonderful kingdom of childhood and all that.'

'Listen, Henny, let's go in and see Mim like we used to when we were kids. Maybe if we tell her we're sorry and didn't understand she'll love us.'

'Love us – you heard what Paul said. It's not Mim who is weak on love.'

'Please, Henny, let's go.'

But Mim's room was dark and no light showed under the door. They turned the handle and whispered, 'Mim... Mummy dear, can we come in?' There was no answer from the bed where she slept, or feigned sleep. They closed the door again softly and like fright-ened mice, returned to their own nest and in silence threw off their clothes, donned pyjamas and climbed into bed. When she put out her light, Barbara heard Henrietta sniffling, with her face turned to the wall.

'Move over,' she said and climbed in beside her. She remembered that there had also been unhappy times in their childhood. But she didn't remind Henny.

CHAPTER TEN

The M.G. roared into the quiet street and hummed to silence in the Shorman driveway. Wednesday was a dull day of little sun. Feet scuffled down the hall from the kitchen to knock on Mim's door.

'It's Barbi. I've got Paul and Sims with me. Can we come in?'

The reply was brief and bright, 'The door's open, dear – come in.'

Entering first to hold the door for Sims who was balancing a tray, Barbi was overwhelmed by the atmosphere of a space in her own house which seemed to belong somewhere else. The room was no longer Maddy's old bedroom but her mother's working den, set around arrangements of recognisable furniture. An unexpectedly ordered chaos had taken possession under a heavy aroma of paint that swirled like a fog past her face out the open door. The single bed in the far corner was made, but the bedspread was obliterated by canvasses corner-weighted with books. Paintings and charcoal sketches leaned everywhere, even against the tiny pink roses of the papered wall. A worn length of splattered green oilcloth covered a corner quarter of the mushroom carpet and dead centre of this island her mother sat like a gnome on a kitchen chair in front of a rickety easel. A table level with her right hand balanced a wooden tray of squeezed tubes, brushes in turps and a two-ounce Vegemite jar of medium.

Barbara said in a small voice of amazement, 'We brought coffee makings. Paul has the electric jug and a bottle of milk, but we couldn't find any biscuits.'

'I have the biscuit tin here, behind you on the bureau. It's my tin, you know. You and Henny gave it to me for my birthday two or three years ago, because of the Vermeer portrait on the lid. Put the jug on the floor, Paul.'

Barbi let the door go and swung round. There was a thermos on the bureau beside the tin, plus a packet of Jatz and butter and cheese and four apples and an orange in a basket. She stood very still.

Sims leaned over to put the tray in his hands on the floor beside Mim and rose slowly, his eyes on the portrait on the easel. 'You've got that child, Mrs Shorman, got it exactly.' Then he swung round slowly, as if his will was imposing silence on an already silent room. His eyes remained on the bed. 'The canvasses need stretching,' he said. 'I'd better stretch them for you. If we can't find anything in the shed, we can buy what we need at a place I know in Richmond.'

'Thank you, Sims,' Mim said, and put her brush into the bottle of turps. 'Let's have the coffee first.'

Barbi flopped to the floor by the tray and unscrewed the lid of the coffee jar. She couldn't look at Mim. 'No sugar,' she announced. 'I would forget the sugar.'

'I'll get it,' Paul said.

Barbi raised her eyes as far as the enormous black eyes shining out of the receding mauve face of the easel child and shivered. 'Did you see that little boy on your trip, Mim?' As soon as she asked it, she realised it was her first question about the trip beyond banalities, and shivered again.

With his back to her, Sims said, 'You didn't inform me your mother was an artist, dear girl, nor did Paul, which has been my loss since every bit of art is a free diamond in the coal of society.'

'She keeps her art hidden,' Barbi said flatly, since a state of nerve-wracking bitterness had overtaken her usual joy. 'She never shows us anything any more – hasn't for years. We just happened to find her at it today, that's all! You can ask Henny or Dad or anybody. It's Mother's private escape.'

Mim said, 'About this little boy – I'll tell you. After the conference in Beirut, we were taken to the Gaza Strip to a school there in one of the new refugee camps. The whole place was no more than tin shed huts and old canvas for shelter from the sun. The teacher asked me to tell the children a story and I told them *The Three Bears*. It – it was wonderful. They knew it. There was one little boy – this little boy, he was himself and yet he was all of them, all the hungry children in the world. He just sat in front of me. I – I couldn't forget his face. I brought it home with me – that's why I have to paint him. I – just have to.'

During the recitation, Paul came in and put the sugar down and himself alongside it in a massive sprawled heap that left Barbi little elbow room. Sims prowled softly behind them, letting his eyes flit from picture to picture on the bed, mentally measuring so that he was able to speak effortlessly into the silence when it came. 'I think I'd better borrow a couple of stretching frames from old Mixas. He has a heap collecting dust in his back room. Some of these have been rolled up a long time.'

Barbi jumped up and handed each a mug of coffee. Paul took his on the floor. 'Who's old Mixas?' he asked Sims.

'A Greek in Richmond,' Sims answered. 'I work for him occasionally – lumping his gear. He has a gammy leg – arthritis. When it takes him over he sends for me.'

'You know the world,' Paul grunted. 'The whole damn world.'

'Maybe one day the whole world will know Sims,' Barbi snapped.

'Could be,' Paul agreed, but there was no spirit in him. 'I just said the whole bloody world, didn't I?' He stared at Sims for a sign of discomfiture, for any sign at all until, his eyes bored into the back of Sims' head turned Sims to face him with a question.

'Mind if I go with Barbi to see what's available by way of strip? The master of this house must have a shed.'

'There's nothing,' Barbi said. 'We cleaned it out.'

Mim spoke. 'As far as behind the playhouse.'

'Señorita,' bowed Sims. 'Allow me to escort you to your play-house.'

Paul stood up to open the door for them and did not resume his place on the floor. 'I wanted to say I'm sorry about last Sunday,' he said awkwardly. 'It was rotten of me. I'm not famous for keeping my big mouth shut.'

'It was a family thing, Paul. You just happened to be one of the family.'

'I don't think so, Mrs Shorman. I'm not family, not even at home.'

'You write poetry, don't you, Paul? Barbi told me.'

'I do it like Sims talks. It's no good but it makes me lightheaded to get what it says out of my system.'

'I like this room. I like painting here. Does it seem so strange to you?'

'No, it doesn't,' he said, suddenly convinced. 'I can understand, but Barbi can't. That's, that's why we came. I thought maybe I could get a chance to apologise—'

'You, Paul?' She seemed moved beyond speech and paused a long time before continuing. 'You can't understand or apologise for any-body else, dear. You can only stand by in case they need you. You and Sims did that for Barbi. Thank you. Why don't you sit down?'

He collapsed to the floor again. 'Ouch,' he grunted, 'I'm too bloody thin on the rump.' He reached for one of the heavy satchels, his eyes avoiding the face of the child on the easel that Sims consid-ered so wonderful. 'I'll show you a couple of the things I write,' he added, but did not add that he thought it only fair since both efforts were so bloody bad, yet somehow relevant.

She read his handwritten poems gravely, not once but several times before she handed them back ahead of the voices of Barbi and Sims returning. 'Thank you for showing me,' she said. 'You catch the core, the essence, if you like, of meaning – like the eyes of this child I'm painting. Did you know that's why you won't look at it? Barbi won't either, not yet.'

Paul thought Barbi looked stupid coming back into the room ahead of Sims, whispering as if she was visiting a hospital bed before she launched into patiently explaining as if her mother needed protection of some sort, 'Sims sorted right through the junk, darling, but nothing is any good. Can we go to that friend of Sims in your car, Paul?'

'Sure,' Paul said loudly.

'Would you like to come, Mim?' Barbi begged anxiously. 'We wouldn't be long and you'd feel better for the air.'

'No thanks, darling,' Mim said. 'I've had a nice visit with you and I'll get on with my work again now. Thanks, Sims, I can see you're going to be most useful. I didn't know art was within your overall province.'

'Every bloody thing is,' Paul grunted, rising to his feet.

'I'm glad for Sims; to be narrowed down is death, in a way,' Mim said.

Barbi bristled. 'Paul knows that. He's bolshie today. We don't know what's the matter with him.'

Staring at her, Sims launched into rhetoric with the ease of an experienced barrister. 'One of the safety valves sadly neglected in our obnoxious times is the privilege of being what we are when and how we feel inclined, but the lying attitudes of conformity overtake us, step by step as we grow, so that on the brink of maturity one becomes the victim of muddled minds. We sense, we feel, but we don't really know ourselves. So when our inside unexpectedly protrudes, we cover with a snail's shell of irritability, my dear girl.'

'Thank you, dear philosopher,' Barbi laughed, flashing beautiful eyes of diamond sparkle towards Sims' face. She was wearing with bravado the unsuccessful white polo-necked pullover and her face under the mop of light brown hair seemed elflike and pale.

By the door, Paul grunted, 'Gawd, I've left the bloody M.G. parked in the driveway and a car's pulled up.'

Barbi flipped out into the hall like a seal and returned again. 'You've got company, Mim. Guess who's getting out of a taxi? Aunt Harriet!'

Mim said, 'Thanks for warning me, dear. And thanks for the coffee.'

'Are you going to open the door?'

'I'd prefer you to – if you don't mind.'

'Okay, but we're off.'

'Will you be home for dinner?'

'Well, we thought we might have fish and chips with Sarge and then go to the library. Will you be all right?'

'Certainly. Your father is at the Seminar. There's a reception. Take Sarge a couple of jars of jam from the cupboard.' The doorbell sounded with insistent melody.

'Whatever are you doing, Linda dear?'

'Painting, Aunt Harriet.'

'There's something going on here. I know it – don't deny it because I know. Barbi scarcely spoke, put me in here and ran.'

'Auntie, have you been reading the stars again?'

'I woke up with the feeling in my bones. If the stars are correct, it is no more than proof. I woke up fearing the worst, even before I opened the paper. What's going on? I'm not going to be put off. Is Layton having an affair?'

'Oh, I shouldn't think so, Auntie. Affairs are very costly for a man of Layton's age and reputation.'

'Mim, how very unlike you to say a thing like that – Layton being such an attractive man, such a calamity could happen and you have been away. Catastrophes happen even in nice families, even professional families, and my dear Linda, even when men have as nice a wife as you are.'

'Thank you, dear.'

'You haven't answered my question.'

'Sorry.'

'So it is Layton, I knew it in my bones. You must have had a dis-agreement. Is he leaving you?'

'No dear, unfortunately. Layton is not leaving me.'

'Speak up, Mim. You know I dislike people mumbling. Did you say unfortunately?'

'Yes.'

'There is no need to raise your voice. I know you are upset. I can see that.'

'How? Do I look upset, Auntie?'

'You look peculiar painting at afternoon tea time. The whole family is upset. I could tell from Barbi home from the university at this hour. I feel it in – it is a faculty I have. What is your trouble, Mim – it – it's Barbi? Are you faced with a – a pregnancy, Mim dear?'

'Me? – Oh no.'

'Mim, don't be deliberately facetious. Naturally I mean one of the girls. I must say, until this past year I have always found Barbara most sensible, but I wouldn't trust that Paul Carlister she is running around with as far as I could throw him, and as for that Catholic boy Henrietta is interested in – well, you know what I think about that! I spoke very plainly to Layton about it. It is one thing to be as understanding about modern girls as you are, and quite another to allow them to choose their own company indiscriminately. Fortu-nately my mind is at rest about Eliane as whatever it is has obvi-ously happened since your arrival home last week. I must say I am very relieved that Eliane turned out to be so shy and ladylike. Un-der the circumstances, I have always been frightened for Layton's sake that men might try to take advantage of her. There is always considerable risk in adoption, particularly of a child like Eliane, and Layton has always been so generous in supporting your choice. It is one of the things I particularly admire him for – many men would not have agreed to such an adoption.'

Harriet stopped for breath, remembered first causes and decided to return to the point of her discourse by instituting a dramatic pause. Mim filled the space with amicable comment.

'I'm glad to hear you say that, Auntie. It's very interesting.'

'Mim, which of the girls is it?'

'None of the girls are pregnant, Auntie, if that's what you mean.'

'I am most relieved to hear it. You had me very worried, very worried indeed for a moment, because I understand such misfortune to be a frequent occurrence nowadays – modern morality being lax to say the least.'

'Oh well, Auntie, that's a bit hard; morals, I suspect, are about the same as they always were, except for the Pill.'

'What?'

'I said, you are overlooking the influence of the Pill.'

'Mim, this is no time to be – well, frankly – coarse. You know very well I prefer to leave discussion of the Pill to the medical profession who understand it.'

'I have no wish to discuss it with you, Aunt Harriet.'

'Then why did you bring it up? What are you doing, may I ask, Mim?'

'Mixing paint, Auntie – it's messy, isn't it?'

'Not to start again I hope. It's afternoon tea time and I would like a cup of tea. I feel a little faint after my trip over, in fact before I left I had one of my dizzy turns after my telephone conversation with my last remaining brother. Thomas was very rude, Mim, very rude indeed. He told me to stay home and mind my own business as he was doing. I must have a cup of tea, I really must.'

'You'll find everything in the kitchen, Auntie. There is, or at least there was a chocolate cake in the white cake tin.'

'Mim, are you actually suggesting I make it myself?'

'Yes, Auntie. You see, I'm not leaving this room at present.'

'Not leaving this room – not leaving this room?'

'That's right, not today anyway.'

'Where is Barbara? I really must see Barbara at once.'

'She's around somewhere. Try the garden. I haven't heard Paul's car go yet.'

'Is that whose car it is? Well, she ran to the kitchen when I came in.'

'Then she'll be getting some homemade jam to take to a pensioner friend in Richmond.'

'A pensioner friend in Richmond indeed.' Harriet looked around for a place to sit down. The room was disgustingly untidy. Mim must be ill, so she tried again.

'My dear, tell me this. Has the doctor been?'

'Not that I know of, why should a doctor come? Nobody is ill.'

'Now that I very much doubt – you won't come out? You won't help me find Barbara?'

'No, Auntie. It's too late anyway; listen.' The roar of the M.G. re-entered the silence of the street and puttered away into the distance. Harriet settled uncomfortably into the only available chair in the room and addressed Mim's back.

'I had to come to make final arrangements with you to go out to the Sanitorium at Healesville on Thursday.'

'Didn't Layton tell you I wouldn't be able to drive you, Aunt Harriet?'

'Won't be able to take me? But you always take me. I'm ill!'

'Not really, Auntie. It's just your nerves. You've often been before. You know the place.'

Harriet caught her breath, recovered and began to sniff. 'I can't understand. I just can't understand. I'm seventy-five years old and have always been good to this family. Thank God I have been able to be – thank God I have my financial independence. What it must be like for gentlewomen who are dependent I dare not think – being reduced to the pension plus unkindness must be intolerable. One's own family turning on their own relatives, once they are elderly. I'm very hurt, very hurt indeed and insulted – I really can't understand it. You say nothing is wrong and you treat me like this. It can only mean one thing – you are refusing me your confidence as well as being rude in your own house. What have I done to deserve it – can you tell me that Mim – or is that too much? Well?'

'The reason I am staying in my room, Auntie, has nothing to do with you. It has only to do with me. Usually when you come visiting I drive over and get you myself, or send somebody else for you, so naturally I wasn't expecting you today. Also, I thought Layton told you on the telephone I couldn't come over. It just happens I'm spending a few days in this room painting.'

'Layton was most abrupt on the telephone – most abrupt. He wouldn't call you for me. I asked him several times. I thought it very strange. I am Layton's aunt and I have always offered all my help. How could I suspect you would treat me like this?'

'Auntie, go and get yourself a cup of tea – you're getting all worked up.'

'Not until you tell me this: why didn't Layton tell me not to come?'

'Yes, indeed, why didn't he? As usual he prevaricated, dear Auntie – his university manner, you know, courteous and indecisive on the telephone. Someone is in the kitchen now, Auntie – I heard the tap – it rumbles in the pipe occasionally. I suggest you go and ask whoever it is to make you a cup of tea, or pop the kettle on yourself.'

'So Layton is home. Well, the very least he can do is drive me home again.'

'Layton won't be home until at least ten-thirty. He is attending a Seminar. It may be Henny. Sometimes Greg drops her at the corner when she doesn't want to bring him in. If it is, she might have time to drive you home in my car.'

The blown-up huff of Harriet rose like a hen from a nest of chicks to leave the evil room. Panting, she arrived at the door of the kitchen, which was closed.

Henrietta was arranging the contents of a white confectioner's bag on to a pink plate. The assortment of cakes was limited, exclusive and as dainty as the two cups and saucers it accompanied on the doilied tray. When she looked up at the opening door and the flurry that was Harriet, dismay jammed her mouth into a straight hard line of disappointed anguish. Mephistopheles, with all his temptations, she might have faced with strength proper to her moment of planned confession. But Aunt Harriet!

'Your mother said it might be you in the kitchen and that you would take me home immediately in her car,' Harriet moaned, throwing herself towards Henrietta in a great sway that intentioned a fainting spell.

Henny moved quickly to pull out a chair to receive the weight of Harriet's descent. The pretty cups rattled and the kettle boiling vigorously, with its whistle so carefully removed, spat out a jet of boiling water. Her mind a sudden black blank, all Henny could utter was spontaneous common sense.

'Oh, sit down, Aunt Harriet, and have a cup of coffee.'

Having sat, which was recovery of a kind, Harriet regained sufficient composure to gasp between sobs, 'Only a cup of tea and two aspirins will help. Get me tea, Henrietta.'

Henny had never seen Harriet cry, or Uncle Thomas, or Molly or any of her father's family, including Pops himself. So, having turned off the kettle, she stood with her mouth fallen open like a staring street urchin regarding the phenomenon of tears on the face of Aunt Harriet. She indulged herself for an absorbing minute before she said, with a sense of disgust from which she wished to extricate herself, 'I think I had better go and get Mim.'

'Oh no, no,' shrieked Harriet. 'She won't come. She's turned against me. Now I'm old and have to go to the Sanitorium for a rest she has turned against me. She doesn't want to see me and she won't take me on Thursday. I don't know what I have done to deserve such treatment after all these years. I've done everything I could for this family. She says she's not ill, then why, why should she treat me like this? No wonder your poor father couldn't tell me on the telephone and how was I to know? I came over in all good faith. How was I to know?'

Henny was looking in all the canisters for a tea-bag and didn't answer. Succeeding at last in her search, she deliberately took out another cup and saucer to make Harriet's tea and, moving the pretty tray to one side, placed the drink at her Aunt Harriet's right hand. 'Here's the sugar,' she said. 'You don't take milk, do you? I'm sorry I haven't got an aspirin.'

With trembling hands, Harriet pushed her heavy handbag towards her niece. 'Get them for me, dear,' she sighed. 'I'm in such a state I just couldn't find them. I'm sure I couldn't find them.'

This mission accomplished, Henrietta excused herself to get the keys of the car. She did not knock at Mim's door but hurled herself into the room and hissed at her mother's back, 'I came home on the tram all by myself to see you. I even bought us a special treat and now she's here blubbing in the kitchen. Where are the car keys? I'll take her home.'

'Thank you, dear,' Mim said. 'The keys are behind you on my bedside table.'

Henrietta threw her arms wide, her golden eyes sparing her mother's face to glare at the ceiling. 'And,' she paused for effect, 'I'll be right back. Don't you move.'

'No, dear,' Mim replied. 'I won't move, that is sure.'

Harriet had finished her tea along with the prettiest two of the four little cakes. She was on her feet waiting by the dining room door, with one ear cocked under her mink hat. 'I don't want to rush you,' Henny said rudely, 'But I have a dinner date. We'll go out the back door. I just hope Mim's bomb doesn't go skittish on us.'

'Did you see her?' Harriet breathed tearfully.

'Uh-huh,' opening the door.

'How was she? What did she say?'

'I only got the car keys Auntie. I had to pop into the lav as well.'

'Really, Henrietta!'

The door closed with a bang and Mim heard with sympathy the screech her middle-aged Peugeot produced slithering up the driveway.

Returning, the car took the driveway with quiet precision and was carefully stowed away for the night.

When Henrietta appeared in Mim's room, she was carrying not only the pretty little tray, but one of the nest of lounge room tables beneath it. She was wearing the paisley jersey housecoat Mim had brought her from Paris, and the perfume of her skin and hair mingled with the aroma of strong black coffee.

'Well, at last I've got you alone to talk to,' she announced as Mim reacted to thin bread and butter sprinkled with hundreds and thousands beside two cakes on a pink plate. 'Would you believe it, Mim, poor weeping Harriet gobbled up the best two of the treat I bought.' She giggled more like Barbi than herself. 'I hope you like the replacement.'

'Don't be disrespectful, Henny,' Mim said. 'She's an old lady.'

'That's precious, coming from you. You slaughtered her.'

'I did no such thing. I simply refused to give in to her once.'

'Is that what you're up to with us?'

'This coffee is delicious, Henny. Your domesticity is improving.'

'Well, what is the idea of the sit-in then?'

'I'm painting. From now on, I intend to paint. I have a gift for it and as Molly says, one shouldn't bury a talent.'

'It's different for Molly. She's divorced. Anyway, I always thought your talent was for running things around here.'

'Thanks. I agree with the running part of it.'

'Well, running a home is all Maddy seems to want. She seems satisfied with George and the children.'

'So?'

'In spite of women's lib, sexual freedom, the Pill and all the other female get with it.'

'And you?'

'I go along with Maddy except for the religious angle. It's religion that bugs me with Greg. It's inconsistent for me to start believing in myths at my age.'

'Inconsistent with what?'

'You know quite well what I mean: with my life, my outlook, every damn thing about me.'

'Well, then?'

Henny spread out her hands in a gesture of despair. 'I planned this talk with you so carefully but you're not helping at all,' she accused. 'Can't you understand? I want Greg. When he touches me my flesh aches. I don't want to lose him by sleeping with him. I want him for keeps, but he's scared to marry me unless I change and marry in his church. I'm frustrated, Mim! I'm desperate.'

'Henrietta, is it lip security you want from me? You should know perfectly well by now that I believe in the power of myths and that I accept life as inconsistent. Both are part of the evolutionary process.'

Henrietta sat back on her heels, astounded. 'You never told me that before.'

'You didn't ask me before.'

'You don't care if I change then?' She was not only hurt, but gnawed by a further confusion she would not have believed possible. 'You really don't care at all.'

'Not at all,' Mim repeated. 'Providing, of course, you look at the problem straight.'

'How do I get it down to that?'

'By not mixing the Christian faith as such with whether or not you adhere to one or another of the institutional factions that have grown out of it.'

'Why shouldn't I have my principles? After all my years in an Anglican school.'

'Which didn't count for tuppence when you fell in love with a boy who spent all his years at a Catholic school. If you both understand and practice the true Christian principle, no question of giving up should arise on either side.'

'Barbi thinks that, not that she ever darkens a church door any more than I do.'

'Then I take it that as you don't believe in myths or in the practiced inconsistencies of the Christian story, or in going to church, it would be better to be honest and admit you considered going to the

Catholic Church only because you are in love with a boy who does. If you love him that much and you know it, then I have no objection.'

'There is still how much he loves me.'

'More important, I think, than holding out to be an Anglican.'

'But he is holding out because he is a Catholic, or because his mother is.'

'Or because he has been conditioned by his life's circumstances. If you love him enough it shouldn't matter. You will have to give somewhere, whoever you marry. There is more to the Christian story than meets the eye, you know. Perhaps Joseph had to be an older man to be big enough to accept illegitimacy in his wife. A young man might have been too proud. Also, perhaps, nobody else would believe Mary's story. She could have become an outcast.'

'I don't think I really believe in the virgin birth – in the angel and all that.'

'A Christian believes in the teaching of Christ, which shows the way to personal revelation, a metamorphosis of self, through love of God and one's fellow man. In the beginning such an idea, such a thought was couched in mystery and wonder. It had to be protected and made holy. And so did the parents of Christ.'

'But in the Catholic Church you have to believe, really believe in the virgin birth – or you can't join. There are other things too.' She spoke with a kind of desperate authority, as if she had secret knowledge she hoped her mother could dissipate.

'What you have to believe,' Mim said, 'is that the voice of God can and does speak to people, particularly to selected people, and that if you happen to be one of them, when the voice speaks you have to believe it and act on it to the best of your present ability, even if you can't understand why or how. You go forward according to your inner voice, step by step, without prior knowledge. That is the meaning of faith. Mary had the vision, the inner voice, if you like, and she went forward in faith. So can you – so can anybody. But you have to have heard the voice or seen the vision and accepted the idea inside yourself. It can't come from anybody else, individual or institution. Can you see what I mean? I can't do it for you.'

There was a long silence. Outside a blackbird whistled twice.

Henrietta said, 'Maybe the trouble is that I haven't had the go-ahead sign, Mim. Do you really get it when you are in love?'

'Not just physically, you mean? Yes, I think so. You reach the higher third. When it is a unity, I mean. When it is only physical, it is an illness like the measles.'

'Contagious?'

'Hmm, contagious – at your age, easy to catch.'

'So you suffer delusions, see yourself as a new Joan of Arc, able to defeat any obstacles, any bridges – in fact like a fever?'

'It can be a fever both ways, Henny. The difficulty is to tell the difference – to see it straight.'

'You mean to know whether you have the measles or the real thing? How do you see it straight then?'

'Sometimes by knocking off everything else – all the trimmings.'

She was really quick – Henrietta. 'In my case the Joan of Arc act? The all for love aspect – beautiful bride making the great sacrifice of changing my religion for love – the dramatisation?'

She lifted her head in a sudden gesture of abandon that floated her hair momentarily into a shimmering halo, then she lowered her face to her bosom so that her shoulders seemed to shrink as she sighed. The blackbird sang again in the oleander shrub outside the window. Mim mixed a dab of yellow ochre into the blob of white paint.

'I would be better to dramatise myself on the stage, wouldn't I? I imagine it would be easier for me and cause less damage all round – I could let my inner voice go forward, as you say, step by step, without prior knowledge and get it all out of my system – except, of course, that I can't.'

'You could try,' Mim suggested, ignoring the dramatics.

'No, I can't. It's the one thing I can't do. The stage is not for me – Barbi wants it, have you forgotten? I'm the one for love and marriage – the one like Maddy! Barbi is like Elie– she wants a career – she has chosen a career on the stage!'

Mim smiled and it was a mistake to smile when Henrietta was being heroic. The smile piqued Henrietta to her feet with the smooth, controlled movement of a panther. She threw both her arms wide.

'You don't believe me,' she accused. 'You don't know that Mike Parsons, the director, pleads with me to audition. He tells me I am a natural, that the part is made for me, that I am wasting myself with books and religion. He has been haunting me, Mummy. Gregory hates him absolutely, has forbidden me to speak to the man!'

'But you do speak to him, don't you?' Mim said.

Quite suddenly, like all dramatic moments, it was over. Indignation like iced water froze Henrietta into a bad-tempered little girl facing her mother on a charge of stealing her sister's doll. She pushed her lip out.

'Barbi's a fool. She can't act. Do you think I'm going to tell her that when I depend on her for everything else?'

'Protection is all very well,' Mim said, 'Up to a point. Then it becomes domination.'

'And domination forces independence.' Henny paused, regarding her mother with shrewd, fierce eyes. 'Which, of course, I could not achieve through marriage to Gregory, but which Eliane has achieved running away with Mark. Which is why you are sitting here, isn't it – because Elie has achieved personal independence by running away with Mark?' She shook her shoulders but this time did not throw her hair. Instead, she put out a hand to touch her mother in a quick gesture of embarrassed love.

'I'll have to dress now, Mim. I'll be back.' At the door she returned to pick up the tray. Her mother had eaten all the bread spread with hundreds and thousands.

CHAPTER ELEVEN

On Thursday afternoon Sims and Barbi decided to walk to Richmond, since Paul had not turned up with his car.

'What exactly is it Mark Carlister does?' Barbi asked Sims.

'He's a bio-physicist; that is, he's in the science of the future. He did both biology and physics, and that combination may discover mere animal-man's connection with the Milky Way. One day Paul's illustrious brother will be an important brain behind the space boys.'

'Eliane did biology. That's why I took it on, Sims.'

'I puzzled my top-layer about that,' Sims admitted. 'You put over your interests as Arts and Theatre.'

'Eliane's honours were history. But she told me you needed Biology or Chemistry as well to be educated.'

'To know what it means to be educated, Barbara!' Sims corrected. 'To be really educated you need the lot: Chemistry, Biology, Physics, Maths, Sociology and History and Art and Philosophy plus... More than the puny brain of any of us can absorb at this stage of the grand evolutionary process.'

'You leave out languages. Is Spanish your idea of slumming out of the big stuff then?'

Sims laughed, not so much at what she said, but because all the time he was with her he found himself wanting to laugh. From his height she was so small and game. Already they had come all the way down Nicholson Street on the pavement and she still floated in the face of the wind as if she did this kind of three-mile walk every day of her life, instead of making use of a heated M.G.

In his subconscious, happy little bells rang in celebration of some kind of victory for Sims, which, in the enjoyment of the moment, he had no time to define. He had, instead, an impulse to pick Barbara up in his arms and carry her for a bit, which was an idea both ludicrous and delicious at the same time, and made him laugh louder. So he was unprepared when Barbara stopped in front of a shop window to allow his laugh to finish before she let him know she had sensed the meaning of his mind.

'I'm not tired, Sims,' she said. 'I never get tired when I'm interested. And I really do want to know why you took up Spanish.'

He was instantly serious. 'Navigation and discovery of an era; an easy sociological history of the mistakes made by ignorance and greed, plus a desire to read *Don Quixote* in the original.'

She looked him straight in the eyes until her own dropped when a tiny flush of colour deepened the pink of cheeks already responding to the walk and the cold, blustery wind. She walked on again, speaking.

'Thank you, Sims. I'm really not much of an actress, am I? I only think I am.' She took his hand quite naturally and the bells inside Sims' head clamoured for recognition while she finished talking out her problem.

'I've wanted to talk to you for a long time – to the real you, not the Sims you dress yourself up in at the Union and at the footy. You're different. You don't think like the rest of us and yet you belong. Belonging has nothing to do with money or comfort, or even being in the same house. We did a dreadful thing to our mother. We let her down over something she has spent her whole life trying to build up. I would like to tell you, Sims.'

She felt the pressure of his hand as he nodded. He could see the great green foliage of the Fitzroy Gardens looming up ahead. They would walk through the Gardens hand-in-hand. He realised how many times he had walked under the trees alone. But he did not speak.

'You see, Sims, our sister Eliane is different. She's adopted. She was adopted in Honolulu straight from the hospital where she was born. Mother already had my eldest sister Madeleine and then five years later, back in Australia, Henrietta and I were born. Mim, my mother, always said that instead of giving Daddy a son to concentrate on, she gave him two more daughters to divide the load. Funny I should remember to tell you that,' Barbi giggled. 'It's straight out of my childhood. It was always a great family joke.'

'Did it divide the load?' Sims asked.

'Well, no, no, Sims, now you ask, no it didn't. Daddy still concentrated on Eliane the most. But I never thought of it that way. You see, she was always clever, got prizes at school. She deserved them too – she worked harder than the rest of us ever did, but she was so nice about it. She always made time to help everybody and Mother most of all. But it's true, Daddy did concentrate on her study and put it above everything else. Maybe that's the answer, Sims – it could be.'

Sims looked into the approaching trees and squeezed her hand with the lightest possible pressure because he could not ask what the answer was while he was ignorant of the question. She seemed to notice vaguely and prefixed her preoccupation by admiring the trees.

'I love the Fitzroy Gardens,' she said briefly. 'You see, Sims, something happened to Eliane when she was about eighteen that changed her relationship with Daddy, but not with Mim. It was after she got her matriculation with high honours. Daddy had a conference in Boston and, as a treat, said Eliane could visit some old friends in Honolulu who had a daughter her age. So she went with Daddy by air and the friends picked her up at the airport and he flew on. Then a month later she picked up the ship Mim took from Sydney to San Francisco to join Daddy. Later they all flew home together. We didn't know it at the time, but Mr and Mrs Carlister and Mark were on that ship.'

'Am I to presume without Paul?'

'That's right. But of course we didn't know the Carlisters then, we only met them later, when Maddy got engaged to George. You see George is Mr Carlister's nephew and now as well as that, when Mark Carlister married Ruth Evans, he married a Shorman, in a way, because Ruth's mother is Auntie Molly's sister and Auntie Molly is Daddy's cousin on the Shorman side.' She stopped and stood puzzled and silent on the path under the trees, and then she turned and looked up at Sims and her eyes were full of tears like an exasperated little girl.

'What's the matter with me, Sims?' she wailed. 'I don't even know what I'm talking about now.'

He put one arm over her shoulder. 'We'll sit down,' he said gently. 'Over there on the bench. It won't be too cold for a little while.' He kept his arm around her along the back of the seat, and she felt all the big, thin warmth of him between her body and the wind.

'Now,' Sims said, 'State the problem, state it clearly and with precision. Just the problem.'

'I can't,' she whispered. 'It isn't clear and I can't state it.'

'Then think of what it isn't. Is it Paul? Yes or no?'

'Oh no.' She was incapable at that moment of feeling the tension relax in Sims, and waited.

'Okay then, it is your sister Eliane.'

'Yes, and Mark Carlister.'

'Who is married to Ruth of the mantilla. I met her with Paul at the footy last Saturday.'

'At the footy – for heaven's sake! And just after she knew...'

'The problem then, is your sister Eliane and Mark, who is already married to Ruth – is that it?'

'They ran away to Paris together and my mother knew when she came home from her trip and didn't tell us. And when we found out she expected us to trust Eliane and keep on loving Eliane like she was doing herself.'

'And you didn't?'

'We turned on Mim. We were mean and horrible. Every one of us put our own interests first and said Mim had let us down by not stopping the affair. Everyone except Paul, that is.'

'Paul, was he there?'

'That's how I found out. Ruth had a letter from Mark and Paul told me and I told the family. I didn't even go to Mim first – that's how rotten I am.'

'If you were rotten,' Sims said mildly, 'you wouldn't give a damn.'

'But I blurted it out at the lunch table.'

'Paul blurted it out to you and I expect Ruth to Paul.'

'It had to come out, Sims, sooner or later. It wasn't Paul's fault. He was upset because Ruth was so hurt.'

'Upset for Ruth, but not for your sister? He wanted help from you then, for Ruth!'

'Maybe he did, Sims, I don't know. He didn't ask. He just seemed to understand more than I did, which I didn't expect. He explained to me that it was terrible for Ruth because Mark and Eliane had fallen in love all those years ago on the ship between Honolulu and America. He said his mother had tried to stop the marriage but couldn't and that my father succeeded where she failed. I was furious on behalf of Daddy, who has always loved Eliane so much. That's why I spoke out. That's why I told them all. It seemed incredible to me that Paul should equate his mother with my father. I think I expected Mim to deny the whole affair in front of Paul.'

'How could she if it was true?'

'She just sat there, Sims. She just sat there and listened to us, one after the other, telling her off. Then she got up and went to that room where you saw her yesterday and afterwards Paul lost his temper and told us all the love she'd spent on us would go into her painting, that we'd lost the best thing we'd ever had. He was tremendous, you know Sims, he was bigger than all of us, even Daddy, when he said that. So we all hated him for it.'

'That doesn't surprise me,' Sims said.

'He... He didn't even blame his own mother.'

'Why should he? Mrs Carlister is no worse than a snob and that doesn't make Paul one. It makes him the opposite.'

'But Eliane – my sister Eliane is not like us, Sims. She's part Hawaiian. To Paul's mother she is brown! Paul was right. For us it was a terrible failure of love and trust. In a way it was complete failure of everything our life stood for, Sims.'

'No,' Sims said. 'I can't agree. Your mother held on. Paul held on. I don't know about the others, but you haven't gone under yet.'

She said, 'You'd hold on, wouldn't you Sims?'

'I never had the chance,' Sims said, getting up. 'One day I might. Let's move. I don't want you cold.'

'Thank you for listening, Sims.'

He turned roughly towards her, as if all the protectiveness he felt was driven out. 'Don't thank me for listening, Barbara, don't thank me for that.'

'But you have listened, Sims,' she persisted. 'And I feel so much better. You've been wonderful.'

'I wanted to listen,' Sims snapped. 'I wanted to shut my big mouth and listen, Barbara. Don't get grateful.'

But he held her hand again as they crossed over Clarendon Street, past two ladies in tweed gaberdine who stepped aside to let them by as scruffy members of the 'who-knows-what-they-do-or-might-take youth'. They went down Gipps Street, unaware of the scandalised eyes that followed their swinging stride in the direction of Richmond.

Suddenly, Sims was able to ask quite simply, 'Will you have dinner with me on Saturday night, Barbi, just the two of us at a small Greek place I know?'

'Aren't you working this week, Sims?'

'Not this week.'

'Then I'd love to. What time?' She did not even suggest by tone, let alone ask if he could afford to take her out.

'Around seven. Paul has offered me the M.G. if I want it this week... Any time, he said... I'll ask for it.'

'I don't know, Sims,' she said. 'Don't count on it. There's something the matter with Paul. He's abstracted or forgetting all the time. He won't remember he offered you the car. We can go on the tram.'

'It's all right, Barbi,' Sims said. 'He'll be out in the Porsche.'

She glanced at him quickly, but he did not stop his fast stride to old Sarge's gate. When they finally arrived she was breathless.

Old Sarge's house was deadly cold. The old man sat in his armchair and did not stir at the sound of Sims' stride down the hall ahead of Barbi calling in a fun-high falsetto voice.

'Make way for company, Sarge. Attention – a lady for coffee.'

But at sight of the old man, Sims pulled up abruptly and his voice turned sharp.

'Sarge... What's up, Sarge?' he demanded. 'Sarge, what's the matter?'

A tremor seemed to run through the old man and he put out his hand feebly towards Sims.

'Glad...to see you, son, been waiting... They've killed my boy...army lorry...accident up near Cairns. They've been to tell me... Son... Two came... One of them welfare officers and a padre... A decent pair, they wuz... Coming back later... I told them you'd fix things up fer me... Would have been out in two months, Jimmy would... Shouldn't have let him get into the regulars... Pushing it too far, it was...' His voice trailed off and over his head, Sims stared at Barbi. Tears poured down her cheeks, but she spoke calmly.

'You get that fire going, Sims, while I make coffee – something hot. And put a blanket over him, we have to get him warm.'

At the front of the house, the M.G. roared to a halt. Paul had caught up with them.

At four-thirty that Thursday afternoon, Layton Shorman called up his cousin Molly and asked, 'Could I call around for an hour this evening? Harriet has been to see me and I'm hoping you and Thomas can give me some advice.'

'Certainly, Layton. Thomas is home and loves a talk with Mim.'

'I'm at the university, Molly. I'd prefer to come straight out now.'

'I'll tell Thomas. We'll be expecting you.'

Stepping into his car, Layton reflected that Molly was certainly the female equivalent of the man of few words. She did not commit herself easily, nor would she be committed. Of course, Layton knew it was a case of a highly intelligent woman who was once badly stung. Not that Molly's unfortunate marriage had lasted long, even with the two children. Molly, being a Shorman, hadn't put up with the man for long, and hadn't married again. As a matter of fact, Layton had always considered Molly rather suited the role of divorcee. She wasn't quite a career type, although she'd worked for years. Molly had a lot of Shorman pride in her.

As he backed out the Ford from his parking space, his secretary appeared abreast of his driver's window. He noted that it hadn't taken her long to follow his earlier than usual departure. Her smile was disinterested, but pervading enough to remind him where she lived.

'Can I give you a lift?' he was forced to ask. 'I'm dropping in on a cousin of mine in Heidelberg on the way home.'

She hopped around the car and into the seat beside him with the alacrity of habit.

'I didn't know you had relations in Heidelberg,' she said. He immediately regretted his offer.

'Not really Heidelberg,' he said. 'Nearer Eaglemont, but I can drop you on the line at Ivanhoe.'

'Thanks,' she said brightly. 'How's Mrs Shorman? Is she tired after her trip?'

'She is – surviving,' he replied, quick to take advantage of a family lead-in. 'How is your little boy going in the new pre-school?'

As expected, she took off non-stop while he nosed the car carefully into the traffic headed towards East Richmond.

After he dropped his passenger, the car purred Layton back into the relief of silence and he almost missed the turn-off to Molly's unpretentious street of war service homes which were, he supposed, the predecessors of the present suburban blocks of villas, picked out of a dozen small-roomed styles to be paid off in thirty years. Funny, Molly hadn't moved and that Thomas had built an apartment for himself on her property. He was sure old Thomas could afford to live where he pleased; Layton would have thought Brighton or even Frankston with a sea view for an ex sea-faring man.

The street was tree-lined green with eucalypts and branched with lillypillies, the neatly-fenced front gardens small. He remembered all those blocks were deep, running downhill with a view towards Mount Macedon. When he parked the car and stepped out, he intended to check the numbers, but recognised Molly's house almost at once as the straight across hard white weatherboard box with the bright blue door dead centre. He walked up the narrow cement path and was surprised by the verandah of black and white Dutch tiles and the resonance of the doorbell. It was, of course, some years since he had visited Molly and Thomas.

Inside, he followed Molly down the hall on rich red carpet that flowed into the living room where Thomas waited beside an open wood fire that burned under a white mantel. Beyond Thomas a wall of glass window kept out the cold and let in a distant view of the first twinkling lights of evening.

'How splendid,' Layton said smoothly. 'I hadn't remembered you had such a view.'

'We're like the Chinese,' Thomas said smugly. 'Keep the best inside.'

Molly indicated a black leather lounge opposite Thomas. 'Do sit down, Layton,' she said. 'Will you have a dry sherry?' She moved with grace in her black velvet slacks to a carved cabinet and poured drinks into glasses from a crystal decanter on a silver tray. Layton noticed that where the window ended, Thomas's two-level apartment began, neatly connected to this room, with an inside open covered deck. They were indeed Chinese, even the garden was enclosed from outside view, and sitting, Layton noticed the magnificent ivory chess set on the inlaid games table between two wing-backed armchairs close to the heat of the fire. Mim had told him old Thomas and Molly played chess, but he hadn't realised it was in comfort like this.

Thomas grumbled, 'What's the matter with Mim? We haven't seen her here since she got back... She hasn't phoned Molly either... Must be two weeks.'

Layton looked into his sherry, then up at Molly. 'Mim is indisposed,' he said. 'She's been in her room for a week, or that is to say, in the room where she paints.'

'Where I was,' Molly said. 'Why?'

Preliminaries would be useless, Layton surmised, so he said briefly, 'It's a family thing and will resolve itself. Mim is tired after the trip. Anyway, I didn't come to talk about that.'

'Then why did you come?' Thomas snapped.

'I came to talk about Harriet and a suggestion she has put up to me. As her brother, I wanted to consult you, Uncle Thomas.'

'Have you talked to Mim? Does she approve of Harriet's suggestion?'

'At present, I can't talk to Mim about it.'

'Why not?' This time Thomas shouted.

Layton looked from Thomas to Molly and discovered her staring into the fire, her mouth set thin.

'Why not, I said,' Thomas repeated with equal blast. Molly's hand, long and white from wrist to fingertip, moved to rest on Thomas' knee. She spoke into the fire without lifting her head.

'Surely you can tell us why it is impossible to talk to Mim, Layton?'

He bristled. 'I had hoped not to have to, Molly. Mim has taken some sort of stand since a row we had last Sunday. It was a family row and Mim has taken it out on the lot of us ever since. She is painting in that room and refuses to come out. She hasn't cooked a meal or done anything else.'

Thomas whistled. It was a soft, piercing, sailor's whistle and it jarred Layton with a suspected quality of jubilance that brought him close to the kind of uncontrolled rudeness he despised in other people.

'I am sorry it has proved necessary to burden you with my problem concerning Harriet,' he said coldly. 'But since I cannot discuss the matter with Mim, I assumed I could bring the matter to you. Mim and Harriet are not on speaking terms.'

'I told Harriet not to butt in,' Thomas said.

'You did what?' Layton demanded.

'She phoned up this week, Monday or Tuesday I think it was. She told me there was something the matter with Mim and I told her to mind her own business. So she's not speaking to me either. Seems to me she's on to you because you're the only one left. What's her proposition?'

'She has offered me the old family home in Mont Albert. She says she's too old to manage it any more all by herself and wants it over in a deed of gift, as I'm the only male heir.'

Molly stood up to pull the curtains across the window against the falling dark. Inside the room the fire crackled, dancing lights on the furniture before she switched on a lamp and reseated herself.

'On what terms?' Thomas boomed.

'Just that we take over the house as it stands.'

'With her in it?'

'There's plenty of room. The house has seven bedrooms. Harriet would have her own bedroom and sitting room.'

Thomas began to laugh – chuckling at first, from somewhere inside himself – before he shook with bodily gasps that left him mopping at his eyes with trembling hands.

Molly cried, 'Thomas!' and ran to the kitchen for a glass of water. When she returned, Layton was on his feet staring at Thomas, who pushed aside the glass of water and shook his head from side to side with his hand over his mouth like a giggling child trapped until the paroxysm passed. Molly put the water on the mantel and poked the fire and Layton marked much concern in her about Thomas. He was old, but she had made her life around his company and one day soon he'd die. However, when he went, she'd be well off. She'd rent that modern apartment of his and have all she needed. She'd deserve what she got for looking after him for years.

But Molly's eyes were full of tears when she said to Layton, 'You'll get the house anyway, when Aunt Harriet dies, Layton. Nobody else wants it.'

'I wasn't suggesting—' Layton began.

Suddenly, Thomas contained his laughter and spoke. 'You want the house now, don't you, Layton? You want it now when it can help your career. Harriet knows you want it now and anything else you can get to help your career. You feel you're entitled to it and you're right. That house and all the other property should have been sold when my mother died, because it was Mother's money. It should have been evenly divided in four and your father and Molly's father and I should have had our equal share with Harriet. But it was tied up by Father for Harriet because she promised not to marry and to look after the old man until the day he died at eighty-nine. Eighty-nine is a good age. By the time he was eighty-nine your father and I didn't care any more and Molly's father was bitter from running the business and Harriet had grown so much like Father none of us could stand her. Only your wife has been kind to her, Layton, and take it from me, Harriet's terms involve your wife. It is Mim that Harriet wants. She wants the attention of Mim for the rest of her life. It is Mim she wants in her house, not you. Think about it, man, Harriet was around when Mim looked after your mother before she died. Another couple of years and those pretty twins of yours will be married. Harriet is five years younger than I am and I'm eighty. That gives her a long time until eighty-nine, long past your retirement, probably long past the time Harriet's money is any use to you. Think about it, Layton.'

'I shouldn't have come,' Layton muttered to Molly. Thomas heard him with the acuteness of the elderly deaf.

'Probably did you good to come. Might help you to see straight. Probably should have come before. When Mim's been here without you, I've her word for it that you've been busy. And I've taken Mim's word about poor old lonely Harriet as she calls her as well, and minded my own business there too and Molly's kept her mouth shut about Harriet, but there's a limit, boy. This time you asked for it, eh?' He stood up unsteadily. Then he rallied his reserve of dignity. 'Now, if you'll both excuse me, I've said my say,' he grumbled and stalked off.

Layton stepped forward, but was restrained by Molly's hand on his arm.

'Let him go,' she said.

'My God,' Layton remarked, with feeling.

'He has a bad heart, you know,' Molly sighed.

'I'll go,' Layton said. 'I'm sorry I came – for your sake, Molly.'

'Oh, don't worry about me, Layton, or about Thomas. He will take one of his little pills and lie down for half an hour or so. Then he'll come back. I never appear to notice his turns so he is not obliged to apologise, which would be worse for him than the attack.'

'You have developed patience over the years.'

'Not at all. Compared to Mim, I don't know the meaning of patience.'

'That depends on the point of view. Although one would scarcely believe it, this last week Mim really has had very little to whinge about, you know.'

'Whinge is a word we use easily, Layton, especially when there are things concerning a person we don't wish to see.'

'Well, after all, Molly, putting the whole family into a state of crisis is no mean accomplishment. And I'm only a university executive, not a psychologist.'

'For which you have to thank Mim, Layton. You've been lucky. Sooner or later most people have to be their own psychologists.'

He took her up sharply. 'I presume you mean women in particular?'

Her eyes narrowed. 'I mean wives in particular.'

'You thereby intend to exclude Harriet.'

'And myself, Layton. I run my own life as I see fit. Like Harriet, I am free to go all out after anything I want.' Her eyes fell on the chess board and she continued. 'It is like a game of chess. Harriet and I may lose the game, but we have the freedom to play it our own way. Mim does not have our opportunities. Most wives don't.'

'I'm afraid I fail to see what you mean, Molly.' Layton's voice was determinedly light as preparation for his departure. 'I wish you would come and see Mim. She'll be pleased to see you. She puts off everybody else except the girls. She'll get over it given time, of course, and the sooner the better, but meantime I do wish you'd talk to her.'

'No,' Molly said flatly. 'If Mim wants me she'll get in touch.'

He tried again. 'The girls are finding the situation a bit drastic, you know, and Maddy can't do any more.'

'If you mean the house, Layton, get in some help.'

'Get in some help... Me? I wouldn't know...'

'Know where to start?' she finished for him. 'No, of course you wouldn't. Ask Maddy then.'

'Getting in help is hardly the solution, Molly.'

'It's an alternative to washing your own shirts, Layton. I presume they are accumulating.'

He started in the direction of the hall and she followed quietly to slip past him and open the door. Her bedroom door was open and the smug neatness of her single bed assaulted him with the pressure of a hammer.

'Goodbye,' he said briefly. 'I hope I haven't held up your dinner.'

'Oh, Thomas and I eat at all hours,' she laughed. 'And sometimes don't bother to eat at all. We have both given up institutions.'

She added goodnight when he was halfway down the path and he realised with something of a shock that she would not care if he did not put the imprint of his foot on her property again. So that was cousin Molly and Uncle Thomas at home, minding their own business in favour of any move Mim cared to make, whether or not it included Harriet, whom they both detested. Well, now he knew.

But getting into the car he remembered his mother had liked Thomas and disliked Harriet. After his father's death she had ceased to insist on Sunday dinner with Grandfather Shorman and Harriet in Mont Albert and later, when he brought Linda back from Honolulu to the house in Kew, she had made a great fuss about entertaining Captain Thomas, as she called him, whenever his ship was in port.

A sense of depression fell upon Layton driving home, which he knew to be a feeling of guilt from thoughts of his mother who had given her only son all she had in return for very little. He had found her stiffly restrained with righteous over-sensibility when her offer of the house had brought him back to Kew with two little girls. She had wanted to move out and then, because her health was poor, had gone away for six months to give Linda time to redecorate and furnish the house.

'Because it's her home now, son, it must be her home and yours.'

The twins could not remember his mother, but she had been a good grandmother and Maddy and Elie remembered her with love. To Eliane she was still very real; once, Elie said, like a golden locket of her very own. And she had helped Mim with the little girls and babies day after day and retired to her room at an early hour on those nights she was not in charge of the children. People had asked with attempted humour how he managed a mother and a wife in the same house and he had replied with forced humour while his inner self wished the mother away.

He had not understood her personality even as a youth, and in his early maturity before marriage found her actions towards him insipid and fussy. In his adult household located in the house she had given up for him, he had watched her spoil Eliane with small, considered attentions and come close to hating her. At the time of her death, when the twins were three years old, he suspected that she knew he had no feeling for her. He had hated himself at her funeral as he watched Mim weep. He knew that Mim had a great pity for his mother, which was somehow wordlessly reciprocated. They had, in some subtle, undefined way, protected one another as women, not against any threat he knew of, but for a purpose that he believed embraced the children who provided their joy. Unlike Mim, his mother had showed no pride in him. Instead he had felt her ambition for him to be a demand without limit, an expectation with the force of compensatory justice. To Mim, his ambition was his own affair, the limitation of his own determination. Until the death of his mother he had felt trapped. After her death, his way seemed set and he moved forward steadily of his own volition, underneath his own compulsion, announcing to Mim his ambition and the expectation of his marriage as the clearly defined head of family in what he felt to be the proud and proper Shorman manner.

Molly returned to the living room fire to find Thomas already back in his chair beside the chess table. Ignoring him, she set two new logs to the blaze and poked viciously at the scattered coals beneath them.

'You're annoyed,' Thomas stated.

'Why did you do it, Thomas?'

'I liked his mother. You must remember your Aunt Ellen. She was a nice woman.'

'Is that a reason to tell Layton he's entitled to Harriet's wealth, so he'll force poor Mim into a wretched prestigious house that was literally the death of your mother?'

'And, in a way, Layton's mother. Layton is like the old man.'

'Grandfather? I don't think so. He's not mean, only spoiled. Aunt Ellen spoiled him. Surely you know that he was all she had when Uncle died.'

'Then it's time he grew up, isn't it? This is his chance. We'll see whether he's only spoiled or not.'

'At Mim's expense.'

'Mim's taking a stand, Molly. That's what he said. He said in his bloody superior way that Mim was taking some sort of stand. It's a wonder he didn't ask you to go over and talk her out of it.'

'He did, but not in the way you suggest, just to go over to see her. I refused, but I want to go, Thomas. I think the family row must have been about Eliane and Mark Carlister. I think Mim knew about them before she came back. I think perhaps Layton and the family failed her. I'd like to go to her, Thomas, but I can't… Not until she asks me. Because of Ruth – I can't go because of Ruth, do you understand?'

'I'm sorry,' Thomas said. 'I should have kept my mouth shut. I've hurt you.'

'Yes,' she said. 'I'm hurt and it surprises me like an old wound rubbed on the outside and the inside hurts. And none of it is really my business. Neither Ruth nor Mim are my business.'

'But I am,' Thomas grunted.

She recovered quietly. 'You're an old brute, Thomas, but I'll make us some toast and tea and we'll finish the game.'

Thomas sucked in his breath as she walked from the room.

'Yes,' he muttered. 'Yes, Thomas, you will finish the game.

CHAPTER TWELVE

Taken apart by an estate agent, the old Shorman house in Mont Albert would be termed a 'boom-style mansion', formidably solid to the last 'Hawthorn' brick in the tower. The least that could be said of the inner accommodation would employ the word generous and a lavish description would focus on the marble fireplaces, tiled hallways, wrought-iron balconies and the magnificent polished staircase. The mansion, thus viewed, would be considered more than a gentleman's residence in the modern sense, owing to the inconvenient enormity of kitchen and bathroom, which gentlemen of the first quarter of the present century still provided as employment for polishing handmaids.

The furniture in the Shorman house was an antique dealer's dream in mahogany, rosewood and teak. The drapes of beige brocade hanging on polished rings from equally polished circular rods sheltered the reception room from the least suspicion of glare, and the tapestry seats of the chairs showed no sign of fading. The curio cabinets shielded with reflective glass doors the rows of Venetian glass, and mirrored the chandeliers and ornaments arranged on delicately balanced tables. The rugs on the parquet floor were Chinese and round like the belly of a lacquered secretaire.

Thomas Shorman paid off his taxi in front of the home of his youth and stood outside the wrought-iron gate breathing a little harder than he had expected. The old garden, reduced to a mere tenth of its original size, harboured enormous trees that now eroded the front lawn to a mere pretence of green, but the rhododendrons and azaleas held their ground in a blaze of colour for which he felt grateful, a sentiment that surprised him. He hated the house but his mother had loved the garden. His nautical eye for all things ship-shape noted the fences and paintwork to be in good repair, in keeping with the lavish homes recently built on the final sub-division sites, for which he expected the solicitors extracted a fortune on behalf of the trust that looked after the house and Harriet.

Walking up the path, his mind dragged up words.

'To my youngest child and only daughter Harriet Shorman, spinster, my house and all there-in and estate to be administered in trust for her benefit by Messrs. Dombey, Potter and Potter in consultation with my sons for as long as she lives,' and on and on and on in the detail of how and by what means. The last will and testament of John Shorman, father of four, worked out to the last comma.

He rang the doorbell with the hard pressure of fury. There was no answer. Harriet lived in the rear of the house, he'd heard, in the small den beside the breakfast room, so he walked around to the back. The side gate to the kitchen garden was barred, but an Italian cutting the hedge let him in. He followed the man to the kitchen door, which was also locked. The gardener pounded hard with the impression of much practice.

'The old lady – she does not hear,' he explained to Thomas. 'Mrs Shorman, you know Mrs Shorman? When she come, she have own key. Very nice lady.'

When Harriet finally opened the door, Thomas walked past her into the kitchen and put his small suitcase on the large laminex table, which tended to make the old leather bag look shabby.

'I think I'll make myself a cup of tea before I take my case upstairs,' he explained. 'Why didn't you answer the front doorbell when I rang?'

'I can't go all that way to the front door every time it rings. You know I'm not well. I should be in the hospital. I would be, only Linda can't take me just at present. What – are you doing – Thomas?'

He opened one cupboard after another, closing each with a bang. 'Looking for tea – where is it?'

She began to whine, 'You have no right coming here, upsetting me, Thomas. You'll just have to go.'

'Go?' he said, 'I've come to stay.'

'You've what?'

'I've come to stay in my old home. Why not? I was born here, brought up here. There's plenty of room. I've decided to live in my old home for a period of time.'

'You can't.'

'Who's to stop me? I've got every right in the world.'

'My lawyers will stop you. The very idea is ludicrous.'

'On the contrary, it is ludicrous that I have not moved in before. You forget, Harriet, that your lawyers are solicitors for the estate, are family lawyers.'

Harriet's eyes flashed and then grew shrewd. 'So you've quarrelled with Molly at last,' she sniffed.

Thomas shivered. The kitchen was a barn since the installation of electrical equipment replaced the old fuel stove he remembered as an ever-singing kettle. He supposed it was a long time, probably past Harriet's memory, when you just walked into this kitchen and drank hot tea with the gardener in an atmosphere of winter warmth.

'Where do you live?' he demanded. 'It's obviously not here.'

'If you must know, I use the butler's pantry beside the breakfast room. I have – my apartment's there. You can come through and I'll make you tea, but just because you've quarrelled with Molly, you can't stay you know, Thomas. I keep this house in trust exactly as Father left it and he didn't leave you in it.'

He followed her down the passage past the rear stairway, blocked off with a bolted door. When she opened up the old breakfast room, the heat overwhelmed him with the full strength of an electric space-heater. The old oak furniture was gone in favour of a television, a green velvet suite and a glass-topped table. He lowered himself into the chair nearest the door before Harriet closed it. She went into the butler's pantry on his left and he noticed another new door off to the right. That would lead into the old den converted to her bedroom. She would have a modern bathroom there too. He called into the rattle of teacups in the butler's pantry, 'Do you need all this heat? It's a wonder you don't die of contrast after you tour your trust. Who else besides that man cutting the hedge helps you maintain this place?'

She did not reply until she reappeared with tea and biscuits on a tray. Her cheeks were flushed pink from the heat and he recalled how pretty she had been as a child, with dark eyes in a small pointed face under fine, fair curls. Father's darling! The price she'd paid for that privilege was evident in her answer. She was a dead seed in the centre of an enormous nut.

'I have had various difficulties with gardeners,' she said haughtily. 'Tony is the last of several migrants in need of employment. From time to time he works very well for Linda.'

'I see. Who else?'

'At present I do not have a housekeeper or a chamber maid, which makes life exceedingly trying for me, Thomas, and no doubt accounts for the state of my health. I hope now that Linda has returned someone will be found to assist me.'

'No housekeeper in her right mind would take on all this.'

'Really, Thomas, you are incorrigible. Working for me is a sinecure. Miss Smith from the shop in Toorak supervises the quarterly cleaning, repair and maintenance of the contents of the house, and Black and Abernathy have a yearly contract for painting and redecorating inside and out.'

'The accounts handled by the solicitors, I take it.'

'Of course. This house is a trust, Thomas.'

'It ought to belong to the National Trust.'

'Don't be ridiculous.'

'You could call it the Shorman Bequest. They might make you a dame of the British Empire for the gesture.'

She regarded him with distaste, like a fly, but his buzz worried her. 'If you've finished your tea, Thomas,' she said icily and rose to her feet.

'Are there any spare bedrooms on this floor?' he asked. 'I prefer to avoid the grand staircase if possible.'

'None of the bedrooms are available for occupation. The rooms upstairs are kept locked.'

'Then where do you expect Layton and his family to sleep?'

Harriet's face wrinkled into a hundred little furrows that squeezed tears from her eyes to fill them. She sat back heavily into the chair she had just vacated. 'You – you beast, you haven't quarrelled with Molly at all. She's put you up to this. I know it – I know it in my bones. I've ached all morning. You just get out of here. I'll have to phone my doctor. I think I'll have to go into the Clinic without waiting for Mim to take me.' Her bosom rose and fell dramatically as her words unmanned her reserves into real tears.

'Go to the Clinic. Don't mind me,' Thomas said. 'For once you needn't worry about the house when you go. I'll be here.'

'Get out!' she screamed. 'You get out, Thomas Shorman!'

'I'm not going, Harriet, and if Layton moves in I'll be here permanently.'

'Who told you?' she whispered.

'Layton told me, who else? He sees the advantages. One day he'll hand the place over as a hospital or a home for the National Trust, fully maintained, and get a knighthood out of it. Why not? He's young. He'll outlive you and I by many years. Why shouldn't he make the most of being a Shorman? Why shouldn't Molly?'

'Molly – did you say Molly?' Her voice was a whisper.

'She could get a good rent for her place in Heidelberg.'

'She's put you up to this, I can see it. I can feel it—'

'In your bones,' he finished for her. 'You're getting old, Harriet, and repeating yourself. As it happens, neither Molly or Mim know anything about your proposition. Layton and I are the men in the family and we will decide.'

'You can't,' she moaned. 'The solicitors of the trust wouldn't let you.'

'If that is the case, Layton can't move in, can he, except if you and I agree?'

'You?'

'If you and I approach the trust, our wishes will be respected.'

'I won't do it.'

'Surely, Harriet, you don't think that Mim Shorman would take over this house if she thought Molly and I wished to indulge in our right to live here? If she thought I wanted to spend my few remaining years in the house I was born in and Molly's father was born in? You have a choice, Harriet – to get Mim at your beck and call, you take Molly and I to look after Mim, or else you make some other arrangement.'

'Other arrangement?'

'Like living as a respectable old lady your age should: in a villa unit, something the size of this nest you've made for yourself. Somewhere warm and comfortable where you don't need three bolts on every door and where you're not looking after a museum!'

'I hate you, Thomas,' Harriet hissed at him. 'I just hate you.'

It was not the first time Thomas had been hated by Harriet. 'Better than hating yourself, dear sister,' he said affably. 'I think I'll take a walk around the old place. Where do you keep the keys? Oh, never mind, I'll take a look at what's easy.'

Harriet sat very still, listening to his feet shuffle heavily towards the front of the house. Then she heard him open a door and step from carpet to the parquet of the lounge and cross over to the window. Her mind's eye saw him pull the thick, tasselled cord of the tapestry drapes to let the winter sun flood the crystal chandelier with tiny sparklets of light that would speckle the upholstery of the chairs and streak the wallpaper as surely as rain. Now he would be looking out at the azaleas that Mim always wanted to pick in great shaggy bunches to distribute in every available space. Thinking of Mim filled the room with people, with the presence of the inhabitants of the house in Kew. Barbara and that untidy boy of the Carlisters. Henrietta and the fair boy who lolled beside her at the airport. Maybe even that mad-looking boy called Sims and Madeleine with all those children and, of course, Layton who was going to use her to become Sir Layton. The nerve of Layton to tell Thomas. Sir Layton indeed! He was arrogant enough as it was. Arrogant! She recalled his voice, smooth as jelly, telling her he would consider her proposal. Consider her proposal, not even surprised, let alone grateful, and he would let her know! And he hadn't told Linda, only Thomas, so that it was Thomas staring out of her beautiful bay window at the azaleas her mother had planted. Her mother who hadn't loved her as much as the boys. Well, her father had made up for it. He'd left her all this and Layton wasn't going to take it away from her. She wouldn't let him. No, not even for Linda would she let him. She'd pay him off, that's what she'd do. Because he'd have to be paid off. He was Shorman like she was herself and her father before her, and if you cheated a Shorman, her father said you had to pay for it. Layton would feel cheated to lose so much. Her father would and she would and therefore Layton would. Besides, if she gave him money now, it would only come from investments he would one day inherit as her only male heir. She couldn't change his status, but he wouldn't inherit so much if she gave the house to the nation for a birthday honour for herself. Well, why shouldn't she have the honour? Her father would want her to have it, rather than Layton. He had considered Layton a spoiled pup. He had indeed. The only young relative he'd had any respect for was Molly.

Harriet sat upright in her chair, as if suddenly stung. Molly! She would not have Molly in her house. Never Molly living in Father's house! Rather give in to Thomas.

She found him standing as she expected, staring listlessly out of the great bay window. 'Thomas,' she said, and he turned. They stared at each other across the magnificent room. The light of noon behind Thomas twinkled the shimmering glass and danced like a fairy in the blue centre of fringed carpet. Sixty-five years before, as a little girl of ten, she had faced him like this, her light voice thin with venom.

'I am going to tell Father as soon as he comes in.'

'If you do, I'll cut your hair off.'

'You won't dare.' He had known he wouldn't dare, but maintained his stance. He was huge with menace, and she said, 'I won't tell if you give me your ivory penknife.' She had wanted a penknife, which she couldn't ask for because she was a girl.

He wondered, standing there with his whole lifetime behind him, what had happened to the penknife and was astonished when Harriet whimpered, 'Years ago, you gave me a penknife in this room. I don't know why you grew to distrust me, Thomas. I used to think it was because of Mother, and then after that I thought Layton's mother turned you against me, and after you gave up the sea I thought it was Molly. But you always were my favourite brother and now you're the only one left anyway.'

He growled from his chest. 'Just what are you getting at, Harriet?'

'I think you are quite right, Thomas. This place is too huge for me and I think I would like to present it to the National Trust as you suggest and live in one of those nice villa units you spoke of. You can phone the solicitors for me and we'll fix it this afternoon.'

He did not trust himself to smile. 'Don't you think you'd better fix it with Layton first?'

'I'll give Layton a cheque instead,' she said airily. 'It's the same thing.'

'You think so?' It was too easy and he prickled with suspicion as she added, 'I'm sure Linda will help me find a place and move me in.'

'Poor Mim.'

'What do you mean, poor Mim? The trip was too much for her. Just at present she is indisposed, that's all. She always helps me.'

'Oh sure, sure,' Thomas agreed, suddenly tired. 'Only sometimes I wonder why she runs around in that broken-down bus of hers helping us all.'

Harriet's eyes narrowed. 'Are you suggesting, Thomas, that I don't appreciate Linda? Are you suggesting I buy her a new car?'

'Anything that saves her time, Harriet, while she's young enough to use it, that's all I mean.' He stared for a long minute at the watch on his wrist.

'All right, I will,' Harriet snapped. 'I'll buy her a car and that ought to save her time. Do you think we'll have time this afternoon?' She drew abreast of him and began to pull the curtains back across the windows.

He looked at her closely, feeling ten, twenty, fifty years older as she swelled from a sick old lady to a virago with new purpose. Time and time again he'd seen his father do the same thing – succumb only to revive with shrewd renewal. He sensed she was thinking how old and weary he looked, how many more years she was sure to enjoy, how she had better hurry him up in case he faltered.

'If we phone now we'll be able to contact Mr Dombey, the senior partner who handles my affairs. You look unwell, Thomas. I must say, you have gone down lately. I expect it's your heart condition. You had better go home and sleep in your own bed after our business is finished this afternoon. What kind of car does Linda drive?'

'A Peugeot – an old Peugeot – 403. Couldn't you leave the car, Harriet? One thing at a time – give you something to do next week while you're waiting for Dombey to fix this business up. It'll take time.'

'Are you trying to back out, Thomas?'

'No, no,' he said, hoping the real measure of his fatigue didn't show. 'We'll get an appointment with Dombey and then call a cab and go.'

'What about lunch? We must have lunch first. I couldn't possibly—'

His moment of panic was real. He couldn't face lunch in the house. He'd give himself away. 'If there's time before the appointment, we'll stop somewhere, otherwise after.'

'I feel quite excited,' Harriet said at the telephone. 'Shall I tell Mr Dombey myself? No, you're a man, Thomas.'

He explained carefully to Mr Dombey, balancing the solicitor's interjections against a terrible desire to get it all out to the other neutral ears. In case she changed her mind. Until Mr Dombey said, 'I think you better come straight in, Thomas. Come straight in. I'll order some tea and sandwiches.'

Outside in the fresh air of the street, waiting, the tension left Thomas. When the taxi arrived and Harriet came out, she was wearing her mink hat tilted to one side like the head of a bear with two paws across the eyes. He had recovered enough to joke as they set out, 'You know, Harriet, that's a beautiful hat, but it's too big for your face. Buy yourself another one and give that to Mim's girls. Henrietta, I'd say, would do it justice. Mink needs a dash of elegance.'

He paused, regarding the stiffness of her profile with conjecture. 'In the young, I mean. You'd suit a smaller one.' As she straightened the hat he noticed the blue veins on her thin pink hands and then regarded his own, gnarled with arthritis.

'I prefer Barbara to Henrietta,' Harriet snapped. 'But I disapprove of that Carlister boy she is running around with at present. Layton should put a stop to it, and I have told him so.'

'Mim doesn't seem to mind the boy.'

'As I informed you, Thomas, Linda is not herself at present. She should never have gone on that trip. It is my opinion, and Layton agrees with me, that various social service societies in this city take advantage of Linda.'

'We all do,' Thomas murmured. 'And you know it.'

'I have just said that I will buy her a new car. Surely that will satisfy you. I shall ask Mr Dombey to arrange it for me.'

'A new Peugeot 405 will set you back $5,000, Harriet.'

He imagined her lip curled around her reply, which was soft as a purr. 'I will take it off the cheque I intend to give to Layton. It's the same thing, isn't it?'

At noon on that Friday, old Sarge insisted on getting up and dressing himself. Sims had made all the necessary arrangements with Victoria Barracks. Jimmy's body would be flown to Melbourne since old Sarge, as the only relative, was too old to fly to Cairns. Sims on the telephone had been decisive and terse. Jimmy's funeral was to be on Monday. Sarge was satisfied with whatever Sims said and did, provided he got no 'lip', as he called suggestions 'from those bastards'. He wanted everything decent for Jimmy, he told Sims. Nothing else mattered.

The old man wanted everything to 'go' for Sims too, not that Sims was his boy, like Jimmy. Jimmy was his own kind, and Jimmy was the last of the lot. It was a helluva thing, and he knew it was the end for himself. But Sims had a future and he wanted Sims to have a go with that girl he was so stuck on, that Barbi Shorman. She was good for Sims, somehow, fitted like good boots. S'truth Sims wouldn't want that girl connected with boots. Sims had kept him in bed all morning and when he wasn't fixing things on the phone he had been talking non-stop. Keeping his mind off... Old Sarge knew he'd been doing that, talkin' on purpose... Keeping his mind off that bloody business. Sarge didn't know how he'd found out that Sims had a date to take Barbi out on Saturday night. He hadn't been sure at first, his mind was so muddled, but he'd been sure when Paul came to see how he was, came in two cars, he had – a blonde driving the other – and left the M.G. for Sims.

'Take it today, Sims,' Paul said at the door, after he'd paid his respects again and left food. 'Ruth fixed it,' he told Sims. He'd left the M.G. and gone off with the blonde in the other car. Sims had explained about Ruth... Too much money and not enough to do, some of these young whippersnappers. She had a little boy too, Sims said... Had a little boy. Well good-o, anyway, it had given Sims his chance with Barbi and he wasn't having Sims stay home, hovering like a fly every time he turned over, instead of taking his chance.

As he dressed he wondered if Sims would have a little boy one day. Cripes, it was one of the things he'd hoped for Jimmy... A little boy one day, a little boy. He pulled himself together and was dressed when Sims came into the room.

'I don't sleep at night, layin' in bed all day,' he growled at Sims. 'It's not as if I'm sick or somethin', son. I just got knocked off me pins... A helluva thing like that, a bloke don't expect it.'

He ate the food Sims gave him that Ruth fixed, and in the afternoon some of his neighbours called and then Barbi came and made tea, but wouldn't stay, and all Sarge could do to make Sims take her home in the M.G. was unsuccessful. She went off again on the tram while Sarge was getting ready for bed. But he heard Sims say he thought old Sarge was better and that unless he phoned he would see her tomorrow night. So Sarge was happy for that... Bloody decent they all were, as that Paul would say. He'd hadn't a ruddy hope of ever understanding what made them tick, but he'd make sure he got to bed early tomorrow night. Five-thirty maybe, right after his tea, that'd do. What the hell had he got to stay up for anyway?

The bed sagged as he lay awake in the dark.

Back in Ruth's car, Paul drove slowly and beside him Ruth waited for him to speak. She had been a little frightened for herself and Rollo and her car, waiting in this part of Richmond, and felt ashamed of it, and yet somehow exhilarated that Paul should have come to her to ask for food for poor old Sarge. He drove all the way to the edge of the Fitzroy Gardens and then pulled the car up. In his car seat behind them, little Rollo clapped his baby hands – a true apartment child, he loved a park.

'My Gawd, Ruth,' Paul cried out. 'Why the bloody hell should a thing like that happen to that poor old man? He hasn't got anybody else but Sims… Do you realise that, Ruth? Jimmy was literally all the people he had in the world.'

'It was terribly hard for you to go to see him, wasn't it, Paul?'

'He looked awful, Ruth. Miserable. Sims said he was much better, but I don't believe it somehow… He looked awful. Sims says the funeral will be on Monday. Jimmy's, I mean… Military.'

'Will you go?'

'Me? Gawd, I never thought of that. Gawd, Sims'll have to go.'

She was quick to feel the distress in him and ached to alleviate it if she could. 'Don't worry about it now, Paul. You can decide over the weekend.' She thought of his car in front of the house in Richmond and of the food he had asked her for. 'You have done all you can. I was glad you came to me to ask for the food. I… I was proud.'

'Don't be, Ruth. I was there, that was all, driving round and round your place. I've been doing it all week. Food for Sarge and Sims was just an excuse, Ruth… I wanted to see you… I just didn't have the guts to come in.'

'Paul.'

'Well, it's true. And now after that lot I'll take you and Rollo home.'

She seemed to wilt beside him. 'I don't want to go home, Paul… I don't want to go home,' she whispered.

He turned to face her, one thin hand on the wheel and the other thrown carelessly over the back of the seat, fiddling with the minute dividing possibility of the upholstery.

'Don't cry, Ruth… For Gawd's sake, don't cry.'

'I'm not crying… You've been so… So wonderful. I won't do that to you.'

But her eyes grew enormous and swam towards him mistily so that the shine of then was blended silver blue and black like deep, clear water and beyond them the circle of her hair illuminated her features into a precipitous immediacy of golden light. Drawn violently by an indescribable tenderness, all that was awkward in Paul melted away and his lips fell softly on Ruth's lips like a benediction.

Her lips responded and the moment of pity swelled into passion; in Paul a stillness deeper than he had ever known; in Ruth, fulfilment recognised as never before. For them both, the whole world of life-hope opened clear beyond meaning and failure.

So that the withdrawal, equally unexpected and sudden, was fiercely brutal.

'Oh my God, Ruth—'

'Don't say you're sorry, Paul. You couldn't help it. You did it out of pity for me.'

'And now need the pity for myself.'

'No, Paul.'

'Yes, Ruth. You know as well as I do.'

'I've been so stupid, so stupid, Paul. I couldn't wait. I had to grab the reflection I saw in Mark—'

'Of Mark, you mean.'

'No, I mean just what I said. I do not flatter myself. I didn't know it could be like - like it just was, Paul. You must believe me. I didn't know, even you see how it could have been with Mark and Eliane.'

'It won't work, you know, Ruth, not for us, not now.'

'I know, and yet I'm not sorry, Paul. I'll never be sorry. I don't want you to be sorry either.'

'All afternoon I've been resisting your hair. I've been wanting to stroke the back of your head. I never even suspected my intentions and God knows I'm not above making a pass on any ordinary occasion that offers, but I am sorry, Ruth. This isn't ordinary. I'll always be sorry. But I - I'll try not to spoil things for you. I'll take you home now - back to Mum and Dad - they'll be waiting in their peculiar, blind innocence.'

'My empty house is also waiting, Paul.'

'Not for me. There is no place for me in Mark's house, not now, anyway.'

'He couldn't help it either, Paul. I can see that now.'

'Oh, that. He should have taken his chance when he had it first. He had to drag you in. I ought to hate him for touching you.'

'Don't hate him. He was... lonely.'

'Did he tell you he was lonely?'

'No, but he was. Withdrawn, always withdrawn. I thought it was his disposition, his work. I thought scientists were always like that.'

'In my book, Mark always had everything.'

'You think he has me?'

'Sure he has you – right until five minutes ago, he had you and when I take you back, he'll still have you. He's always had everything he wanted. I never had his choice and I don't have it now. Mark has hemmed me in since the day I was born. I'm not even sure I don't want you because you're his.'

'Paul.'

'It's bloody well true, isn't it? And you don't know whether you want me because I'm like him or because you might find what you missed in him in me. It's not good enough – not even for an off-beat type like me. Even the second-best has some pride. You have to understand, Ruth – you of all people – you have to understand even if nobody else ever does and it's true that I've been making a fool of myself hanging around the Shormans. I have always missed what that family has, a sort of aura of belonging that attracts everybody and makes outsiders want to dissect them. I thought I'd get in through Barbi – dear, kind, good-natured Barbi, like George got in through Maddy.'

'And Mark through Eliane?'

'No. For some reason he couldn't get Eliane. He was stopped. So he has waited for his chance and taken what he wanted like he always does.'

'Paul, you're wrong. Can't you imagine? Mark – at our age, yours and mine, on that sea trip suddenly surrounded by what you call the Shormans' aura, Linda and then Eliane, introduced by Arthur, held back by Olwyn.'

'What did you say – introduced by Arthur, held back by Olwyn?'

'You heard last night, Arthur already knew Linda Shorman and they re-met on the ship. And Arthur approved of Mark and Eliane, just as Mrs Shorman did – and Olwyn did not.'

'Dad always approves of Linda Shorman. He told me once no finer woman ever lived.'

'Perhaps for him it's true.'

'What? But that's farcical, it's bloody outrageous. It's suggesting that Dad loves Linda Shorman, that I might have been her son.'

'And failing that, both you and Mark have this – this attraction to get into the family.'

'Don't be mad. It's illogical. Anyway, Eliane is only adopted, so it doesn't hold.'

'I know it's illogical and yet it fits – I think it's true. You heard what Arthur said last night, that if I don't want Mark after this, not to let anything in the world interfere with my freedom, not any-thing. Not even Rollo. I think I know what he means now,' Ruth said softly.

'It's bloody fantastic to think of the old man holding a torch. He's so – oh, well, I don't know – would you think Mother knows then?'

'No, probably not. But I suspect she substituted Mark just the same, subconsciously at first.'

'And Dad never had to tell her because Linda Shorman wouldn't have him.'

'Or he couldn't ask her.'

'Don't give me that. It's not true. If he loved her, he couldn't help himself. She must have loved Shorman.'

'Or the children.'

'Are you telling me Mark was better off for all that concentra-tion, or Maddy, if her mother loved someone else?'

'There was also Eliane, Paul, and she was different.'

'But she would have been with Linda either way.'

'No, not if Doctor Shorman named the other man. Nowadays it is possible to get a divorce after five years separation, but before that you had to prove insanity or desertion or adultery. The mother got the children if adultery was proved against her. If I give Mark a divorce, I will get Rollo and Mark will support us both, but Linda Shorman would not have had her children, except, at best, from time to time, at the dispensation of the Court. Olwyn, as the woman wronged, would have had all the sympathy, support, plus Mark!'

'The big guns were all on Shorman's side.'

'So perhaps he didn't even know.'

'What are you going to do, Ruth?'

'Give Mark a divorce.'

'Proving adultery or making him wait for five years separation?'

'If possible, incompatibility – otherwise Mark and Eliane must choose. I won't force adultery on Eliane.'

'Even though the dirty word is true?'

'She was forced and Mark was forced. You and I could have an affair and ultimately get away with it. But Eliane, because of her heritage, would never live it down, would live with it all her life just like she would have suffered if Linda had left her when she was little.'

'You've never even met her, Ruth.'

'I've lived with her, Paul, day and night for a week.'

He put his hand on her hair and stroked it softly, but he did not kiss her.

'Listen, Ruth, there's something I want you to know. That – that aura we were talking about, you've got it. The Shorman women may have it, sure, but for me you'll always have it most of all. It's love, Ruth, but it's bigger than ordinary; it's a kind of integrity of life, it can't be reached but it can't be hurt either – it's out the other side of sex. Someday you'll make a real home out of it, you'll bring Rollo up in it. Mark will feel it and Eliane and poor old Arthur. I'm sorry you had to marry Mark to bring it out, but I want you to know that in giving Mark to Eliane, you've given him back to me and in some funny sort of way you've given me Arthur too. And I don't care if you cry now, Ruth – go ahead, I'll wait.'

'I'm not going to cry,' Ruth said. 'I... I'm almost happy, like when I was a little girl. I want to go home now. I want to take you and Rollo home and make dinner for you both. Please come, Paul.'

CHAPTER THIRTEEN

On Saturday morning, grey skies presaged a Melbourne winter day, cold without rain or wind but also without clear or clean light. A cloudiness closed in the city, inhibiting the dispersal of smoke and fumes. Swishing traffic threw up loud echoes from the highways to penetrate the inner, tree-protected streets. The dogs were restless.

Mim Shorman woke to find every bone in her body ached in sympathy with emotional turmoil of her mind. She was chilled by the draught of cold air blasting in through the two inches of open window between her bed and the smelly paint at her easel. Unhappiness engulfed her as she stared at the ceiling while her eyes, dark with physical and mental hurt, slowly filled with tears. Old people grew alone like this, she thought; cut themselves off for some almost imagined, idealistic personal hope and then, because of it, grew morose and temperamental.

It was one week tomorrow since she had cut herself loose from her family to paint in self-imposed solitude, accompanied by spasms of often vicious and always guarded home-truth conversation. Her back and her arms ached from the strain of absorbing herself in one determined pursuit after years of physical variety. It was like the terrible tiredness of sitting all those hours in the plane; it hardly seemed possible she had returned only two weeks ago.

Well there was one thing. Now she knew that with tension you could ache after a week even painting, yes, even after you had longed for weeks and months and years for a week just to paint as you wished, without interruption. Not that your love of art or anything else would work for you under this strain of isolation and bitterness, this guilt forced by the resentfulness hanging about a house shouting her neglect. Mim wondered as she lay in her bed how she had held out so long. What had she expected would happen? What adjustments did she still expect might be made? What did she want her family to do for her? See themselves, that was all, see themselves as she, the mother, had seen them at dinner last Sunday. But that was impossible. She knew that now. She could not even see herself as Layton saw her, or Maddy or the twins. No, not even Eliane. So how could they see themselves in any way but their own?

Well, could they see one thing then, just one thing? Could they just see that she was a person; not a slave mother, not a heavy listener that wasn't supposed to answer back, not a manipulator to advance causes she did not believe in, but a person, somebody real, who wanted to get away from them all and paint sometimes? That was what she wanted. That was it. She wanted that not just for herself, but for each of the family to see it for each of the others. They had to understand that they shouldn't use her or anybody else as an extra hand to further their own demands. She wanted Layton and Maddy and Henny and Barbi to give the same right to Eliane.

Suddenly, lying there in her bed, Mim Shorman wanted to scream, wanted desperately to scream and could not. Once before, as a schoolgirl in a boarding school headmistress's office, a kind little Scotswoman had told her about her parents' death in an accident. She had gone rigid then, unable to scream. The soft, burring voice of the headmistress still rang in her ears: 'We'll take her away for a bit, I'll take her away myself, for a little holiday.'

After the tremor and then the memory was over Mim knew she could not last any longer. She would have to give up, and if she gave up she would have to go away, and she knew that going away would answer no question but that a breakdown would be worse.

But as she got out of bed she remembered Barbara coming in last night to tell her about old Sarge's grandson and how much Sims had done and how strange Paul was acting and how she and Sims were worried about him and how Sims had Paul's car because Paul had Ruth's and how she was going to dinner with Sims because Sims... All in one sentence, one voice, all in high flight, all Sims. Mim stood still. Sims. Sims Flavin. So that was it... Maddy and George, Eliane and Mark, Barbara and Sims. The flow of the world towards love had enveloped Barbara.

Which left Paul. Mim closed the window, turned up the heat and sat down on her bed again, thinking of Paul instead of herself and yet identifying with him as it seemed he had done with her last Sunday afternoon. Barbi and Sims would be another desertion for Paul and yet recalling the visit last Wednesday, Mim fancied Paul knew and was unperturbed about Sims with Barbi. The distress in him was for something else scarcely accepted and yet mature. Mim thought of the poetry Paul had shown her and knew it was not for Barbi, not even for love, but a deeper search to the inside of himself.

For the second time Mim's eyes swam with tears, but this time she pulled herself up sharply. You did not offer pity to the young. They found their own answers, in their own way. If you could, you offered practical service like a cake for old Sarge. Thinking in this way, Mim found her own answer and knew what she must do. To-day and tomorrow she would finish the new and the two revived canvasses. Then she would come out of her retreat for the funeral of Sarge's grandson. After that, the next day perhaps, on the Tuesday, she would ask Sims to help her get the canvasses stretched and framed. If he and Barbi invited her to go with them, she could offer to visit old Sarge and then maybe Sims would come back to dinner. She would have to warn Layton.

But Layton was already gone; had pulled out for a nine o'clock start on the golf course; had told her last night he had let them put his name down for a four in the competition. He had been late in after the dinner and seemed surprised to find her still working. He had answered her query – 'Yes, the dinner went well,' – and then almost tentatively named friends and colleagues who had sent wishes for her recovery. She had wondered what from, but had not asked since indignation, and the irony that usually pursued it, seemed to have burned out of Layton and left him perplexed. Nor, in the absence of his habitual clipped speech, had she inquired about Harriet. Layton had allowed himself to show tiredness and had looked awkward standing in the doorway for his final words. 'You'll be right for tomorrow... I take it the girls will be around.'

It was already evident that the girls were around, she could hear one twin in the bathroom and the other in the kitchen. Since Layton's car had gone out, another had come in. In the back playhouse the high trill of little Mimi began to dominate the play of her brothers. Maddy, then, was also in the kitchen. Mim plugged in her electric jug for coffee and began to dress. She was startled when the piano began to sound a decided, determined and distinctive assault on Beethoven's 'Sonata Number One Hundred and Eleven'. She drew in her breath. Maddy had come home to practice. Only Maddy could touch that sonata, only Maddy who Eliane said had given up music for a house.

Four hours later, after lunch, which had been served to her on a tray set up as for a feast by Henrietta, Mim welcomed Maddy to share her coffee.

'That was delicious casserole you brought over and, as Henny remarked, the cheesecake was out of this world. But for all that, dear, your music has made my day.'

Maddy looked a little smug around the mouth as she answered, but Mim noticed her eyes were tired. 'No doubt the music drove the twins out to the park with the kids. All the same, I'm grateful. Henny really was ecstatic about the food... You'd think she hadn't eaten for a week.'

'Maybe she hasn't.'

'Don't you worry, Mim, Henny looks after herself. She's going out with that theatre director type tonight and told me she'd kill me if I breathed a word to Barbi. And poor Barbi going around in some kind of dream.'

'She's fallen in love with Sims Flavin.'

'You're joking... That strange, weird friend of Paul Carlister?'

'He's not so weird as his appearance would have you believe. I like him, almost as much, I think, as Paul.'

Maddy laughed. 'Well, you must admit you are almost alone on that one too.'

The laughter died abruptly on her lips as she realised what she'd said, but a new determination in her made her brazen it out. 'Not,' she added, 'that I meant the remark like you probably think I did. When are you to give all this up, Mim? You look dreadful today, all washed out.'

'On Monday morning, I think,' Mim said. 'I'm not quite sure of the time yet, but I think around ten.'

Maddy was surprised into a premature admission. 'I was coming over to practice again on Monday morning.'

Intently observing her mother's face for the effect of her words, Maddy was shocked to see the lines of weariness and the tears that waited to flood her expressive eyes. Mim really was just about at the end of her tether. Just the same, she smiled out of some secret resource that she had before she answered.

'You know you can come whenever you like, Maddy, the house is yours. Are you going to play somewhere on a grand?'

'No,' Maddy said. 'I'm not. That is, not yet. But I will be.' She rustled her fingers together between herself and where her mother sat and the expression in her eyes exhibited a disgust for stiffness in hands that had once been outstandingly supple. 'I'm going to take up my lessons again, and I think I will teach a few top-grades after school. But I'll practice here, three hours, three days a week on the grand. That's if you don't mind.'

'I don't mind,' Mim said. 'Actually, it will answer my need. I will paint in here three days a week for three hours. The same three hours. Mimi will play.'

'Mimi will be dropped into nursery school. I'm all organised, Mim. I'll drop the boys, then Mimi, then arrive and begin. It will be rather good to think of you painting in here while I work.'

'You are a good organiser, Maddy, much better than I ever was.'

'I have everything in the house that opens and shuts and as dear sister Henrietta pointed out to me last Sunday, I'd go nuts in a thing-o house full of pseudo antiques instead of modern cons.'

'I hope she didn't say that in front of George.'

'I told George. He took it rather hard, but he's bearing up.'

'Even over Parkville?'

'The house was a pig in a poke for a family of five. A second look with the kids in tow convinced George. And, of course, the place wasn't anything like worth the money and when we went over there last Sunday after we left here, Mrs Flair-Jones said they hadn't really decided yet whether they'd take the Georgian unit... He'd told George he'd signed up and poor old George believed him. Last Sunday certainly was a day. George and I were exhausted when we got home. The only lucky thing, as I pointed out to George was that you'd refused to go straight to Arthur Carlister without further consideration. I still can't get over Paul taking such a stand against George and acting like he did in our house. He's odd, I know, and as George says, terribly spoiled, but even so... Well, he is Arthur's son.'

'Maddy,' Mim said sharply. 'Have you thought about Ruth? Have you put yourself in Ruth's place?'

'Why no, Mim. Why on earth should I? She's not a bit like me. I know Auntie Molly thinks she's Christmas, but for all that she really did grab Mark Carlister the minute he got home from Cambridge.'

'Do you think that makes it any easier for her now, or for Paul?'

Frowning, Maddy stood up. Almost immediately, she dismissed the consideration of herself in Ruth's place, her marital experience was with George, who was as unlike Mark Carlister as she was unlike Ruth. But Eliane! Eliane and Mark Carlister, the two this whole hassle was about, they fitted. And if they fitted, it would be all or nothing for them, particularly for Eliane. That left Ruth, who had never belonged there at all.

'So Paul was doing for Ruth what you did for Elie,' Maddy stated. 'I see what you mean, but I can't see what we can do about it.'

'We can stand by for Paul as well as Eliane. That's all we can do.'

'And what about Ruth? It seems to me she's hurt far more than Paul.'

'You know, Maddy,' Mim said, 'I think Paul might bring Ruth to see me. If he does, that will be my chance. I hope he does.' She picked up a large brush, dipped it into the turps and wiped it clean.

'You ought not to sleep in here, Mim.' Maddy sniffed, wrinkling her nose. 'Thank God music is a clean art. I'll leave the door open and switch on the fan.'

Henrietta returned from the shower as a glossy advertisement for a black lace bikini and brassiere to find Barbi still undecided about which dress to wear. There was, however, no sign of the white turtleneck jumper and the black pants. Henny coughed at her sister's reflection in the mirror to gain attention.

'I've never known you to be this fussy before, every time I opened my mouth to speak to you, you'd come in here to mull over your gear. What's up? I never knew Paul to care what you had on.'

Barbi swung around, two bright spots of pink glowing on her cheeks. 'It so happens I'm not going with Paul. I'm going out to dinner with Sims.'

Henrietta shrieked, 'Sims, but you amaze me, you really do. All this sugar for Sims. Whatever for?'

'Because I want to. Actually, Henny, you don't even know Sims – not really, I mean... He's... Well... I don't know what he is, but I have to be right, that's all. I don't want to be overdressed.'

'You never are,' Henny began and then stopped, embarrassed. Barbi had the stupid wide-eyed Christmas angel look, the countenance half heavenly and the other half sexy doll. No wonder she had been so hard to get at all day. Henrietta felt herself cut off and therefore draped herself with lavish abandon across her bed, from which vantage point she proposed to pursue an ironic interrogation. But Barbara, blissfully unaware of any but her own unfamiliar star-tracks of thought, counteracted the attack.

'Paul has lent Sims the M.G. for the whole weekend,' she said.

Henny sat up. 'Oh no, Barbi, not you. You can't do that. It doesn't go with you.'

'But I want to, Henny. I want to go to dinner with Sims more than I ever wanted anything.'

'More than the famous actress bit?' Henny demanded.

'Don't be silly, Henny, what's being an actress got to do with it?'

'It's just that I want to know, that's all, and expect you to have the decency to tell me. I've been trying to get through to your dream castle all day, just tell me. Is this more important than the actress bit? Yes or no?'

'I just told you. Yes, yes, yes. Much more important.'

'I can't believe it,' Henny gasped. 'It can't be true.'

'Why, you know perfectly well when I failed the audition I lost interest in the whole business. That crowd's too tough for me, Henny. I don't know what gave me the idea I was the type in the first place. I guess you did. You must have... Who else?'

'Me? Did you say me? Well that cops it. Me!'

Barbi nodded vaguely and turned again to the mirror to stare intently at the ruffled reflection of her hair. She was amazed when Henrietta swung her round with glee and pushed her backwards to sit on the bed among her dresses, insisting that she listen with at least a measure of concentration if she wanted to be allowed to rise again.

'All day long, my dear sister, I have been trying to tell you that my date tonight is with Mike Parsons. He's divorced and he's a wolf and he's after me and the party's at his place and... I wanted you to know.'

'For Heaven's sake, don't go on my account, Henny.'

'But I'm not. I'm going on mine. I'm going to wear my kaftan and my golden sandals and be the belle of the ball, as Mim calls it, while I look over the field.'

'What about Greg?'

'Tomorrow morning I am going to church with Greg, honour intact, and we will make a decision. I have a feeling it will be a final decision. But that's tomorrow... Tonight I am borrowing Mim's Spanish shawl.'

'You must be mad, Henny,' Barbi gasped. 'It's freezing cold.'

'And, you'll be glad to know, Mim's car. I am also borrowing Mim's car.' She spun around once within the limited scope of a room with two beds and threw her arms wide. 'I want that part, Barb. I want the lead in that play.'

'If you want it, I'm sure you'll get it, Henny,' Barbara said, easily moving back into the orbit of her own sun. 'I've decided to wear this dress. It's sort of blue-green like the sea, don't you think? Can I borrow your woollen cape with the hood?'

When the doorbell rang it was Henrietta who tripped down the hall to answer it. She came back screaming for Barbara, in through the open door of Mim's room.

'From Elie,' she panted. 'From Elie... it's a telegram from Elie.'

Mim froze the brush in her hand, released it again and put it down. At Henrietta's shoulder Barbara's eyes stared at her with undisguised apprehension.

Mim said, 'Read it out, Henrietta.' Her voice was very soft.

'It doesn't say much,' Henny began and then read from the paper in her hand...HOPING TO COME HOME NEXT WEEK STOP APPRECIATE REPLY TO SAME HOTEL LONDON STOP ELIE. That's all. It's addressed to you, Mim.'

Mim Shorman felt her shoulders collapse with a trickle of nervous tension that ran all the way down her arms to the tips of her fingers. At the same time, her throat seized like wrong-lane saliva swallowed to prevent her from speech without a splutter. Luckily, she coughed as her eyes filled with tears. It took her a little time to recover and, side by side, the twins waited, their faces unexpectedly alike with overawed expectation. The resemblance between them was, for all that, superficial and in spite of herself, Mim was amused to notice Barbara like a doll, short-skirted in simple shimmery blue with her curly hair pulled neatly back in a sedate neck bow and Henrietta... Well! Henrietta was a member of a ballet, perhaps, or the princess in the Christmas pantomime, all gold threat embroidery on velvet, even to her slippered feet, her long, straight, golden hair centre-parted for the long exciting fall. Elie would have said both hair-doings done especially as foil for the shine behind the make-up of the eyes. So Elie would have said... So... Elie would have said.

'I think the answer to the telegram is up to you,' Mim told the wide open blue of the twins' eyes. 'You and Dad and Maddy work it out.'

/ CHAPTER FOURTEEN

Ruth settled herself into the deep car seat Thomas had just vacated. The Porsche smelled faintly of the Rhodesian pipe tobacco the old man smoked. Paul stirred uneasily in the driver's seat as he asked where he was to go, and loving Ruth, refrained from adding the question that persisted in his brain – where bloody well could he go from his strange, overpowering passion? He was suspended in time, transformed to the lightness of air and moving in a sphere that would never be reconciled with his ordinary life. Saturated with the presence of Ruth, he was isolated into himself by the pressure of his longing to touch her. For reassurance of her response he felt his body was ousting his brain.

Beside Paul in the Porsche, Ruth sighed as if she was in his arms again. She felt calm with Paul, calm and right, and her answer to his query was practical: 'Let's go somewhere and eat.'

'Eat?' Paul said, surprised. 'Did you leave Rollo with Molly so we could eat together?'

'Only partly – there's something else I want to do, somewhere I want to go later, but first we can eat together, just you and I. There's a place down Burke Road we can go to.'

For a small moment or two he drove softly, purring the car to warmth before he trusted himself to speak again. 'I still can't get over how you came down,' he said out of his wonder that he should be so accepted. 'Sure, like you said, we'd talked of taking old Thomas for a ride in the Porsche on Saturday and this is Saturday. But I drive up and there you were waiting; I pull up and there you are, you and Rollo and we put him in the back seat and you get in. It was as if…' He stopped and she finished for him.

'As if I knew you were there. Why of course I knew you were there. I've known every time you drove by. I think I even knew last week, let alone today.'

'I don't know if I can stand it, Ruth, let alone face it.'

'Well I can. And it's strange for me too. You see, it's never been like this before for me either. Never, not even once.'

'You had Rollo.' She noticed his knuckles clenched white against the wheel and straightened her shoulders defiantly against the support of the seatbelt. There was flat bitterness in her voice.

'I begged for Rollo. That's all I thought the whole thing was for, just that for women and some sort of male urgency.'

'Oh my God, don't say that.'

'It's true and I must say it. Don't you see, Paul, I can't not tell you. Last night I just didn't have words, only some fierce, terrible, speechless joy. I was happy all night, as if I were covered with music. Can you understand that?'

'For me it only lasted until I left you,' he said. 'Then I hit the bloody night air. There's something in the Bible about it, isn't there?'

'You're not to think of things like that. It was real and it was beautiful and bigger than both of us. It started in the kindness of your heart and that was wonderful too and I just won't think anything else and you mustn't either. Please, Paul. Somehow without realising it I made a rotten mistake and because of it, I'm going to give Mark a divorce and then I'm going away and while I'm away you're not going to be tied. Neither of us are.'

'I hurt, Ruth,' he said. 'I'm all buggered up. I'm all bloody inside.'

She put her hand on his hand. 'Lots of people are,' she told him quietly. 'Not just you and me, lots of people, only I didn't know how it was before. Maybe if we know we'll come out of it some time. Maybe we can, there's always the chance.'

He agreed miserably. 'Yes, I suppose there's always the chance. Anyway, we've got to play it that way. There's nothing else we can do, not a bloody thing. I wish I was smart, Ruth. I wish I could promise a brilliant degree like Sims is bound to get so I could offer it to you for sure in a couple of years. But it wouldn't be any use. I'll probably end up on the road.'

'Promises are stupid, Paul, and useless. I don't care what you do. That's why you have to be free... You of all people know you can't control love, your own or anybody else's. You just have to accept it where it is real. I guess that's what Mim Shorman thought about Mark and Eliane and why I want to go and see her tonight after we have had dinner.'

'No,' Paul said.

'Yes, Paul, I want to tell her Mark can have the divorce. Then I can tell Arthur. From what you've told me, things have been hard for Mim Shorman.'

'Yeah, I reckon so,' Paul admitted. But somehow his agreement offered him no comfort; if Mim Shorman was hurt inside like he was then what the hell could he do to ease her situation? Suddenly he thought of Sims and the face of his friend loomed up at him as if reflected in the wet pavement; Sims looking at Barbi without any defences up. Sims loving Barbi. And in between, himself, big bloody fool Paul, hanging around to break into the Shorman ménage. Well, it might not help Mim Shorman much but he could do something about Sims anyway, he could do something about Sims. He turned suddenly and smiled at Ruth.

'Okay, Ruthie,' he said. 'If that's what you want. After we've had our dinner I'll take you to see Mim Shorman and then come back for you later.'

'But Paul, what'll you do?'

'I'll go and see Sims. You know, like I told you, Sims never had a family and he never seems to expect anything for himself. There's a couple of things I gotta get straight with him.'

Paul parked the car with precision under the Shormans' enormous plane tree on the nature strip, and Ruth winced because she knew he was parking from habit, having forgotten his intention to move away again immediately. Then the deep passion of his kiss mingled with the tenderness of his hand on her hair and for that instant, with her body straining against his, Ruth forgot she had come to see Mim Shorman. As she drew away from Paul she felt almost ashamed. But Paul said, 'I adore you, Ruth. You must never forget that, not for a minute.' He walked with her as far as the Shorman steps, but when the doorbell was answered went back to the car.

Ruth had never before been in the room Mim Shorman led her to. She knew it as Aunt Molly's recent abode, where the door had always been kept shut to reinforce the privacy Molly felt she needed. Other doors in the house had been casually, easily, left open. They were still open that evening but somehow nothing was the same. Ruth, through shadowed glimpses by means of the hall light, sensed a disorder she could not see.

'Come in,' Mim said. 'I'm painting. I am very fond of this room. I took it over when Maddy was married. I offered it to Eliane but she preferred to keep her own little corner next to the twins. Layton thought perhaps the twins would spread out, not realising how it is with twins.'

'So you got it,' Ruth finished as she walked in, following on for something to say because she could not help wondering what was so wonderful about the room, which displayed muddled clutter beyond sense or quietude, being papered and carpeted like Maddy Amber, yet with a slept-in bed under a modern striped spread while smelling of oil paint and turpentine and something else less definable, perhaps coffee, perhaps even sweat.

Mim switched on another light and removed a roll of unstretched canvas from the armchair.

'Sit down, Ruth,' she said, 'and excuse the muddle.'

Ruth's response was quick, driven by an inner urgency, emotional rather than rational.

'It's such a contrast to the rest of your house. That's why you like it, I suppose. Molly slept here, didn't she?'

'Yes, she did. But you didn't come to see me about Molly, did you, Ruth? Paul brought you?'

'Yes, he'll be back to take me home in an hour or so.'

'He didn't come in.'

'No. He's gone to see Sims.'

'Will he come in then later?'

'Oh yes, I think so.'

'I'm glad. I've been expecting him, I think. He's been on my mind all day.' Mim paused.

A shiver ran through Ruth and she felt unreal, as if she was no longer responsible for herself, while strangely Mim Shorman seemed to float in some alternative place between reality and illusion. She watched Mim seat herself before an easel and bend her head over her hand; watched her raise the hand and place two fingers across her lips in deep thought and then pick up a tube of paint. Ruth's eyes fell on a purple child's face painted on board leaning against the wall near the easel. The eyes of the child moved out at her and she felt bruised as her voice spoke out, high and excited, even shrill.

'I did something I'm sorry for. I pestered Auntie Molly about her divorce. She'd never really told anybody the details, not even Uncle Thomas.'

'Oh, I suspect Thomas has a good idea anyway. Molly is fond of you, Ruth – she loves you more than you know. She won't mind you knowing or she wouldn't have told you.'

'But I shouldn't have asked. I suppose you know?'

'Enough – what I pieced together. You see, I had a reason to help her once. When Les died, she came to me and I know the circumstances of his death. Will you sit down now, Ruth, and let me talk to you?'

'But I—'

'You have come to me, Ruth. There is something I'll tell you, the other side, my side.'

'Because of Molly?'

'Yes, in a way it's only fair to you because of Molly. There's one side and there is the other. Because of Molly I owe you the other.'

'I don't understand.'

'The woman who did not get a divorce.'

'You?'

'You are surprised. Why, because it is me?'

'Yes.'

'Well, I'll tell you as quickly as I can. When I was not long married and had my first baby, I fell in love with another man. It was very simple. I went to a reception and met a man and fell in love. If anyone had told me such a thing could happen to me, I wouldn't have believed it. He was also married, with a little boy, and it was the same with him. Luckily he was only on a business trip of one week to Honolulu where we were living at the time.

'He had three days left. So I met him one night, saw him the next night at another party, and the third afternoon and evening before he went away we spent together. We had dinner and rode around in a taxi in a kind of desperate bliss. Nothing else, because we knew if there was anything else we could never give each other up. I let myself into my home after midnight. My husband was asleep in bed and had been drinking heavily, which was most unusual for him. I woke him up – I had to, I don't know why. He was a bit sarcastic and asked me where I had been. I told him and he said he believed me, because I had never abused his trust. In the morning the incident was dismissed and he never mentioned it again. Life went on as usual. I kept myself too busy to think with a round of social engagements. I had an excellent Nanny with Polynesian parents, called Mera. Maddy, who was about eighteen months old at the time, adored her. In the mornings the three of us went to the Club to swim. I felt guilty at first, I have to admit this, that I found it so hard to forget a man I had only known for three days, but after a while because I felt I had done the right thing, I put the whole affair right out of my mind.' Mim paused, then looked at Ruth for a minute before she went on. 'You know, somehow it is easier to think you have done the right thing when you are young. Besides, not long after that, Mera went back to her village because her mother was sick and I just looked after little Maddy myself. I really liked that better than anything else anyway.'

Remembering, Mim paused so long that Ruth started to speak. 'Mrs Shorman... Please...' Mim ignored her interception and went on.

'At that time, we had a lot of moves to consider because Layton was beginning to feel he'd had enough of lectureships abroad. He'd been in England and America, and of course Hawaii, and felt that for his own advancement he had better get home. When he was offered an appointment here at Melbourne University I could see that he wanted to accept it, although he discussed the terms point by point. When finally the decision was made, both of us would have preferred to leave immediately, but of course, Layton had to finish his term and we had to pack up. When we were ready to go in advance of our booking Layton suggested that as I loved the islands I might like to spend a week or so with a friend on Kanai, which I was thrilled to do... But the day before I was to go, a note came for me asking me to come to a private hospital to visit one of my servants who was ill and asking for me. I was spending the afternoon with an American friend, so I asked her to come with me to the hospital. She agreed, and then asked if the servant was Mera. I hoped not because I loved Mera, but Coral said she'd be having a baby for sure. "They all do this to you. They ask you to adopt the baby and then you give them money."

'So I took some money in case and we went. It was a surprisingly nice private hospital, staffed by Anglo-Indians, and as soon as I announced myself, the receptionist took me into a doctor's office where the Indian doctor explained to me immediately how sorry he was to have to tell me that after all our kindness, the poor girl was dying. I stared at him and he patted my hand and said he could see I was shocked and would I like to sit for a moment before I went in. It was only that she was so insistent that she see me. He couldn't refuse her and had to ask me to come. I said of course I would like to see her right away.

'I will never forget that hospital room, a small private room at the end of a corridor. It was all white with one of those iron beds taking up almost all the space. I think it was the loneliest room I had ever been in before or since. A nurse stood beside the bed and the deep rich colour of her skin made the arm of the patient on the white counterpane look like alabaster. The nurse went out almost immediately and so did the doctor. For a moment I almost ran after them, but instead stood swaying at the end of the iron bed. I don't think that at first I even heard poor Mera trying to speak. When I realised, I moved up to the bedside table and looked down into her face. As I said, her skin was like alabaster – so fine and pale you could see the bone structure. There seemed to be no life except in her eyes, which were brimming with tears.

'"Sorry, so sorry," she was whispering. "Had to tell you – so sorry."

'I didn't know what to do, so I tried to take her hand but it slithered away from mine like a piece of silk. I simply couldn't speak because my breath was all choked in my throat and my ears seemed to be ringing as if somehow I was really somewhere else. So I put my hand on her forehead and watched as her lids fell over her eyes. Then in panic, I rang the bell. I don't know how long I just stood there until the nurse came to smile at me with bright efficiency. I don't remember getting out the door and starting down the corridor. The doctor's voice waylaid me.

'"How long?" I demanded of him. His answer was one of those expressive movements of an Indian's hands.

'"She has spoken to you?" he asked. I nodded. "Good. Come now to see the baby – is so beautiful. Missus Shorman – you will see." He took my arm and I went with him lightly, like a woman in a dream. I have an idea he talked all the way to the nursery, but I am not sure. Nothing was real; not even the baby was real. She was a doll, a perfection of porcelain.

"'You will like to hold her – yes?" the doctor said.

"'No," I breathed at him. "No, I will come back tomorrow."

"'Good," he said. "That is better." I think I left him standing there. In the waiting room my friend Coral rose from a chair to meet me. To give myself time, I turned to the reception desk. "I'll come back tomorrow," I said to the girl.

"'You may as well take this, Mrs Shorman," she said, and handed me a letter that I put in my handbag as she added, "We were going to send it."

'Coral said, "Geez, Linda, you look awful," and I answered, "I feel it. She's dying."

"'Let's get some coffee," Coral said. "There's a place we passed not far back – didn't they warn you?"

"'No, just took me straight in."

"'Ye Gods," Coral gasped, and although she later insisted on two aspirins with the coffee, she didn't mention the hospital again until we were in the car. She just talked about similar experiences she'd had with Indians and Japanese. She'd been too long in Hawaii. When we were in the car again she asked me, "And there was a baby?"

"'Yes, the most beautiful baby I've ever seen."

"'What! Now you be careful, Linda, and don't be a sucker. What'd they ask ya for?"

"'Nothing."

"'Then I wouldn't go back if I were you."

"'I promised to go back tomorrow."

"'Boy, I wouldn't go for a million bucks."

"'But the girl is dying, Coral, the doctor said so."

"'Makes it tough," I remember Coral replied. "Just the same, I wouldn't go – send them a cheque or something."

'But I went back to the hospital, Ruth. I went back because when I got home and took the letter out and looked at it, I found it was addressed to my husband, care of the university instead of home, and an account rendered bill for all Mera's expenses.'

Mim began to mix paint again, with her head turned away and didn't speak again until Ruth cried out, 'The baby was Eliane! You took that baby. How could you?'

'It was my fault.'

'Your fault – you're joking!'

'No, I told you I fell in love, didn't I? I told you about that one night. Well, it seemed Layton knew. He came home and started drinking. Then he went upstairs to Mera's room.'

'How could you be sure it was that night?'

'I took his word for it.'

'And came home and based your life on it?'

'Yes.'

'I don't see how you could.'

'I loved him, I had Maddy and I couldn't desert Eliane.'

'But how could you ever trust him again?'

'I had to learn to trust, Ruth. That's why I had the twins.'

'Does Eliane know?'

'Yes.'

'Does anybody else know?'

'I haven't told anybody else.'

'Why did you tell Eliane?'

'Because her father insisted she should know, because if I hadn't told her, he was going to.'

'Why?'

'To stop her marrying Mark. She was so clever and so beautiful and only eighteen and he didn't want her to get married.'

Ruth stared at Mim's painting. Incredibly, like the parts of a diver's suit, the whole fell into place and became a neat pattern of undeniable answer. A shiver ran through Ruth and she bit her lip, as if she could stop an inevitable sentence that had to be spoken.

'You mean, don't you, that Mark was Arthur's son; that your husband blames everything on you and Arthur for falling in love? It was Arthur, wasn't it?'

Mim Shorman smiled at the canvass and dabbled at it with a thin brush, putting her head a little to one side like a bird.

They all did that, Ruth thought, but it wasn't a Shorman thing. Molly didn't do it, and she herself didn't. It was to do with waiting. Mim wouldn't answer her – she'd said all she was going to say. She had finished. They had come to Arthur and she had finished speaking and she wasn't going to ask Ruth to keep her secrets like Molly did. She wasn't going to say she was trusting Ruth. She'd just handed her Arthur and Eliane and herself and Doctor Shorman as new people and that's all Ruth would get.

But Mim said softly, 'I didn't want you to think divorce is the most important thing.' Startled, Ruth jumped to her feet. She had forgotten altogether her own problem. She was thinking of Arthur and young Linda Shorman and a younger Mark and Eliane and somewhere, at the back of her mind, herself and Paul.

'It's all stinking,' she cried angrily. 'Absolutely stinking – the whole thing. And it's incredible that you should have gone along with it, all these years. What good has it done you?'

'I ask myself that question, Ruth.'

'Yet you just sit there and paint.'

'I have to do something,' Mim said. 'For years I have been trying to put the paint on in the right places, but the canvas sucks all the paint in like blotting paper—'

She was talking about love, Ruth thought, but she wouldn't say so. She'd never say so. And how was Ruth to know whether love was the paint or the canvas? Well, she wouldn't ask her, she had asked enough. She'd asked enough of everybody. A terrible weariness crept over her, releasing her from anger and unclenching the two fists her hands had become. She stood beside Mim Shorman, drained to the stillness of the staring point. Then, without further speech, she sat down, accepting.

Paul had still not come when they finished the coffee Mim made from the electric jug. Neither of them were hungry enough to taste the biscuits that Maddy had put into the container on the tray. Finally, Ruth said, 'I just can't understand it, something must have happened to Paul. He said an hour and surely if Sims was out he wouldn't stay longer with the old man, unless something's gone wrong.' The crescendo tone from normal to tense in Ruth's quiet voice alarmed Mim.

'He hasn't much of a sense of time, Ruth,' Mim said. 'None of them have.'

Ruth bridled immediately. 'It's not that. Something must have happened.' She was suddenly decided and sure, and Mim noted with surprise that the quality suited her.

'If you don't mind, I would like to phone Arthur.' Standing, Ruth was much taller than Mim and her stance slumped just a little when she mentioned Arthur, so she added, out of the new fairness she felt she somehow owed. 'You see, Paul and I decided that after I told you about giving Mark the divorce we would go together and tell Arthur.'

Arthur came straight over and Mim, on the pretext of getting more coffee, sent Ruth to open the door for him. She heard their voices murmuring in the hallway and as the moments passed realised that Ruth had taken her chance to talk to Arthur and also, Mim fancied, express to him her fears about Paul. Because when the two of them entered her room, Arthur remained standing and she saw how strained he was; a tall, thin, middle-aged rich man uncertain of his next move. She was relieved when Ruth made it for him by continuing a conversation already begun.

'I've been telling Arthur I think I'd like a grand tour around Australia, the North and the West and Queensland. Drive, maybe... I like driving. We have such a lot of land without borders or passports, no strange currency, or language or regulation difficulties.' Addressing Mim, Ruth was protecting Arthur. She was also taking his interest for granted as a daughter would and Mim sensed he was strangely soothed out of his sense of loss.

'You have a very nice daughter, Arthur,' Mim said as she put a cup of coffee in his hand. 'I put your sugar in, but you can have whisky if you prefer.' His hand rested for a brief moment on Mim's hand and Ruth noticed the searching look of Arthur's eyes on Mim's face.'

'Just the coffee, thanks,' he said. 'You look to me as if you need your sleep. Ruthie and I will push on, she seems to think we should look in at Sims's digs on the way to pick up Paul. He's got Ruth's car.'

'Is Olwyn well?'

'Only just. She wants to go up to Queensland to Surfer's next week for a rest... You know how it is, the winter and...everything.'

They were skirting around the main issue, Mark and Eliane and the divorce. Arthur turned to Ruth, 'Do you remember how peeved Olwyn was when I refused to buy that house at Coolangatta? Well it's up for sale again. We can think about it, Ruth, maybe you and Rolly could come up for a bit and help us decide.'

'But you wanted that farm,' Ruth said. 'For Rolly, you suggested, and Paul.'

'There's no reason why we shouldn't look there too,' Arthur agreed. They were negotiating a father and daughter relationship that would outlive the divorce. Both of them knew it and Mim also knew. The unspoken pact between them would also institute an escape system and might even invent the mechanism to make it work. And somehow Paul was with them in the room, although he had not come back so that Mim was able to bring him easily into the conversation.

'Before you go, Arthur, there's something I'd like to tell you about Paul, just a little thing but I think you might like to know. I owe a strange debt to Paul and perhaps so do the rest of my family. The day they all found out about Mark and Eliane, Paul felt responsible and told my family to just watch out in case all the love I'd been pouring into their affairs was not transferred into my painting. He was very nearly right, Arthur, except that I wasn't there and one after the other starting with Layton, every member of my family told me what he said. Paul knows that art is human love returned and re-expressed. That's why he writes poetry.'

'Paul,' Arthur said, deeply moved. 'Paul writes poetry?'

'Last week, because he couldn't really understand my painting, he showed me some. It was very good. Sims, I believe, collects what he throws away.'

The pang of her own unexpected jealousy surprised Ruth, who said tersely, 'Does Barbi write poetry too?'

'Yes,' Mim said. 'And I think Sims is collecting hers too. It seems to me he will.'

From somewhere within himself, Arthur grunted aloud, 'They always act like such scruffy ruffians in public, those two. It's a disguise, I guess.'

'There are lots of disguises, and you know, Arthur, I've discovered that inside I'm the same kind of elephant as those two. So are you, even if you don't know it yet.'

'Don't leave me out altogether,' Ruth said. 'But don't put me in altogether either.' She was pleased to feel Arthur's arm on her own again.

'That qualification puts you in as far as you ever need to go with me, Ruth,' he said softly. She knew his eyes were again on Mim Shorman's face.

Going to the door, all three found they laughed gently with each other.

CHAPTER FIFTEEN

Early on Sunday morning, the roar of a car woke Layton, and, he suspected, the whole neighbourhood. He had scarcely dozed off again before another car disturbed him. Now thoroughly awake before his normal hour, he rose to hear what he took to be family shufflings around the house. Doors clicked. Feet ran past his door down the passage. As he knotted his dressing gown, it occurred to him that Henrietta was going to church again with that beautiful Greg; to early Mass, no doubt, as she presently appeared to be investigating this aspect of religious practice. Layton did not take a serious view of student participation in any form of mysticism, considering the manifestation a passing phase, but he found Henrietta invariably amusing in her comments. Since he was awake, he decided to go to the kitchen in the hope of sharing a cup of coffee.

Henrietta was not in the kitchen. Instead, Layton was startled to find a crumpled heap of young man half hunched, half sprawled over his kitchen table. One of the youth's hands seemed detached from the sleeve of his clothing and moved strangely like a naked automation with the fingers spreading and clenching. In spite of surprise, Layton noticed it was a good hand, long and thin from a large, tight-skinned wrist. Squared shoulders apparently as bony as the wrist supported a head of hair as beautiful as any girl might claim. Although Layton cleared his throat, he elicited no response from the detachment of this youth.

Anger engulfed Layton. Who and what in heaven's name would his daughters bring home next? The boy must have heard his approach; was he to excuse himself walking into every room in his own house? God, what a week. Ever since knocking at Mim's door after that damn lunch last Sunday. Yes, and he'd stood that same day in his own lounge room doorway, second in command to that young Paul Carlister holding forth. Paul, well that was it then. This head at his table belonged to Paul's friend, the one they all talked about... Sims, Sims Flavin. Suddenly, he remembered the hand of all things; the boy had come to dinner while Mim was away and afterwards he'd looked him up at the shop... Sims Flavin, one of the best brains of the current lot... One of the top line-up for awards. This bundle of bad manners!

'You're Sims Flavin, aren't you?' Layton demanded with loud authority. The hand stilled to move back into the sleeve and slowly the bowed head rose and turned. Two deep-set, glazed eyes held Layton's. The blue-white face twitched at the nostrils. He was sick, Layton surmised. Or maybe doped or boozed. He repeated his question, 'Are you Sims Flavin?'

'Yes.' No apology, no attempt to rise, a silence and then, 'I'm waiting for... Barbara... She... is telling her mother.'

Fear hit Layton in the pit of his stomach. 'Barbara?' he demanded sharply. 'Tell her mother what? Or, as her father, am I not to be informed?'

'She only said she wanted to see her mother.'

Layton moved to stand over Sims where he sat and the measure of his controlled fury registered in his voice. 'And what, may I ask, are you waiting for, or do I expect too much?'

Not a muscle responded in Sims. His answer, when it came, was flat. 'I'm waiting for Barbara, even if it's a long time, she'll come back.'

The anger flowed out of Layton. The boy was sick. 'Must you wait in our kitchen?' he asked reasonably. 'Wouldn't you be better lying down somewhere?'

The form in the duffle-coat shifted, pushed the chair back and rose up to fill the space between table and sink. Both Sims' hands, white at the knuckles, gripped the chair as Sims spoke to Layton standing equal. 'I'm big with words, Doctor Shorman. Usually words are my defence. But not now. Now I'm waiting for Barbara. She said to wait here and I am. As soon as she can we are going back to the hospital. I came to get Barbara. Mister Carlister and Ruth are waiting there. I've got Paul's M.G. – he lent it to me for the weekend. I told Paul's father I had it and why, and he said keep it, Sims, keep it forever, Sims. That's what he said. Paul didn't know his father loved him like that.'

In amazement, Layton watched the tall figure slump again into the chair. He couldn't drive, Layton thought, he couldn't drive anywhere... He was in a state of shock. What in God's name was happening around here? Why didn't anybody tell him anything? He put his hand on Sims' shoulder. 'Sims,' he said as gently as he could. 'Sims, could you tell me what's happened? Was there an accident?'

Sims made no reply, so Layton knew he would have to go and find Mim and Barbara. But at the kitchen door he changed his mind and came back. 'I'd better make coffee,' he muttered to himself. 'And give this boy some. I'd better make everybody some. I guess Henrietta has already gone to the church with that boy of hers. That would be the first car out front. So that leaves three of us and... Sims.'

He had four mugs and the milk bottle out on the sink and had just turned off the electric jug when Mim and Barbi came into the kitchen.

Mim said, as if it was an hour and not a week since she had been seen in her kitchen, 'Oh, thank you, Layton, you have made the coffee.' She was walking light as she always did in a crisis when it seemed as if her will was detached from her body.

Barbara, dressed in jeans and a white polo neck jumper, walked straight over to bend her head above Sims. 'Sims, dear,' she said softly so that Layton winced as he turned to answer Mim.

'Well somebody has to make him coffee. He is certainly in no condition to drive, that's certain.'

'I've offered,' Mim said and took over the coffee, to which response Layton lowered his voice to mutter, 'I'm glad something has dragged you out of that room anyway,' before demanding in his normal voice, 'What the hell has happened, anyway? What's happened?'

Barbara heard him and turned immediately. Layton saw that although she may have been crying she was quite calm. 'Don't you know about Paul, Daddy?' she asked. 'Hasn't Sims told you?'

'No, he hasn't. I gather he's in a state of shock.'

'Not quite, sir,' Sims said, standing up. 'I expect, sitting here waiting for Barbara, it only just hit me... If he dies, I mean. I had things to do up until now.'

Exasperated, Layton turned again to Mim. 'Can you tell me, dear, in as few words as possible, what has happened?'

'There has been an accident,' Mim replied quietly. 'Paul Carlister was found gassed last night.'

'Gassed. Good God,' Layton exploded. 'Why would he do that?'

Sims' voice cut in, cold as a knife. 'Mrs Shorman said an accident, Doctor Shorman.'

'But gas?' Layton repeated. He saw Barbara take Sims' hand and then reply for him.

'Paul tried to pull old Sarge out of the house, Daddy, and got gassed himself. He should have got help before he even went in, but he never did know one smell from another. He just barged in and must have tried to turn the gas off in the kitchen thinking old Sarge was asleep in the bedroom at the front. But Sarge was sitting in his armchair and Paul tried to pull him out before opening up... That's what the neighbour thinks, because Sarge was fully dressed and had been dead some time...'

Sims put his big hand over his mouth like a gesture to stop vomit. He seemed to gag before he spoke. 'Can't we go, Barbi? I said I'd bring you back.'

Mim put black coffee beside Sims on the table and stirred sugar in. 'Drink this first, Sims,' she said. 'And eat as many biscuits as you can stuff in – you needn't taste them. You too, Barbara.'

'I'm no eater, Mrs Shorman,' Sims protested.

Barbi said, 'Please, Sims,' and he sat obediently and began to sip the coffee. Barbi sat opposite him with a mug in her hand. Mim opened the biscuit tin between them and the big hand dipped in. Sims' eyes rested on Barbi's face.

'I should have called in like you suggested... I should have suspected what he was up to, going to bed before six so I could get out easy. And I didn't think Paul would come... You know that, Barbi... I thought because of Ruth...'

She answered him before he could continue. 'And you were right, Sims. I'm sure of that. You see, Paul did have dinner with Ruth and then he brought her here because she wanted to talk to Mim. Paul didn't come in with her, but he was coming back to get her. He was filling in time and that's how he found Sarge..'

Layton grew belligerent. 'There are various things I don't understand.'

Mim put her hand on his arm. Simultaneously, Barbi and Sims stopped speaking to stare vaguely at him and Mim said, I'll explain to your father later, Barbi. He doesn't know about Sarge and Jimmy. Sims, I've told Barbara I'll drive you to the hospital if you want me to... not, if you prefer to drive.'

With a sudden strange gesture, Sims took Mim's hands in both his own. Layton felt outside this odd movement of hands like a spectator watching the Indian rope trick. 'I can drive,' Sims said simply. 'I know the M.G. But I'd like you to come. Ruth and Paul's father said they would like you to come.'

'No,' Mim said. 'You two go... I'll be waiting... Please tell them, Arthur and Ruth, I mean, that I'll be waiting. Phone just as soon as you can.'

Layton tried to speak again, but she bustled them down the hall and out the door. He heard the roar of the M.G. as it sped down the street. Mim came back to the kitchen and he admonished her.

'You shouldn't have let that boy take Barbi – he isn't fit. One of these days you'll hold hands with and trust young people too far.' He put her coffee mug into her hand. 'Now, will you please sit down and tell me what I want to know?'

Mim settled into the chair vacated by Sims. 'Sims rents a room from the old man called Sarge in his house in Richmond. Sarge is an old pensioner living in a little house he bought for his only daughter when she and her little son were deserted years ago. Since his daughter died, Sarge brought up the boy himself, and, I gather, very much to the tune of the glory of the A.I.F. Anyway, Jimmy got the call-up and in spite of Sims and Paul, volunteered for Vietnam. Then he volunteered to finish time as a regular and signed up as a mechanic. He was a nice boy and he was close to his grandfather and the old man just about lived on his letters.'

Mim paused and sighed as she shifted in her seat. 'Anyway, Layton, sometime last Thursday, two officers – a social worker and a padre – called on old Sarge and told him Jimmy had been killed the day before in an army lorry. The old man took the news as he considered an old soldier should, promised to get in touch with the officers to make funeral and other arrangements as soon as he had consulted with Sims, and showed them determinedly off the premises. Then he collapsed in his chair and there Sims and Barbi found him.'

'Barbi,' Layton burst out. 'Why Barbi? Isn't Barbi running around with Paul? That's what I understood.'

'For some time now the three have been running together, Layton. You saw how it is with Sims, didn't you, here in this kitchen this morning?'

'So that's why young Paul...'

'No, Layton. Paul had already lent Sims his car to take Barbi out to dinner last night. And all day Friday the three of them had tried to look after old Sarge, never left him alone. Sims made all the funeral arrangements with the army on behalf of the old man.'

'Well,' Layton admitted. 'From what I can gather, Paul is very decent about lending his car. But it doesn't explain anything.'

'Paul has been using Ruth's Porsche all week, Layton. He's been trying to look after Ruth since she heard from Mark. He was with her all day yesterday.'

'What the hell are Arthur and Olwyn thinking about to let such a thing happen?'

'They probably had no idea, any more than you had, Layton.'

'And when did you find out?'

'Last night, some time after nine Paul brought Ruth to see me, but he himself went off to Sims' place, according to Ruth. He was to come back for Ruth in about an hour, as he had Ruth's car. He didn't come back, nor did Barbara and Sims in his car, or Henrietta, who was out with mine. You didn't come home, either. A bit after eleven, Ruth began to get nervous about Paul and phoned Arthur.'

'So Arthur was here as well.'

'He is very fond of Ruth, Layton, and she of him. He came right over to get her.'

'I suppose her little boy was in Olwyn's care anyway.'

'I gather Olwyn has cracked up a bit, which is not surprising. Anyway, Molly had Ruth's little boy last night.'

'Molly! Who else, with the exception of myself, has been in on this?'

'You were at the golf club all day, Layton, as well as having dinner.'

'A man has to have some relaxation from this madhouse, don't you think?'

'Yes, I agree that is true from your point of view. I am only explaining as you asked me to. Little Rollo was at Molly's house because Ruth and Paul went out to Heidelberg to give Thomas a ride in the Porsche, which it seems he fancied. Rollo went to sleep and Ruth decided to let him stay until today. You know, Layton, I think maybe Molly wanted Ruth to come and see me. I think perhaps that's why Paul brought her over.'

'Considering Eliane, what could you possibly say to her?'

'I told her the truth as best I could.'

Layton looked intently down his nose, avoiding Mim's eyes. His manner held unexpected dejection, like that of a man who contemplates no relief from sadness, yet persistently demands it.

'You don't feel you could tell me about Eliane as well as all this other?' he asked, almost humbly. 'It's what I really want to know.'

Mim sighed. 'I'll try, Layton,' she said wearily. 'It's a sad little story, and not very long considering all the years between. Eliane and Mark were like two people possessed when they met again. They shone; they spoke each other's thoughts instantaneously. To be near them was to enter an enchanted, appalling place. They were two halves of one divided and taut to the weakening point. They sensed each other with that hyper-reality that only lovers possess. Everything was beyond coincidence.We went to post a letter; there was Mark. Out of all the shops in London, we walked past the one he happened to walk out of. Eliane was distraught and kept asking me odd little questions apropos of nothing, unlike her, without any visible sign of interest in my reply. Then after two days she had dinner with him alone, just a high tea sort of meal before he left for Paris by the nine p.m. plane. She asked me to come, but I just couldn't; there are some things you just can't do. I went to our hotel room and I didn't even go out to eat because I was afraid she might not, or would come back... Well, she came back, smiled at me like a little lost child, went into the bathroom for a shower, got into bed and lay there... She just lay there, not even crying. At last, I couldn't stand it any longer and I told her I was sorry I'd even come to London. Eliane said no, that I mustn't think like that, that nobody could help the situation which was inevitable. Then after a long silence, she asked me the question that sat on her heart. She asked me, Layton, whether if I had my life to live again, I would make the same choice that I made before. There was only one answer that would help her so I gave it... She woke me very early in the morning, about six, I think it was. I hardly seemed to have slept at all. She was fully dressed, with her handbag on her arm. Her face as she leaned over me was extraordinarily beautiful. I remember the exact words she said. She had wakened and known that Mark had not gone, but was waiting. She looked out the window into the street and saw him across the road looking up. She asked me if I could understand.

'I was speechless, Layton. Eliane questioned me with that sweet urgency she has: Could I manage, would I be able to get myself out to the airport the next day? Would I be able to arrange to give her the time she needed until she could write?... I promised and she kissed me and went out the door. I truly thought the love of this family would allow me to give her the time she asked for. There is nothing else to tell.'

Layton sat very still, staring at the table. At last, he raised his head, wiped his hand across his eyes and, casting a glance in front of him, saw that Mim had risen from her chair as she finished speaking. He watched her go to the stove and set the oven, then to the refrigerator to take out a sirloin roast. For a moment, he seemed to peer at her as if she were difficult to see. His voice faltered uncertainly and came out in a whisper that he did not intend. All he asked Mim was what she intended to do.

'I'm putting on the roast, dear, just in case, so there will be food if it is needed. I'll get out the vegetables – potatoes and carrots will do.'

'There's nothing else to tell me then?'

'No, except that a telegram came last night from Eliane. It is for the family to answer jointly, it is not really for me at all. She just wants to come home; I know she would rather settle her affairs from home, if she is welcome. I've given the telegram to the twins and you'll all be together at lunchtime or sometime today, I suppose. It doesn't seem so important now, except that I'm glad Eliane has had this bit of happiness.'

Layton sat quietly on his chair, inexplicably grateful to Mim, and in spite of himself, sorry for seeing her suddenly as a kind of human shuttlecock batted about from court to court. He watched her move deftly about the kitchen, amazed that she should manage to remember to remove a tart from the deep-freeze. Her skin had a grey look in the early morning light and her eyes showed violet circles. She felt things too deeply, and so did Eliane and Barbara – society dumped itself on their kind. Funny that Eliane should strike out for herself. Mim never had. Except this last week, of course, and the week had taken its toll, there was no doubt of that – you just had to look at Mim.

'Have another coffee and wind yourself down, Mim,' Layton said in his accustomed voice.

She put vegetables on the sink and, leaning her back to it, turned to look at him with misted eyes. 'I don't seem to have had much sleep,' she said. 'I went to bed after Arthur and Ruth left... Then I heard Henrietta come in... Then you came and after you the M.G. pulled up – but it seemed like a long time before Barbara came inside and the M.G. left. Then in no time at all the M.G. roared back again. I must have come out of a deep sleep, or a terrible dream to feel this tired, Layton.'

'Comes of sleeping in that room full of paint instead of your bedroom where you belong,' he grumbled.

'I always hear the cars come in, Layton, one after the other when the girls are out. There's one pulled up now. It will be Henny. I'll go and have a quick shower in case the phone rings soon. If Henny has Greg with her, talk to him, will you, and send her in to see me for a few minutes.'

'He's not easy to talk to,' Layton muttered, but she was gone, closing the door behind her. He recognised Henrietta's fast, light footsteps on the side path. Alone and demanding her mother, Henrietta bounded into the kitchen to be arrested by her father's rather startling command, 'Sit down, your mother is having a shower.'

For all the power of unexpected paternal demand, Henrietta decided to demonstrate her disquietude by remaining on her feet.

'Something's going on around here that I don't know. While we were on the way to get Greg's mother, Paul Carlister's M.G. passed us with Sims Flavin driving it like the devil. Barbi had a date with Sims last night and when she got home she wouldn't talk. I tell you, Pops, something's wrong with Barbi when she won't talk to me, let alone when she doesn't give a bugger about acting any more. Something's got to give around here and if I can't see Mim I'll take on sweet sister Barbi.' She stopped for a first breath on a high pitch without floundering, but Layton, by determined timing, snapped shut the tirade with sarcasm.

'When Sims passed, you didn't turn and come straight back did you?'

Henrietta threw wide her arms and collapsed on to the kitchen floor like a Yogi. The drama in her voice assumed a new, low, key. Pops was not only an apparently willing audience, but a new one.

'Greg wouldn't come back, his mother was waiting to be taken to Mass and he didn't dare disappoint her. For your information, Pops, and later for Mim's, I've just finished telling him he can get out of my life.'

Layton grunted, 'You can't want him much. Besides, you're far too young to be serious, and the wrong type.'

'Wrong on all counts, Pops. He makes love like heaven and when I'm serious like most days, that's my type too. We make a beautiful couple, haven't you noticed? But I can't see why I have to accept his mother and his church along with good sex in bed. That's not my idea of marriage.'

Layton gained the impression that he was expected to register shock and realised he would have in conversation with any one of the other three girls. He wanted to be annoyed, recalling the gift this one had for getting the best of everything, but he knew he preferred her to amuse him. His advice was brief: 'Concentrate on your exams.' She didn't even consider it.

'You've missed the point again, Pops,' she informed him lightly. 'Which is that I've been seeing myself as the beautiful bride and mother of children like Maddy. And you can skip the lecture, it would be wasted on my past tense since last Sunday.'

'My God, Henrietta, you're not going to drag up last Sunday are you?' A portion of Mim's weariness assailed him. It was not easy to dampen the deviousness of Henrietta, especially with other things on your mind.

Henrietta was up and prowling again. She removed Mim's coffee mug to the sink and placed it behind the assembled vegetables and demanded amicably, 'You don't think George shone up as much of a golden boy last Sunday, do you? He wasn't much of an ad for marriage.' Suddenly, she stopped short and turned on Layton. 'Look, Pops, just how long ago did Mim go for that shower? I want to talk to her. I want to know what's going on.'

'Then sit still on that chair and I'll tell you,' Layton snapped. 'So far, you haven't given me a chance; you've got too little respect for people. And when you do see your mother, keep your problems to yourself since just at present yours, like mine, are irrelevant.'

She dropped into the indicated chair, staring at him wide-eyed. 'You shatter me, Pops. What did you say?'

'I said that your problems and my problems, being merely selfish, are minor to your mother at present. She will be out of the shower and dressing now, because she is waiting for a telephone call on the condition of Paul Carlister who is in a very bad state at the Alfred. Barbara and Sims are standing by with the Carlisters at the hospital.'

Layton's stomach turned over watching Henrietta deflate like a pricked balloon and shrink before his eyes into a horror-struck child, all eyes in a small, white face, terribly still.

'Oh, Pops,' she whispered. 'Was it a car smash?'

'No, he was found gassed in the house in Richmond where Sims lives. The old man called Sarge was already dead when they got them out.'

She gagged, put three fingers across her mouth and spoke through them. 'It's a dreadful old place, Pops. I went with them once and waited while Paul and Barbi went in to get Sims. How awful for Sims.'

She began to cry without sobbing, a splash of silent tears from over-full eye sockets. Layton handed her a tissue from the pocket of his dressing gown and found he was glad to tell her everything he knew, even word for word as far as he could remember, those strange remarks of Sims and Barbara. She listened gravely and without interruption and he was relieved when she wasn't aghast that he himself had thought of suicide, although he could tell she considered such a suggestion remote from the character of the Paul she knew. When he was finished, she asked him to repeat only one thing.

'What did you say Sims said about Paul's father and the car?'

'That Sims could keep it.'

'No, after that, about Paul's father.'

'That Paul didn't think his father loved him so much.'

Henrietta said, 'Barbi knew Paul's father loved him. She always knows things like that. She's better than I am, Pops.'

Layton felt rather than heard the confidence and shivered involuntarily as he asked, 'Why do you think that?' so that she told him with surety, 'I know it. I've always known it. I've always leaned on her. That's why I protect her all the time, that's what I was doing last Sunday, thinking of myself by protecting Barbi when I should have been using my scatterbrains. Haven't you noticed what an act I can put on?'

Layton nodded and watched her sniff and then blow her nose. 'You always fall for it,' she continued. 'It's stinking of me to say it to you, Pops, but it's true. I can do any kind of crying when I want to. But I'm not going to cry now. Barbi wasn't crying, was she?'

Layton was amazed. 'No,' he said.

'Did Mim cry?'

'No.'

'When they cry, they cry by themselves. Eliane is the same. When Elie used to cry, Barbi wouldn't let me go into her room and she wouldn't go either.'

'What are you going on about?' Layton cried, not knowing what to expect next, and apprehensive, in spite of his sophistication, of some new vulnerability Henrietta had uncovered in him. For a moment, he felt her look at him strangely, with eyes that seemed hard, almost shrewd. Then she relaxed and shrugged so that he recognised the truth she had just told him about her act. But all she said was, 'Keep your cool, Pops. I'm talking about years ago, before Elie finally went overseas. It's a long time ago now, when she was at the university. She used to cry a lot then. I used to think you had to get married like Maddy to be happy – you think some funny things when you first hit your teens. Anyway, it doesn't matter. Was Mim putting the dinner on?'

'Yes, the roast is in. She seemed to think we'd be hungry as usual.'

'Is Aunt Harriet coming?'

'I shouldn't think so. She considers your mother insulted her.'

'You couldn't insult her with a hammer. What about Maddy and company?'

Layton didn't know, and said so apologetically, as if for the first time in his life he should have known. Henrietta began to move about the kitchen again; he noticed she was graceful even peering into the oven before she tackled the pile of potatoes and carrots with obvious distaste. There was something incongruous about the way she peeled potatoes that inspired a father's need to remove his child's fragile fingers from danger. Without meaning to, he said, 'Your mother won't be long now.'

She snapped right back at him, 'Then I'd better put a wriggle on, hadn't I? That's the thing I mean about Barbi, she doesn't think you can escape life. She bogs right in. She used to help Sims clean up old Sarge's place. Mim too. Mim sent him jam and cake and stuff.

If Barbi was home she'd bloody well be doing these veggies. Hand them to me, will you, Pops, while I get the roast out?'

Layton stood up as she opened the oven door with the tea towel around her hand. Reaching into the sink he picked up two potatoes and because they were unexpectedly slimy, let them slither from his hand. They fell with a splatter to the floor and Henrietta was startled a step backwards. For an instant she tottered, balancing the roast before she could shove the pan back into the oven. She turned furiously to abuse her father.

'Now I've ruined the tea towel,' she stormed. 'And burned my hand as well. I thought any fool could pick up a potato. It just shows, doesn't it? I suppose you don't ask men to do such things. I should have known, shouldn't I, since I never saw you pick up a potato, or George either come to think of it; only Maddy and Mim and Barbi, with Eliane, of course, always ready to pitch in to help Mim... Not that any of us wanted to help Elie when she needed it...' Once again, she stopped for breath on the high note.

Her anger astounded Layton. She was a virago, fierce and uncontrolled, and for a minute he thought she was going to bombard him with the potatoes as she picked them up. But she threw them, with a gesture so violent it was almost obscene, under the cold water tap in the sink. As she turned the tap, he stared at her back and saw that she trembled in every muscle. He was wise enough not to speak and when she turned again she was calm and moved with a tense lightness to the stove where she opened the oven and removed the roast.

Back at the sink, she arranged the vegetables around the sizzling meat with neat accuracy. After she re-closed the oven door on her effort, she looked Layton straight in the eyes. Her own were blue-black with storm, but her voice was mild enough and without apology as she suggested, 'Why don't you and I just get stoned, Pops?'

Layton was just wondering if his cue was to laugh when the phone rang. Involuntarily, they moved close together as they listened and heard the phone click as Mim picked up the receiver. Together, they opened the kitchen door and tiptoed across the dining room to stand like conspirators in the doorway to the hall.

Mim was leaning against the hall table. 'Yes,' she was saying, her voice raised to a high, clear level. 'Yes, I hear you, but not too well. Yes – Arthur and Ruth with him. Yes, Arthur came out to tell you. Crying – poor Arthur, Barbi, I can't hear you, dear, Barbi don't cry. Sims? Yes, Sims – thank you, Sims, thank God. That's wonderful news. Yes, Sims, that's right, just bring her home now. No, I quite agree – you can't do anything there now. Just... Bring... Barbi... Home.'

Layton and Henrietta caught Mim as she slumped to the floor. 'This time she's just about had it,' Layton said. 'We'll get her into bed – back in her own room. Do you know where to get some Valium or even an APC we can give her?'

'Sure,' Henrietta said. 'In her handbag. Then we'll phone Maddy.'

Mim slept. When she opened her eyes, not only Henrietta, but Maddy and Barbara hovered near her bed. Maddy was arranging a table tray with a serving of roast beef that dominated the room with the aroma of very brown gravy. Barbi was waiting with patience, exhausted past the control point and her words spilled out as her mother stirred.

'Oh, Mim,' she cried. 'Everything is all right now, really it is. We were all so scared and then Paul suddenly said, "Ruth". He wanted Ruth. After, when Ruth came out, she asked Sims and me to phone Molly and after lunch Sims and I are going out to Heidelberg to get Rollo and Molly because Molly is going to stay with Ruth for as long as she needs her.'

'I'm so glad, so glad.' Mim looked at Maddy's hands fixing the tray. 'You see, last night Ruth came to tell me she is giving Mark a divorce.'

Henrietta did not miss her moment. With full dramatic measure, her voice chimed with the resonance of a bell. 'And we – are sending a wire back to Eliane.'

Mim raised her eyes to Maddy's face.

'Don't you want to hear it?' Henny demanded. 'It's a beaut telegram – it's from all heads gathered around the kitchen table, including Sims. Pops stood rather aloof at first, but he's in on it too, isn't he, Maddy?'

Henrietta paused, filling the room with sudden silence. Maddy nodded numbly, holding her mother's gaze while Mim said softly, 'That's a good effort.' Her voice was even and flat.

'Please... Read it.'

Henrietta found that her voice trembled, but she read the telegram as she intended:

'ICEBREAKER BROKEN THROUGH STOP WARM WELCOME HOME FROM ALL STOP LOVE'

oooOOOooo

Kathryn Purnell was born in Vancouver, Canada in 1911. She travelled by sea to Australia with her family as a young woman. During the voyage she met and later married Australian scientist William (Bill) Purnell.

Kathryn embodied the soul and spirit of a creative writer. She maintained an intense interest in everything around her, the natural and spiritual worlds, the everyday and the eternal, diverse countries and their cultures, as well as the human condition (of which she had an uncanny understanding). A gifted educator, she was an inspiration to many aspiring writers to whom she taught creative writing. She believed intensely in the need to encourage women writers, the constraints on whom she felt herself at a very personal level.

Bill Purnell's work in the early years of UNESCO as head of its Science Cooperation Division took Kathryn to Paris to live in the immediate post war years, then to Cairo and later Jakarta. She travelled widely in Europe and later spent time in South Africa. Her husband's ill health compelled the family to return permanently to Australia in the late nineteen fifties, It was particularly in this period of her life, with the common pressures of maintaining a family, supporting a husband in his professional life and finding time to create, that she felt most strongly the constraints and limitations placed on the female creative spirit by the societal practices and beliefs of the time.

But create she did, both poetry and prose work. She also spent much of her time teaching aspiring writers, mostly women. Active in the Society of Women Writers, in 1998 she won The Alice Award, a biennial award for long-term and distinguished contribution to literature by an Australian woman. Other awards included the State of Victoria Short Story Award and the Moomba Short Story Prize both in 1966/67 and The Society of Women Writers Poetry Prize in 1972. In addition to poetry, Kathryn left a fine legacy of prose writings, much of it unpublished. A current project seeks to redress this by publishing some of her novellas, short stories and her singular novel.

ALSO BY KATHERINE PURNELL

PROSE
The Augustinian Correspondence
Honey Eyes
Apollo in January
Sam in July

POETRY
Safari
Pandora
Harpsichord of Water
Otway Country
Fairy Trees: Poems for the Fitzroy Gardens

www.ingramcontent.com/pod-product-compliance
Lightning Source LLC
Chambersburg PA
CBHW070009120726
47909CB00003B/849